To Matt and Max, who have the biggest hearts I know

PROLOGUE

London, 1890

Virginia shivered but didn't dare reach up to gather her damp, wool cloak around her throat. She didn't dare breathe, though she doubted the sound would be heard over the heavy rain pelting the canvas above her, or the churning waters of the wide and mighty Thames. When she'd first arrived in London five years ago, it had also been raining, but the circumstances couldn't have possibly been more different. Instead of a wooden crate on a narrow and shadowy riverboat, she'd arrived in a bright steam engine after an ocean liner brought her from New York to Southampton, and her heart had been filled with pride and ambition, not gnawing guilt and fear.

She'd been the first woman from Atwood, Kansas to earn a college degree, and once she'd completed her graduate work in biology at Cornell, she was offered the once-in-a-lifetime chance to study in London. Her parents had bragged to the whole town that she would spend the next four years studying abroad, working with the most renowned and respected doctor in London. Some had simply scoffed at the news; others had warned that pursuing a man's profession would be her undoing. Then, when she'd returned to her parents' farm after only a year, all of them got to smirk, sneer, and boast that they'd been right. The whispers spread through the farms, the church, the tavern, and dry goods store: *The Carroll girl was ruined in London.*

They had no idea.

The boat dipped, and she swallowed and tightened her arm around her daughter, who was curled up next to her on the single trunk they'd brought from home. There was so much Virginia regretted, so much she desperately wished she could change, but nothing more than tearing her daughter away from their family farm. Even after both of her parents died of scarlet fever, and those who hadn't already shunned her in Atwood turned their backs, Virginia had remained determined to raise her daughter there. She'd managed to keep the land and gotten a job as a nurse in town, and eventually, even convinced herself that she'd never left Kansas at all, that everything that had happened in London had only been a dream.

But then, three weeks ago, she received a letter from Lady Cullum, who had been not only the benefactress of her mentoring doctor but the closest thing she'd had to family while living in London. The letter confirmed the rumors that had only just reached The States, stories of a crisis that was crippling the city.

And you're bringing your daughter here, she thought, guilt slicing her like a knife. *You're bringing your three-year-old daughter into a lethal, quarantined city.*

She closed her eyes, reminding herself that she didn't have a choice. Her parents were gone, and she had become a pariah back in Atwood; even if someone *had* been willing to take her daughter in, they certainly wouldn't have given the girl the love and care she needed. And she'd had to return to London and do what she could to save the city, not only because Lady Cullum, who had never begged for anything in her life, had implored her to, but because she knew what Lady Cullum didn't.

That, in a way, the crisis was all Virginia's fault.

The boat rocked and then stilled, and her heart leapt into her throat. This was it; they had finally reached the heavily guarded border. She heard the booming voice of their oarsman—a burly Scotsman who'd introduced himself as simply "Beck"—but couldn't make his words out over the rush of pounding rain. He hadn't told her what lie he planned to give to the border guards, who would surely be baffled by anyone wanting *inside* the quarantined city. Virginia could only imagine how much money Lady Cullum had promised him to smuggle her in, because once they made it inside, he wasn't getting out again. For a moment, she almost hoped the guards would turn their boat away, but then she felt a jerk as the oars dug back into the water, and she knew they were gliding past the border and into the city limits.

She waited for her veins to flood with relief, but instead, her lungs began to tighten and her throat began to close.

London. God in heaven, she was actually back in London.

Her heart sped up, pounding against her chest, and she clutched her daughter's hand, pulling the little girl closer and inhaling the scent of her hair.

He's dead, he's dead, she told herself. *He can't hurt you now. He's dead.*

It was madness, she knew, to fear a single man when they'd just entered a quarantined city filled with monsters, but she couldn't fight her terror of his memory any more than she'd been able to fight her adoration for him five years ago. He hadn't just been her mentoring doctor. He had been the epitome of all she wanted to be—brilliant, passionate, well respected—and though it made her sick to think it now, beautiful, too. His eyes had been the color of honey—a fierce, burning amber ringed with a band of vivid gold. But one night in his lab, she'd watched those beautiful eyes go black, and the man she'd come to worship as a god had become the devil.

She tightened her grip on her daughter and dug her free hand into her pocket, clutching the leather-bound notebook she'd been clinging to for three weeks. It was his journal, which Lady Cullum had found just after his death and mailed to Virginia along with the letter, hoping she'd be able to find some clues or solutions inside. At first, the sight of his coiled, familiar writing had turned her stomach, but she soon discovered that, strangely, touching the pages made her feel strong. There was something incredibly powerful about clasping the words

7

he'd written with his hands in the palm of her own, as if it restored the power he had taken from her that night, when those hands—suddenly smooth, strong, and ethereally pale—had ripped the seams of her lab coat and severed the fabric of her life.

The journal made her feel safe as well, because having it in her hands was further proof that he was dead, as he never would have let it out of his study otherwise. The story the pages told was common knowledge in London now, not because of the journal but due to one of the doctor's friends, who spilled the truth to authorities before both of them were killed.

According to his journal, the doctor's intentions had been noble; he'd wanted to find a way to extract the evil from human nature, but what he'd produced instead was a serum that did the opposite. The drug not only stripped him of conscience, sympathy, and compassion, it made him impossibly strong and terrifyingly beautiful, like the indefatigable offspring of an angel and a demon, with pale, glowing skin and deep and ravenous ebony eyes. The effects only lasted a couple of hours, but it was enough to change his mind and noble intentions forever. Soon, he began ingesting the potion nearly every weekend, prowling through the streets of London and taking and breaking its people and things like a child might batter its toys. Because he only took the drug while slumming in London's East End, where minor spikes in violent crime were likely to go unnoticed, he managed to keep his secret under wraps for the next three years, but all that changed when he shared his creation with some of his wealthy friends.

The boat slowed and Virginia knew they must have been nearing the shore. Her suspicions were confirmed a moment later when the boat rocked back and she felt Beck leaping out and then dragging them up onto solid ground. She'd begun to smell a difference in the river soon after the border, but when he climbed inside again and peeled the canvas back from her crate, the stench of sewage, filth, and rotting death swept in like a wave.

"This is the building, miss!" he called out over the pouring rain, unlatching the door and extending his hand. "Lady Cullum will meet us inside!"

She nodded and took his hand, keeping her daughter's tight in the other, and the two of them crawled up out of the crate and into the icy rain. They were somewhere near the East End docks, which a month ago would have been bustling, but now all the buildings were empty and dark, dead as the city's trade. Virginia glanced up, unable to tell if the sun had set or not, as the sky was a blanket of fog, rain, and stormy, soot-stained clouds.

"Go to the door that says 'Office,'" Beck yelled, crawling behind them and seizing their trunk. "She said it would be unlocked."

Virginia nodded again and hurried toward the shadowy building, attempting to shield her daughter from the rain beneath her cloak. She found the door, pulled it open, and then ushered the little girl through. The room was dim and filled with ghostly papers, folders, and files.

"Are you all right, darling?" she asked, kneeling before her once they were both inside and smoothing the rain from her dark, unruly curls.

"Yes, but I'm cold."

Virginia pressed her hand to her daughter's cheek. "Go ahead. Just remember to stop once Lady Cullum comes for us with her carriage."

The little girl nodded and closed her eyes, and her damp, clammy skin grew warm beneath Virginia's fingers. She let out a breath and smiled, and Virginia smiled back.

"It shouldn't be long now," Beck called out.

Virginia looked up to see him hauling their trunk inside the room. He sat it down, closed the door, and then pulled a pistol from his pocket, peeking out through the curtains of the window a few feet away.

"I thought they couldn't be killed with guns," Virginia said, rising up. "That they heal and regenerate immediately after being wounded."

There was a name for the creatures, but she didn't like to use it, didn't like to think it any more than she thought *his* name, because it was the name he had called himself that night. Thankfully, when Beck replied, he didn't use it, either.

"They do, and that's what people thought at first, but according to

Lady Cullum's latest wire, they can be killed by either a shot to the back of the head or complete decapitation. Anything that destroys the brainstem or severs it from the body."

He glanced at the little girl then and cleared his throat, looking embarrassed, but she didn't flinch, and Virginia actually brightened.

"That's good," she said, walking over to him. "They aren't invincible." She glanced at the second, smaller gun, sticking out of the top of his boot. "May I have that one then?"

He furrowed his brow. "You can shoot one of these?"

"I grew up on a farm. I've been shooting coyotes and rabbits since I was nine."

Perhaps coyotes and rabbits weren't the same as nearly invincible monsters, but Beck was impressed enough to hand her the gun.

"What else did she say about them?" she asked as she took it from him. "Lady Cullum, I mean. In the wire she sent to you."

Virginia hadn't had contact with Lady Cullum since her letter, as she'd spent the three weeks since then on a train and an ocean liner. She hadn't even written her back, as it wouldn't have been any use; by the time her letter had reached Virginia, the quarantine had begun, and mail was no longer being carried in or out of the city. Apparently, however, she had managed to transmit more information to Beck by telegraph.

"She told me what they do," he replied. "I mean, the way they kill."

Virginia swallowed, glancing down at her boots. "Yes, she told me that, too."

In truth, she'd read that particular detail in the journal. A few months after the doctor shared his secret with his friends, one of them broke the circle of trust and tampered with the serum, altering the substance from a liquid to tablet form. Harsher and more potent, the new product didn't simply increase its user's strength and strip them of conscience, it transformed them into massive, hulking beasts with black, unseeing eyes; razor-sharp teeth; and smooth, hairless skin as white as a corpse. High on his own arrogance and eager to pad his pockets, the doctor's friend began to manufacture and sell the tablet, and only then did the devastating effects become apparent. The doctor and his friends had stolen, raped, and brutalized, but the monsters the new drug created did one thing and one thing only: kill. But that perversion was not the worst nor the one that doomed the city. Once consumed, the new drug altered the user's genes forever. After that, they could become the monster at any time, without any warning and completely against their will.

That was how, in the span of only two months, London collapsed. Half of its people were dead and a fourth of those left were clandestine killers—ticking bombs that could detonate at any given moment. And, as Beck had noted, they had a particular way of killing, a way that seemed quite fitting to Virginia.

They ate people's hearts.

That was what the doctor had done in his lab all those years ago— gouged her hopes, slayed her dreams, and devoured the heart of her life. After that, she'd fled the country, never telling a single soul what her mentor had created.

Or that she'd been the first to face one of London's original monsters.

But he was dead now, she reminded herself, gripping the gun and clenching her jaw as she looked back up through the window. When the crisis broke out and the government captured the man who'd made the tablets, he exposed the doctor's secrets in an attempt to save himself. It didn't work, however. Both men were taken and charged with treason, and an angry mob stormed the jail and killed them before the authorities could. Virginia would never see those burning amber eyes again.

Except, of course, whenever she looked in the eyes of her own daughter.

"That's how they sense them, you know," Beck said.

She blinked. "I'm sorry, what?"

"The monsters. They don't see very well. The way they find their victims is by sensing their beating hearts."

Virginia glanced at her daughter, who had seated herself on the floor against the wall, now warm and content. Lady Cullum's wealth would give them a measure of security, but perhaps there was an additional way the girl could protect herself.

"There—I think that's her."

Virginia felt the relief she had expected when they made it across the border wash through her veins. She turned to the window and followed Beck's gaze as two stately horses materialized through the fog and rain. They were drawing Lady Cullum's carriage, the same coach Virginia had ridden in with her five years ago, only now there were bolts on the doors and thick, black bars across the windows. Two armed men sat on each side of the coachman, and when the carriage stopped, they leapt down into the mud, unlatched the door, and slid it open. A wide, black umbrella emerged, and then finally, Lady Cullum.

The wealthy widow had no relation to the royal family, but one would never suspect it from the way she carried herself. Her firm posture and smooth gaze were nothing short of regal, and Virginia had never known a woman more confident or quick-witted. Even now, in a downpour on the ghostly East End docks, she walked up the path to the office door as if ascending a throne. The two armed men followed close behind her, and once the three of them reached the building, Beck opened the door and extended his hand to help her through.

"Lady Cullum."

"Mr. Beck," she said in her firm, crisp voice as she took his hand and allowed him to guide her inside. "I can't thank you enough."

He nodded deferentially and took her dripping umbrella, while the two other men remained outside the door, keeping watch through the rain. Lady Cullum turned and searched the room, and when she found Virginia, her eyes grew soft and visibly moist, and the thin line of her mouth curled into a smile.

"My darling girl."

"Lady Cullum," Virginia murmured, her own eyes suddenly stinging with tears.

The regal woman swept across the room.

"Silly child, call me Mary."

She embraced her, filling her lungs with her familiar lilac scent, and Virginia closed her eyes and allowed the tears to slip down her cheeks. Besides her daughter, no one had embraced her since her parents died, and she hadn't realized until that moment just how much she'd missed the comfort of someone else's arms. Then, with a jolt, she also realized she still had the gun in her hand.

"Oh, wait," she said, pulling back from the embrace and walking around Lady Cullum to hand the gun back to Beck. "Thank you. I won't be needing it now." She wiped the tears from her eyes and then turned back to Lady Cullum, but she was no longer looking at her.

She was looking at her daughter.

Virginia's muscles tensed. She'd known this moment was coming, but she still was not prepared.

"Is this... your daughter?" Lady Cullum asked, turning back to her.

Virginia swallowed, set her jaw, and walked over to the girl, then helped her to her feet and took her hand.

"Yes, it is."

Lady Cullum held her gaze and then looked at the girl again, and Virginia knew she was calculating her age and doing the math. There was no way she didn't recognize those amber eyes; the secret Virginia had kept from even her parents was now laid bare. The room seemed to shrink and the air seemed to thin around her, but then Lady Cullum spoke.

"What a lovely child," she said, glancing up. "She looks just like you, Virginia."

Those words, combined with the warmth and understanding that shone in her face, filled Virginia's lungs with air and her eyes with grateful tears. She knew Lady Cullum wouldn't ask her any more questions, wouldn't force her to open the wounds she'd worked so hard to close. But others, she knew, would not be nearly as kind or sympathetic. No one else who had known the doctor could find out about her daughter.

Or the strange, inexplicable things the girl could do.

Lady Cullum bent down and extended her hand to the child. "How do you do, my dear?"

Virginia felt her daughter's skin obediently cool as she took the woman's outstretched hand and replied, "Very well, thank you."

Lady Cullum beamed. "What a proper young lady you are." She released her hand and straightened back up. "Well, now that we've all been introduced, we'd best be on our way."

They hurried out through the mud and rain toward the waiting carriage. The two armed men returned to their seats on either side of the coachmen, and Beck—his pistol still at the ready—hoisted the trunk up into the carriage and climbed in beside Lady Cullum, across from Virginia and her daughter.

"I'm sorry you had to arrive this way," Lady Cullum said to Virginia as the carriage lurched and then rattled up to the street and away from the docks.

"There's no need to apologize. How else could we have gotten inside a heavily guarded city?"

"You wouldn't have had to cower inside a crate like some kind of criminal if the Lord Mayor hadn't refused to listen to me, as usual."

"The Lord Mayor?"

"Harlan Branch. He's in charge of the city now." Lady Cullum sighed and shook her head. "The queen, all members of parliament, and most of the House of Lords escaped as soon as the crisis broke out. They relocated to York and made it the temporary capital, leaving the Lord Mayor to run the city until the quarantine ends. I asked him to make a special provision for you to be allowed inside, and he not only refused me, he specifically instructed the border guards to deny you entry."

"But why?" Virginia asked. "What could it hurt to let me in?"

"He said it would be a waste of time," Lady Cullum said with a snort. "That only *real* scientists—and by 'real,' of course, he meant 'male'— could possibly be capable of discovering a cure. In truth, however, I think he simply resents the influence I still have and wanted to show me once and for all that he's the boss of the city."

Virginia's chest tightened. "What will he do when he finds out I'm here?"

"He'll remember that I'm a powerful woman who's not to be trifled with. And then, when you do discover a cure, he'll apologize and thank me."

Virginia flushed, both with admiration for her audacity and with pride for how fervently she believed Virginia could help. But then the warmth dissolved, replaced by a rush of icy fear.

"But what if he's right?" she asked. "I never finished my degree. I'm hardly qualified—"

"There's no one more qualified than you. You were studying with the doctor when he first created the drug."

"But he kept all that a secret from me, and this new drug isn't the same—"

"But it exists because of *his*." Lady Cullum leaned forward, her fierce gaze penetrating the shadows. "You will find a cure, Virginia. And in the meantime, I will do my part by creating shelters."

"Shelters?"

"Yes. For the people who are infected."

Virginia knit her brow, her blood running cold. "You mean... for the monsters?"

"They're people," Lady Cullum replied, leaning back but not averting her gaze. "They have a horrendous disease, but they are people like you and me. If I can create a place where they feel safe enough to admit they're infected and lock themselves away from society with dignity, then we can make the streets that much safer until you find a cure."

Virginia's daughter yawned and laid her head in her mother's lap, and Virginia smoothed her hair with one hand and pressed the other against the carriage wall to keep herself upright, as if she were physically bending beneath the weight of the challenge ahead.

"We can do this," Lady Cullum continued, leaning forward again and clutching Virginia's free hand in her own. "All hope is not lost."

Virginia nodded, her throat dry, and Lady Cullum squeezed her fingers once more and sat back in her seat.

"Together, we will end the curse of Dr. Henry Jekyll."

CHAPTER ONE

London, 1903

Anyone watching might have suspected Elliot Morrissey was about to commit a crime. He was slipping through the shadows of the alley like a bandit, moving with speed, but careful not to draw any attention. No one was there to see him, however; that was the point of taking the alley. For the last two weeks, he'd stayed as far from people as he could get.

So why am I on my way to a bloody music hall? he thought, though of course he knew the answer: As always, it was for Cambrian.

His best friend and near brother had begged him to end his self-imposed seclusion and come out tonight, and though Elliot, like most people, usually found it hard to resist Cam's contagious energy, this time he had given in for a very different reason. When Cam had twisted his handsome face into a miserable scowl and flung his body over the edge of Elliot's bed in mock-despair, Elliot hadn't laughed in spite of himself like he usually would. Instead, he'd turned away, gripping a chair and trying to breathe, because beneath Cam's playful façade was a pool of icy fear—an overwhelming, marrow-deep concern for his friend's wellbeing. And Elliot hadn't seen it in his eyes or heard it in his voice; just as he had for the last two wretched, agonizing weeks, he had *felt* the fear himself.

As if it belonged to him.

Beyond the filthy, ever-present haze of yellow fog, the sun began its descent, bathing the city in sooty shadows. Even from the moderate seclusion of the alley, Elliot sensed the people around him scurrying off the streets. Only two groups of Londoners would dare to venture out now: those who were wealthy enough to afford a weapon or bolted carriage, and those who were desperate enough to provide the services the elite required. Technically, a Hyde could transform at any time, but for whatever reason the change seemed to happen more at night, and those who couldn't protect themselves from the vicious, heart-eating monsters had to hurry to shelter once the sun began to set.

But even people with money, like Elliot, were never safe. Owning a gun was one thing, but killing an active Hyde was another. The massive, bloodless, black-eyed creatures were practically immortal when they were in their monstrous state. A shot to the heart or a stab wound to the lung would heal within moments; the only way to stop them was to entirely dispatch their brains. A Hyde could either be killed by a well-placed bullet to the brainstem or by the surer, but often more difficult, act of decapitation. One of Elliot's father's students at St. Thomas's Hospital carried a katana his grandfather had purchased before the quarantine and claimed he'd used it to sever the heads of more than twenty Hydes.

Elliot wished he remembered more of the city before the disaster. He'd only been four when the epidemic broke out thirteen years ago. When she was alive, his mother had told him stories about "before," painting scenes of a thrilling, vibrant, bustling metropolis as clearly and as beautifully as her watercolor landscapes. But now, Elliot found such images difficult to conjure. It seemed to him that London had never been more than a desolate prison, and that he had never known anything but restlessness, longing, and grief.

As soon as the thought crossed his mind, however, his stomach flooded with shame, a feeling that clung to him like the stench of the

Thames on a mudlark these days. He was one of the most fortunate people in all of London. The Hyde outbreak had left the city half as populous, but the quarantine had doubled the number of people in poverty. The docks were closed, the trains shut down, and the underground railway completely abandoned; hundreds of jobs were gone and thousands of people were destitute. Never before had the gap between the rich and the poor been so wide, and Elliot sat at the very top of the city's social ladder. He lived in a place that was clean and well guarded, that bloomed with electrical light. His home was a palace—literally.

His home was Buckingham Palace.

Cambrian's father, Harlan Branch, was the Lord Mayor of London, a yearlong position he had held for over fourteen years now. When Parliament and the royal family abandoned the city for York, they left the former capital entirely in his hands. His move to the palace was meant to last until a cure was discovered—until the threat had passed and Queen Victoria could come back. But the queen had died, no cure had been found, and King Edward seemed no more inclined to return than his mother had been.

Elliot lived at the palace because his father, in addition to teaching medicine at St. Thomas's, served as Harlan Branch's own personal physician. He'd had the job since Elliot and Cam were little boys, back when the two of them had dreamed of one day becoming their fathers. Cam—bright, charming, and loved—would certainly succeed in becoming a brilliant leader someday, but Elliot had destroyed his chance at a future in medicine. He longed to tell Cam the reason why, to finally let down his guard and share his burden with his friend. Keeping a secret from Cam was like cutting the air off to one of his lungs, but suffocation was preferable to the shame of telling the truth.

A figure passed through the shadows at the end of the alleyway, and Elliot paused and slid his hand inside his overcoat. He wasn't reaching for the pistol holstered beneath his arm—the figure was much too small and moving too slowly to be a Hyde—but rather for the flask of gin pocketed in his vest. He'd downed a hurried glass before he left the palace grounds, but it wasn't going to be enough to withstand the crowd he'd soon face, or to persuade Cam he was cheerfully on the mend.

Steeling himself, he lifted the flask and took a hasty swig. The liquor seared his throat and left a poisonous taste in his mouth, but he forced himself to endure a few more gulps before stopping to breathe. He hated gin, hated its sour burn and rancid taste, but it was the most effective medicine for his affliction.

Ever since the grave mistake he'd made a fortnight ago, Elliot had been able to feel the emotions of those around him—feel them in the marrow of his bones, as if they were his. His father had called him "thin-skinned" and "sensitive" all his life, but now he was more than sensitive; he was an open wound. The feelings of a passerby had the power to incapacitate him, even when the person in question was feeling something good. Once, when he was in Limehouse in the early morning hours, he passed a prostitute performing her services in an alley, and the fusion of her crippling shame and the customer's blind desire was so repulsive and overwhelming he vomited in the street.

Such an affliction would surely be detrimental in any place, but London was an ocean of terror, sorrow, and desperation. The fear and grief Elliot knew before seemed a fairy tale now; no physical blow or injury could ever match the pain he'd found in other people's hearts. Even the servants who lived in the clean, bright safety of Buckingham Palace—people whom he'd previously regarded with the level of interest he held for the furniture—pulsed with fear, burned with anger, and ached with longing and grief. Perceiving the secret burdens of those around him was painful enough, but *feeling* their collective misery was unbearable.

After a cough, he raised his hand and took another drink, sickened again but also calmed by the growing feeling of numbness, which spread through his veins and rose up through his skin like a coat of armor. Nothing could blot out the feelings entirely, but alcohol helped; it dulled the edges, softened the impact, diluted the potency. Drunk, he was slow and useless, but clear-headed, he was exposed.

Perhaps the only trait he retained either way was cowardice.

Slipping the flask back into his vest, he spit the taste out onto the cobblestone street and hurried on. When the alley opened up at Euston Road, he took a left, keeping close to the shadowy, padlocked buildings as he walked. The largest and most noticeable was King's Cross station, which towered over the street like a massive, empty tomb.

It seemed extremely wasteful to leave such a grand place untenanted, but Elliot understood why the city refused to convert it to something useful. The station was a symbol of hope that the quarantine would be lifted, that a cure would be discovered and London restored to its former glory. No one wanted to think that trains would never pass through it again, so it would remain a vacant relic wrapped in locks and chains.

The security was necessary not only to keep out homeless vagrants but also fugitive Hydes. A countless number went undetected, since anyone—except for women, for whom the monster-inducing drug was inexplicably fatal—could be an infected Hyde, but those who'd been discovered hid in careful, moving nests in order to avoid being captured and executed. Common belief was that most of them lived in the tunnels of the abandoned underground railway, which even the police were often too afraid to enter.

The sky behind the stagnant clock on the station's tower was dark now, and snow was starting to fall in ashen clumps through the smoky air. Elliot shivered, which meant the gin was doing its job too slowly, so he took another swig and trudged up the street to *La Maison Des Fleurs*.

He and Cam had come here a month and a half ago for "St. Cambrian's Day," which was what Cam called his birthday since it fell on St. Valentine's Day. The music hall was larger and grander than most, but not elegant. Every inch of the place was drenched in its gaudy flower theme: light fixtures shaped like tulips, wallpaper crammed with garish blooms, waitresses with "floral" names in tawdry petal-pink dresses.

As he stepped inside the oily light and yeasty warmth of the crowded hall, Elliot wished again that Cam had chosen a gentlemen's club. In dim, quiet rooms reserved for men of the upper crust, he'd only be exposed to clouds of cigar smoke and self-importance. Music halls were crowded, bright, and worst of all, filled with women, whose rivers of fear ran so deep he felt he might drown inside them. He'd already known their lives were more precarious than his own, as they were prey not only to Hydes but also to fiendish men, but he'd never truly understood the horror of living that way, of always feeling like hunted game in a world that didn't care.

But Cam, unburdened by Elliot's knowledge, found gentlemen's clubs to be boring. Five years ago, his father had closed every theatre, opera, ballet, museum, and symphony in London, declaring them all superfluous drains on the city's meager resources. Music halls were the only "artistic" entertainment left, and Cam was starved for aestheticism and desperate for the arts.

At the moment, a bevy of chorus girls were dancing on the stage. They were dressed in daffodil-yellow tights and bustled skirts so short they exposed the fullness of their thighs. Their bodices were nothing more than corsets lined with beads, and when they kicked their legs in the air, they exposed bright purple drawers. As they danced, they sang a bouncing song called "Get Away, Johnnie."

I'm a flirt as you'll discover,
All my sweethearts I can tease,
When I stroll out with my lover,
Don't I like a gentle squeeze.

Elliot sighed for Cam's sake.

This was London's "art."

Bracing himself, he pressed through the heady haze of smoke and feeling, dodging bursts of heartache, yearning, and unbridled lust as he passed. He'd arrived early on purpose, knowing Cam would choose a place up front in the heart of the crowd, so when he spotted an empty box hanging high above the stage, he rushed toward the rickety steps in the back and started climbing.

From below, it had seemed the entire second floor was unoccupied, but when he reached the top, he discovered two waitresses on their break. They were huddled at a grimy table, rubbing their feet and crouched over two dark pints of weak-looking stout. Their shoulders and arms were deflated from hours of carrying heavy trays, and their petal-pink dresses looked sallow, pinched, and too small for their frames. Elliot wondered how long they'd been working, and if those pints of stout were the only supper they'd had tonight. The gin had started to work a bit, so their stale fear and hollow dejection wasn't overwhelming, but when they lifted their heads and saw him, a sudden rush of desperate hunger flooded the air between them.

It wasn't lust, though Elliot now knew women could feel that, too, contrary to what his father and friends at St. Thomas's had told him. The waitresses' yearning, however, was not for his looks but for his wealth, for the safety and protection that came with silk hats and silver cufflinks. Swallowing hard against the borrowed burn of their desire, he closed his eyes and walked away from the pair as fast as he could. Once he reached the empty box, he collapsed in a chair at its table, removing his hat and coat and then running a hand through his sweat-damp hair.

At least he wouldn't receive that kind of attention once Cam arrived. Not only was he the son of the mayor, who might as well be king, he was also arguably the handsomest man in London. His sleek hair was jet-black, and his eyes were a piercing ice blue, and there was something regal, smooth, and feline in his bearing. Even as a child, he'd had the air of a jungle cat, like the noble panther Bagheera in Rudyard Kipling's *Jungle Book* stories.

Elliot was tall, strong, and had an agreeable face, but if Cam was a polished, princely panther, he was an alley cat. He'd never possessed much poise or grace, and even before his affliction, he'd been hopelessly incapable of concealing his emotions. His eyes were a raw and mossy green, and his dirty blond hair was perpetually tousled and unkempt, as if it were a symptom of the unruliness within.

But none of that mattered now; he had no one to impress. There were no teachers, medical boards, or employers in his future. The fear and mental anguish of the sick made it impossible to function in their presence, even if his father hadn't refused to continue his tutelage upon learning what he'd done. Perhaps it was a blessing in disguise his mother was gone. Feeling what she'd feel if she saw him like this would be too much to bear.

Elliot raised the flask to his lips, this time in an effort to dull his own internal pain, but before he could take a drink, it was snatched from between his fingers.

"Started the party without me, I see."

Cambrian rounded the table and rested his hand against the back of a chair, placing the rim of the flask beneath his nose and taking a sniff.

"Gin?" he exclaimed in mock horror, sliding down beside Elliot and placing his hat on the table. "Gin is not a gentlemen's drink," he scolded, taking a sip, but as soon as the liquor passed his lips, he coughed. "Good Lord, that's vile."

He laughed and wiped his watering eyes, and Elliot forced a weak, reciprocal smile he hoped was convincing. Two weeks ago, he would have bought Cam's spirited, carefree act, but now he could taste the cold, metallic bite of his anxiety, could feel the wary relief that flooded his heart in his own chest. Some people were better at concealing their feelings than others, and Elliot had learned Cam wasn't good.

He was one of the best.

"I tell you, El." He coughed again, screwing the cap back on. "Keep drinking swill like this, and you'll end up in an opium den."

It was a joke; there were no longer opium dens in London. Perhaps the only positive effect of the quarantine was that it had cut off trade and severed access to the drug. Once a month, the Empire sent in supplies to sustain the city: coal, grains, wine, tea and other essential provisions. But other than that, no person or substance could cross the fortified border. The shipments were brought in by boat at a different hour and dock each time, with armed guards protecting the goods and preventing desperate Londoners from trying to board the ship.

That was where Cam had been before he'd come to the music hall—overseeing and organizing the imports with his father. The Lord Mayor controlled what came in and how it was distributed, but while opium had been eradicated, the Hyde drug had not, which meant—unlike the narcotic—its ingredients were local. For a reason Elliot couldn't fathom, people were apparently still making and taking the substance. According to speeches Cam's father had given at meetings and in the papers, the persistent scourge was due to the sinful weak-mindedness of the poor. Elliot had believed this explanation in the past, but since his affliction, he hadn't found the working class to be any more unsound or depraved than the rest.

"If gin is beneath you," he said to Cam, maintaining his smile as best he could and seizing the flask from his hand. "You don't have to drink it."

"True," Cam replied, leaning back and sliding a silver cigarette case from the pocket of his coat. "But what sort of friend would I be if I stood idly by and watched you indulge in such a filthy habit?" He grinned widely and placed a cigarette between his lips. His teeth were white and very likely the straightest in all of London, but Elliot wasn't blinded by the brilliance of his smile. Beneath the smirk was a real concern for how much he'd been drinking.

"You're one to talk of filthy habits," he said, raising an eyebrow and nodding toward the silver case.

Cam sighed and struck a match against the side of his shoe. "Really, El," he mumbled against the cigarette as he lit it. "You're such an old lady sometimes."

A warm, genuine smile slowly crept across Elliot's face. The familiar banter was comforting, and Cam was calming down, too. At moments like this, it almost seemed safe to finally share his secret, but if he did, he'd never have such moments with Cam again. Over the past two weeks, he'd been an unintentional voyeur, feeling his friend's most intimate, hidden emotions without his knowledge. How betrayed would he feel if he discovered what Elliot knew? Especially the feelings where his father was concerned.

Elliot had hated Cam's father since they were little boys. His own father was cold and distant—especially since his mother's death—but the Lord Mayor was more than hard and removed; he was cruel. Cam had never known his mother, who died in childbirth, so when a Hyde killed Elliot's mother when he was twelve and Cam was thirteen, Cam grieved for her like a son. Elliot's father shut him out, unable to face his tears, but the Lord Mayor beat Cam for crying like a child, dislocating his jaw and even fracturing his arm.

Still, even while Elliot's father was setting the broken bone, Cam laughed and joked about plans to convince the staff he'd been mugged. Elliot had believed his laughter then and for years to come, fully convinced his father's malice had no effect on him. Cam mocked the Lord Mayor when he wasn't around, defied him at every turn, and insisted he was immune to his constant and brutal disapproval.

Now, Elliot knew the truth he'd tried to hide—Cam feared his father more than anything else in the world, feared him in an acute and primal way that stilled the blood. His terror went beyond the simple threat of physical violence. It was a deeper, more constant fear that infected the core of the soul, paired with a strange disgust that Elliot didn't understand.

As if to a certain degree, he felt he deserved to be afraid.

Mingled with the dread was also a longing for his father's love, a feeling Elliot knew too well, and it made the fear he carried even more tragic and hard to bear.

"Look at those girls." Cam sighed, blowing smoke out over the stage. The dancers had turned their backs and were shaking their rumps to the rhythm of the song.

> Get away, Johnnie, I'm sure there's someone by,
> Get away, Johnnie, to kiss me don't you try.
> Get away you naughty man, or I shall kick and strike,
> Well get away a little closer if you like.

"Most of them would have been ballerinas if they'd been born somewhere else," he continued, flicking ash into the lotus-shaped ashtray on the table. "And this ridiculous song was written at least five years ago." A sudden cloud of sadness bloomed and billowed through the air, as tangible as the smoke that coiled around his statuesque face. "Beyond this city, there are new songs, new ideas, new everything..."

But he didn't finish. He simply stared at the girls with sad, glazed eyes, so Elliot took advantage of his distraction and finished the gin. A soft, warm buzz had started to hum in the back of his brain, but it wasn't enough to dull the hunger he felt from the waitresses' table. Their attention had turned to Cam, as he had known it eventually would, and now they were yearning for much more than riches and protection. Shifting in his chair, he struggled to loosen his dampening collar, trying to think of a way to suggest more to drink without seeming desperate.

Thankfully, Cam soon arrived at the same idea. "What are we doing?" he scolded himself, rising up out of his chair and then leaning out over the rail of the box. "Eddie!" he called down to one of the managers on the floor. "My friend and I would like some champagne brought up. We're celebrating!"

Elliot ran a hand through his hair, relieved. "Celebrating?"

"It's Import Night," he exclaimed, sliding back down into his chair. "The best night of the month."

"Oh, right, I forgot. You expecting anything good?"

One of the most audacious ways in which Cam defied his father had to do with the monthly imports sent into the city. The Lord Mayor made all the requests and supervised each shipment, but Cam had struck a deal with one of the sailors on the ship, and every month he smuggled in different items at Cam's request—modern books, art, inventions, and other advancements the Lord Mayor declared to be frivolous. On Import Night, while Cam and his father inspected the provisions, the sailor took Cam's treasures to an old, abandoned ferry, retrieving the money he'd left there and depositing the goods. Later that night—when the Empire's ships and guards had all departed— Cam rowed out to the boat and recovered his hidden contraband.

"He always leaves a surprise or two, but I'm hoping he brought those new, twelve-inch records he told me about. Did I mention they can play for over *four consecutive minutes*?"

He had, many times. "Yes, but isn't that Victor Talking Machine he got you broken?"

"Andrew thinks he can probably have it fixed in a couple of days."

Elliot lowered his gaze to his lap and hoped Cam didn't notice. Andrew Heron was his and Cam's age, and when his father was hired to be the Lord Mayor's personal—and the city's only—telegraph operator, the three of them became friends. Elliot liked everything about Andrew, from his soft laugh to his sharp mind to his feathery ginger hair, but lately, he'd avoided him as much as he possibly could. The task was nearly impossible though; Andrew was at the palace so often he practically lived there, too. Before, he'd been his father's assistant, but now he'd taken his place. Because his father was dead.

And it was Elliot's fault.

"The Lord Mayor will probably keep him busy until ten o'clock," Cam said, theatrically accentuating his father's title like always. "He'll meet us out at the ferry after, probably around midnight."

Elliot glanced at his lap again, and this time Cam took notice. He paused, took a final drag, and snuffed out his cigarette. "You *are* coming with us?" he asked, slowly exhaling the smoke and glancing indifferently toward the stage, but Elliot felt the concern creeping back into his chest.

"I don't know," he replied, though he had already made his decision. Andrew's fresh grief was like a knife in his own heart, and he didn't deserve the grace and forgiveness that shone in his soft, brown eyes.

Cam sighed and turned toward him, his own eyes suddenly warm and void of all jokes and pretenses. "Listen, El, there's no need to keep avoiding Andrew."

Elliot swallowed and stared at the scuffed-up floorboards beneath his feet.

"He doesn't blame you," Cam continued. "Nobody does. You've got to stop hiding yourself away."

He opened his mouth to say more but then a waitress approached their table.

"A bottle of champagne," she said, setting two flutes before them and popping the cork with a practiced hand. She poured the golden, fizzing liquid into their glasses, but Elliot was no longer aware of the drinks.

His world had stopped.

For fourteen interminable days, he'd felt nearly every emotion on the human spectrum, but never once had he encountered anything like this girl. Her feelings were like a bomb that had obliterated his senses; he could scarcely see her face through the dense and astonishing haze of her spirit. Everyone, especially women, lived in a cloud of crippling fear and gnawing incompleteness, but *wholeness* radiated from her being like rays of the sun. She carried a touch of longing and a hint of indignation, but neither emotion could dampen the fiery strength that pulsed at her core, the unapologetic pride and confidence she possessed. What stood out the most, however, was the feeling she was missing.

In a city rife with terror, she was absolutely fearless.

For a moment, the only word his brain could form was "beautiful." There was no other way to describe the impression her spirit made.

When he finally blinked away the shock, he saw her physical presence was as stunning as the rest. Her hair was a billowing mane of thick and tightly wound charcoal curls, held back from her lovely face by a ribbon that matched her dress. She was small with delicate features but also strong and extremely poised, as if she believed she were ten feet tall instead of five and half. Most arresting, however, were her gold-ringed amber eyes, which glowed like embers beneath two fans of silken, coal-black lashes.

"Can I... get you anything else, sir?"

To his horror, Elliot suddenly realized he was staring. "I... no, I mean... thank you." He bit his cheek, appalled by how slow and ridiculous he sounded. For the first time in two weeks, he wished his mind was clear and sober.

"Good Lord," Cam murmured.

Elliot turned to see that he was staring at her as well.

A surge of excitement had shot through his veins, and for a moment, Elliot found himself absurdly jealous.

When Cam spoke again, however, he understood why she'd caught his attention. "You're American," he said, his eyes wide with awe.

Elliot had been too stunned to notice it at first, but Cam was right—the girl spoke with a clear American accent. There were foreigners in the city at the time of the quarantine, of course, but meeting someone who wasn't London-born was very rare. The only other American he'd ever come across was a woman who'd been friends with his mother when he was a very young child.

"Forgive me," Cam added hurriedly, struggling to remember his manners amid such fierce excitement. "I suppose you hear that from customers often."

The girl quirked her lovely lips into a bitter smile, and the indignation Elliot sensed before began to swell. "Almost never, actually," she said, boldly meeting his gaze. "Few of them are aware of what I say, let alone how I say it."

"So much the loss for them," Cam replied, widening his grin, and Elliot felt another preposterous surge of jealousy.

The girl, however, seemed quite unmoved. "Well, I'll be returning shortly if you two need anything else."

"No, wait—stay!" Elliot cried before he could think. The girl's eyes widened as she turned in his direction, and his face burst into flames.

"Yes, please. Stay," Cam said, rising from the table and gracefully pulling out a chair. "We'd very much enjoy hearing about America."

The girl hesitated. "I'm not supposed to sit. I'm working."

Cam glanced over her shoulder. Eddie, the manager, was now approaching the top of the stairs, gruffly informing the waitresses at the table their break was over. "Eddie!" he called, and the man's head snapped in his direction. "Would you mind if this young lady sat and talked with us for a bit?"

"Not at all, sir," he replied. "Iris, sit with the gentlemen."

"But Mr. Dorset," the girl—Iris—protested. "I have other tables. I'll lose money if I—"

His eyes flashed as he crossed the room and angrily lowered his voice. "That gentleman there is Cambrian Branch, the son of the

Lord Mayor. If he asks you to sit with him, by God, you are going to sit."

He gave her another hard look before he walked away, shooing the other waitresses before him down the stairs. After a moment, Iris turned around and looked at Cam, and once again, Elliot felt the world grind to a halt. Her eyes were calm, her smile placid, her cheeks void of color, but flowing from her heart was the purest rage he'd ever known.

CHAPTER TWO

Elliot doubled over, straining his muscles and clutching the sides of his chair. Iris's wrath was murderous, dense, and completely overwhelming; he could hardly contain the raging fire that now consumed his blood. How could there not be a flush in her cheeks or quickness in her breath?

"El, are you all right?" Cam asked as Iris slid calmly and smoothly into the chair he had pulled out.

"Yes," he said with a cough, clenching his fists and bringing them up to his knees. "I'm fine."

"Are you sure—"

"I'm sure. I think it's just a stomach cramp or something."

Cam looked wary but let it go and returned to his own chair. "Thank you so much for indulging us," he said, turning to Iris. "I'll gladly compensate you for any tips you might be losing."

"There's no need, really," she said, her tone as smooth as glass.

"I must insist. You're sacrificing your money and your time. It means a great deal to me, and I am truly in your debt."

She blinked, momentarily betraying her surprise. The puzzlement she felt, however, did not abate her rage, which apparently stemmed from something other than losing her hard-earned wages. "Thank you. You're very kind."

"It's you who is doing me the kindness," he said, his eyes alight. "I'd wanted to introduce myself, but as your manager already said, my name is Cambrian Branch."

Her anger flared, and Elliot tightened his fists.

"Pleased to meet you, Lord Branch."

Cam shook his head. "No, please. Call me Cambrian." Her mouth dropped open a little, and he rushed to explain himself. "I don't mean to be forward. It's just that I find those rules to be unreasonable and old-fashioned. I'll address you however you like, of course, but please don't call me Lord Branch."

Her bewilderment rose again, and this time it did ease a bit of her rage.

"All right," she said slowly, "Cambrian. You can call me Iris."

"What's your real name, though? Not the one from *La Maison Des Fleurs*."

"That is my real name: Iris Faye." Her smile curled as she added, "I suppose I was simply born to be a waitress in this hall."

Cam—unaccustomed to sarcasm not his own—cleared his throat. "Um, this is my friend, Elliot Morrissey. You can call him by his Christian name as well. Right, Elliot?"

Elliot nodded, afraid of the emotion his voice might convey. Her rage had not only flared again, it had sharpened to a point.

"Are you the son of Dr. Morrissey?" she asked, turning toward him.

Swallowing hard, he glanced away and murmured a quiet "yes." He'd never been so uncomfortable or ashamed in his whole life. What must this beautiful, strong, mysterious girl think of him? He was sweating, half-drunk, inarticulate, and drowning not only in her emotions but also in his own.

"How do you know Dr. Morrissey?" Cam asked, knitting his brow.

A flicker of panic shot through Iris like lightening and then was gone, as if her heart had leapt and then immediately steadied. "Everyone knows who he is. He's the most prominent doctor in London."

"Oh, right. I suppose he is. Well, why don't you tell us about yourself? Where in the States are you from?"

She smoothed her dress and tucked a charcoal curl behind her ear. "I'm from Kansas. If you don't know where that is, it's—"

"Right in the middle," Cam said, beaming. "I've studied world maps. Were you born in the country then? On a farm?"

His enthusiasm was so pure it must have been disarming, because her raging fire simmered down to a steady glow, and Elliot let out a breath and rested his hands against his thighs.

"As a matter of fact, I was," she replied. "Born on a farm, I mean."

Cam nearly sighed with excitement. "Do you remember much of it?"

"I was three years old when we left, but I remember almost everything. We lived near a lake—a vast, clear lake that reflected the sky—and behind our house was a grove of pecan trees that seemed to go on forever." Her gaze grew distant and wandered to the wall beyond their heads, as if she were seeing swaying branches rather than oil-stained lamps.

"So, why did you come to London?"

She blinked, regaining her focus. "My mother wanted to come here to work with English suffragettes. She liked that they were more radical than those in America."

"Suffragettes?"

Elliot snapped his mouth shut as soon as he realized he'd spoken. He hadn't meant to, but something about her voice had drawn him in, causing him to forget his shame, her rage, and everything else. He liked the way she spoke, the soft yet sturdy feel of her accent. It was comfortable and clean like cotton—bright and clear like the sky and lake she'd longingly described. The sound of her voice matched the pure, fiery beauty of her spirit; it sparkled and bubbled with light and made him feel almost... happy.

But the spell of her voice was only part of the reason he'd suddenly spoken. He'd never heard the word "suffragette" and didn't know what it meant.

"Suffragettes were women who campaigned for the right to vote," Cam explained. "I've read about them before."

"They still exist, just not in London," she said, her eyes suddenly burning. "What use is fighting for suffrage in an absolute monarchy?"

Elliot's blood went cold even as her anger flared. What she'd said was true; there were no longer legislative bodies or votes in London. The Lord Mayor was the ultimate and only authority, but no one would dare to criticize that, especially in front of his son. He didn't need to look at Cam to know he was stunned as well, but when he spoke, it was clear he'd been surprised for another reason.

"You're extremely well-educated," he said. "I don't mean to sound insulting, but most girls—I mean, most waitresses—"

"The brightest men in this city—in this *world*—couldn't match my mother. She attended prestigious schools in America, and she taught me well."

Her pride swelled, but as it did, Elliot's chest caved in. What must it be like for women like her and her mother to be trapped in London? A place where education, passion, and pride did women no good?

"She did at that," Cam nodded, smiling. "What does she do now?"

Iris's face became placid again. "She was killed by a Hyde a few years ago. Like every one else's mother."

Elliot clenched his fists and closed his eyes, preparing for the terrible wave of grief...

... that never came.

Confused, he lifted his head again and slowly uncurled his fingers. He hadn't expected her grief to be as raw and fresh as Andrew's, but he'd expected *something*. His own mother was killed over five and half years ago, and the thought of her still conjured memories that tore at his insides like claws: her reading to him before bed at night, laughing and running her warm, paint-stained fingers through his hair... her body covered up with a makeshift shroud in the cobblestone street, tubes of paint crushed flat and brushes stained red—not with paint, but her blood.

If Iris's mother was killed like that, she was either callous or lying, and Elliot already knew how much she was capable of feeling.

"I'm sorry for your loss," Cam said. "Is your father still alive?"

The shame that flooded her chest would have caused most girls to avert their eyes, but she stared at them, unflinching, as she said, "I have no idea. It's always been my mother and me. I don't even know who he was."

After a moment, the shame dissolved, unable to withstand the fiery pride that burned at her core. An emptiness remained, however—a longing for something unknown—and Elliot knew this story, at least, was absolutely true.

"If you don't mind my asking," Cam said, tactfully changing the subject. "Since you remember your home so well, do you also recall your journey? My whole life, I've wanted to know what it's like to see the ocean."

She sat back in her chair, her face growing soft and distant again. "I do, and it was beautiful, but also a little scary. I remember one night my mother and I went out onto the deck. I don't know why—perhaps we were seasick and needed a breath of fresh air. I'd imagined the sea would be glittering with reflections of the stars, but the sky was cloudy that night, so everything above and below us was infinite and dark. The ocean went on forever, even farther than the fields back home, and its waves were constant and rhythmic, like an ancient, endless song. I felt so small and frightened out there, but also strangely soothed. There's something almost... *hopeful* about being dwarfed by something so big; it makes you feel like there's more to the world. Like there's... possibility."

For a moment, none of them spoke, moved a muscle, or even breathed. This time, Elliot wasn't enthralled by her voice but by her words, and he wasn't the only one. All three of them were feeling the exact same thing at that moment, a phenomenon he hadn't come across since his affliction. They sat in silence amid a cloud of longing and desperate wonder, sharing the same audacious dream, the same perilous hope.

It was Iris who finally broke the silence, shifting and tossing her hair back as if shaking off the memory. "I'm surprised you two even knew what an American accent was. One of the other waitresses here thought I was from some backwoods part of Ireland for a week."

"Well, we'd heard it before," Cam replied. "Back when we were children. Remember," he said to Elliot, "that woman who was friends with your mother? Her name was Miss... Ferrell, I think."

"Carroll," Elliot murmured, clearing his throat. "Virginia Carroll."

"Right. I remember her and Lady Cullum coming over for tea. It didn't happen often, as Lady Cullum was rarely on good terms with the Lord Mayor. Of course, that was before... well, before things went bad with her shelters."

Elliot recalled the Lord Mayor's tirades against Lady Cullum's shelters. He thought the Hydes were criminals who didn't deserve to be "coddled," and claimed that protecting them was a risk too dangerous to take. As it turned out, he was right: One day a Hyde broke loose in one of the shelters and killed Lady Cullum. After that, the Lord Mayor closed the havens and changed the law, declaring all infected Hydes to be enemies to the city. Active or not, infected people were now to be killed on sight, as were any who harbored, helped, or failed to execute them. Then, only a few days later, Virginia Carroll died as well, killed by an explosion in Dr. Jekyll's old laboratory. This led to the second law that changed the city of London: Only those appointed by the Lord Mayor could seek a cure, as experimentation was simply too perilous, especially for women.

"I should return to my tables," Iris said, rising from her chair. She smiled and moved with a cool grace, but Elliot sensed a terrible storm of emotion building within her. This time, however, it wasn't rage.

For once, it was fear.

"Wait," Cam called. "You forgot, I haven't paid you for your—"

"Please, there's really no need." She paused a moment and looked at them, betraying a sadness that drifted through her storm like a heavy wind. "Keep your money."

She walked away, and Cam took a sip of the champagne they hadn't touched. "What an outstanding girl," he said. "Intelligent, bold, and beautiful, too."

Elliot stared at the surface of the table, jealousy searing his skin. The feeling was ludicrous, of course; Iris hadn't desired either of them for their looks or their money, and even if she had, he didn't stand a chance against Cam. He reached for his own glass of champagne then, and took a long, deep drink.

"The places she's been and things she's seen," Cam continued. "I envy her."

At that, Elliot's jealousy abruptly turned to anger. "She's an orphan who works as a waitress in a tawdry music hall," he snapped, though he still wasn't sure he believed the story she'd told about her mother. "She has no protection and no outlet for her passion or her mind. Her life is an endless cycle of danger, hard work, and disappointment."

He regretted the outburst as soon as he felt the shame creeping into Cam's stomach. "You're right," Cam murmured, almost to himself. "That was thoughtless of me."

Elliot shook his head and sighed. "No, it's not your fault. You meant no harm, and I understand. I envy her as well."

As terrible as it was, he did, in spite of all the advantages he had that she did not. He not only envied the places she'd been, but the fire that burned inside her, the unassailable passion and pride he'd never before experienced.

"I'm sorry, Cam," he continued. "Lately I... haven't been myself."

Cam paused, took another drink, and turned toward him. "I know, El, and I understand, but..." He glanced at the floor and let out a breath. "I would be lying if I said I wasn't worried about you."

Anxiety and affection filled his eyes and the air between them, and Elliot tightened his jaw and stared at the bubbles in his glass.

"You can't hide in your room with a bottle of gin for the rest of your life," Cam continued, reaching over and gently placing his hand on Elliot's. The gesture was meant to be comforting, but Elliot's body clenched up like a fist when their skin connected. The nearer he was to the heat of someone's feelings the stronger he felt it, and actual physical contact was like thrusting his hands in the fire. He closed his eyes and fought back tears, paralyzed by Cam's love.

"It kills me to see you this way, El. You've always been so open and warm, even after Edith..." His grief for Elliot's mother rose like bile. "Even after that, you were *you*—expressive and unrestrained like her and like every brilliant artist. But now you're cold and distant, putting up walls just like—" He didn't finish, but there was no need. He'd meant to say, "like your father."

"My point is," he recovered, "You need to stop punishing yourself. What's past is past. It's time for you to pick up and move on."

Elliot nodded and sucked in a breath, wishing he could explain this was the reason he'd never "move on." The mistakes he'd made would be with him, crippling him, for the rest of his life.

His first mistake occurred one month ago, just after Cam's birthday. While walking down the street, he had passed a bakery with its door hanging open, and when he peered inside, he saw a Hyde crouched over the bloody, heartless body of the baker. Trembling, he drew the pistol holstered beneath his coat, building up the courage to strike before the creature saw him. But at that moment, the monster's ebony eyes rolled back in its head, and its body convulsed along the bloodstained floor. Elliot watched as its body shrank and the color returned to its bloodless skin, revealing a scrawny teenage boy.

A boy he knew.

His name was Will, and he was only thirteen or fourteen years old, the younger brother of one of the palace stable boys, Milo Clements. When the boy saw what he'd done, his shoulders collapsed and started to cry, his high-pitched, wailing sob as raw as a frightened child's. Elliot steadied the gun, knowing all Hydes must be shot on sight, but it was no use—he simply couldn't kill the sobbing boy—so he turned around and dashed back into the street as fast as he could.

It was only two weeks later when Elliot's act of cowardice and treason came back to haunt him. While visiting Milo on the palace grounds, Will morphed into a Hyde and attacked Robert Heron, Andrew's father. The guards shot and killed him, but not in time to save Robert's life, and Elliot knew his friend's father's blood was on his hands. He told Cam and Andrew the truth that night, and they both claimed to forgive him, but nothing could assuage the guilt and shame inside his heart, so the next night, in desperation, he made his second grave mistake.

A few months earlier, he'd overheard his father and the Lord Mayor discussing Dr. Jekyll. The Lord Mayor believed his mistake was not creating the evil drug, but trying to separate good from evil, when what men really needed was to separate weakness from strength. He said he wanted a serum that would remove all human weakness, making the user firm, resolute, and unwavering. Elliot knew where his father kept the notes for the secret project, so that night, sobbing and terribly drunk, he stumbled down to his father's lab, turned the formula into a serum, and slid it inside his veins. The next thing he knew, he was lying on his back on the cold stone floor, staring up at his father's face and feeling a panicked fear he somehow sensed was not his own.

"I know," he said to Cam, sliding his hand back out of his grasp. "You're right. I need to move on. Just... give me a little more time."

Cam searched his face for a moment before he nodded. "Good," he said, as if his apprehension were gone. "Christ, these heart-to-hearts are exhausting. Let's not do it again."

He snapped open his cigarette case again and leaned back in his chair, masking the anxiety that still clawed at his chest, and Elliot drained the rest of his glass of champagne to block it out.

When it came time for Cam to leave and meet Andrew at the docks, Elliot claimed he wanted to stay and order something to eat at the bar so he could sober up. Once Cam was gone, however, he stayed exactly where he was, finishing the rest of the bottle of champagne by himself. When he glanced at the stage, he saw the girls were dressed in even less clothing—dark green tights with no skirts at all and black, strapless tops. Instead of dancing, they now swung from ropes designed to look like vines, twisting and contorting their bodies midair like acrobats. The lighting was dim and grotesque, and the music was ominous and dark, so Elliot put on his coat, grabbed his hat, and stumbled out.

The snow that had begun when he first arrived now coated the midnight sky, painting the sooty air and filthy streets a misleading white. Elliot, however, couldn't feel the bite of the wind or the sting of the flakes. All he could feel was the wretchedness that gnawed at his own heart.

This was to be the rest of his life: getting drunk, lying to Cam, hiding from the world, and bringing shame to his family's name. And that was the *best* prognosis. One day, Cam might finally get fed up with his behavior, or even worse, discover his secret and shun him like his father. He was the only good, true thing Elliot had left. If he lost Cam, he'd have nothing.

And not much of a reason to live.

For just a moment, when talking to Iris, he'd felt as though he could almost touch the edge of a beautiful dream, that he could dare to hope for something better in his life. But it was a cruel delusion—a lie that meant nothing in the end. There were no fields or oceans for him, no strength or fiery pride.

As he walked through the city this time, he followed the streets instead of the alleys. At midnight, few would dare to venture out without a carriage. Cam had taken a carriage both to the music hall and to the docks, and Elliot had planned to get a hansom to take him home, but somewhere between the eerie dance and snowy streets, he'd forgotten.

He ploughed on through the thickening flurry, but eventually, he realized he'd gone west instead of north. Shielding his eyes, he turned around and took another left, but the icy streets and ghostly buildings looked unfamiliar now. His blood was still warm from the alcohol but the numbness was leaving his skin, causing him to shiver beneath his hat and overcoat. The wind picked up and he stumbled against it, sure he was heading north this time, but then he sensed an approaching feeling he'd never felt before, one so strong it pierced the haze of the drink and the cold night air.

It was a hunger unlike any he'd ever known in his life, a raging desire that tore at his lungs and strangled his arid throat. Overcome, he collapsed to his knees and plunged his hands through the slush, gripping the freezing stones beneath. His chest ached and his blood burned as if it were on fire, but with the pain was also a strange and powerful elation, a high that blazed in his brain and made him feel unstoppable.

Only then did he realize what it was he must have been feeling.

He turned to see the Hyde racing toward him like a rabid dog, its bloodless skin as white as the snow that flew through the air between them. Instinctively, he reached for his gun, but between the creature's hunger and his own inebriation, he knew he'd never make a clean shot.

So he leapt to his feet and ran.

Blind fear propelled him forward, but as he pounded down the street, he realized the savage hunger he shared with the Hyde was also making him faster. But no feeling, no matter how strong, could keep him out of its reach for long, so he jumped the fence to a cramped cemetery and searched for a place to hide.

The monster followed, smashing the tops of headstones, crosses, and sculptures, its body healing immediately where the granite sliced its skin. Elliot scrambled through the cluttered darkness and blinding snow, but then he tripped on a raised tree root and plummeted to the ground. He crawled through the slush and huddled behind an enormous marble angel, but the Hyde seized the statue and tore the wings from its body like sheets of paper.

Elliot backed away along the ground, but it was no use. This was it; this was how his pathetic life would end. He would die like his mother, Andrew's father, and thousands of others, but the difference was that his demise would be completely his fault. Closing his eyes, he thought of Cam, of his mother and his father, but then something warm and wet shot through the air and sprayed his chest.

The Hyde roared, and Elliot opened his eyes to see it rear back, crimson blood spewing from a wound across its neck. At first, he couldn't see anything but a blade and a pair of hands, but then the creature crumbled onto its back.

And he saw Iris.

Immediately, the Hyde's throat began to heal where she'd sliced it, so she picked up one of the angel's wings and smashed it over its head. The creature moaned and squirmed along the ground as she rushed to where Elliot lay, thrust her hands inside his coat, and retrieved his gun from its holster. Without a word, she turned and hurried back to the writhing Hyde, shoved her boot against its face, and blasted its brainstem away.

As the shot rang out, the monster changed back to its natural, human form, and Iris stood over the body like a great avenging angel, her black coat and charcoal hair billowing in the wind, snow and smoke from the gun rising and swirling around her head. Elliot sat as still as the sculptures, thinking he might have died after all, but then she slid her knife in her boot and extended her hand toward him, her voice as solid as earth as she said, "Come on, let's go."

CHAPTER THREE

n the years before the quarantine, Elliot had often gone to the zoo in Regents Park with his mother. As young as he'd been, he recalled it clearly—the sounds and smells of the animals, the lush, colorful gardens, and the aquarium with fish from all over the world. But more than anything, he remembered his mother showing him how to paint what they'd seen when they returned home, teaching him how to shift the scenes from his mind to a fresh, white canvas.

But the Lord Mayor closed the zoo a few years after the quarantine, as the isolation and lack of resources made it too hard to maintain. The larger, more dangerous beasts were put down, the aquarium was drained, and creatures in need of special heating quickly died on their own. Now the grounds were locked and barred, and not even beggars or fugitive Hydes would dare to venture inside, as rumors of poisonous snakes, diseased bats, and mutated, inbred descendants of animals left behind abounded. So when Iris approached the back gate, slid between two warped bars, and climbed through a broken window, Elliot hesitated.

"Come on," she called above the furious roar of the rushing wind.

They needed shelter—both from the snowstorm and from more roaming Hydes, so Elliot squeezed through the bars and climbed up behind her through the window, grateful to find the alcoholic sluggishness leaving his veins.

The dark room was empty except for a desk and some yellowing papers, and Elliot guessed it was once some kind of records or finance office. His muscles relaxed, and he let out a breath, but then Iris swept right by him and opened the creaking door.

"Where are you going?" he whispered, though there wasn't a sound or a sign of life except for the whistling wind.

She gestured toward the broken window. "We'll freeze if we stay in here."

Without waiting, she walked out the door, and Elliot picked up his feet and followed her through a pitch-black hallway. The warm glow of her confidence guided him like a lamp, but then she stopped at a large, metal door, and his heart stood still.

"This is the Reptile House," he said. "We can't go in here."

Bitterness bloomed in the darkness as she muttered, "Stop joking around."

She gripped the doorknob, sending a bolt of panic through Elliot's veins, and before he could stop himself, he reached out and grabbed her by the wrist. Her heart exploded with fear and she jerked her arm away, clutching the gun she still held in her other hand. Elliot froze, stunned that a girl who'd singlehandedly killed a Hyde could be afraid of *him*. She'd just seen proof he wasn't infected, as the only people Hydes *didn't* hunt were the dead and other Hydes. But then he remembered that monsters weren't the only threat women faced.

"I'm so sorry," he said, raising his hands. "I shouldn't have done that. It's just that I don't think you realize how dangerous this place is. The zoo is filled with poisonous, diseased, and mutated creatures. The Reptile House especially."

Even in the darkness, he could see her knit her brow. "You weren't joking," she murmured in disbelief. "You really don't know."

It was Elliot's turn to look dumbfounded. "Don't know what?"

"Here," she said, gripping and turning the knob. "Let me show you."

When she opened the door, Elliot jumped—not because of what he

44

saw, but because of what he heard. The thunderous sound of beating wings erupted beyond the doorway, as well as the rustle of branches, leaves, and the tinkle of running water. The Reptile House he remembered was a cold hall of bare cement with cages along the walls, but now the floor was covered with soil, and all the cages were gone. Instead, it was filled with ferns, bushes, and even some mid-sized trees, protected by a ceiling of glass and lit by the light of the moon. A tiny waterfall trickled into a pond to Elliot's right, and a wooden path stretched from where he stood to the back of the house. But the strangest sight of all was the multitude of birds. Pheasants flapped through the braches, quails skittered across the ground, and ducks and geese splashed up and out of the pond at the disturbance.

"Bloody hell," he murmured under his breath before he could think, but when he glanced at Iris she didn't seem to be offended.

"You really didn't know about this," she marveled, closing the door.

"No," he answered, starting down the path. "What is this place?"

"It's the Lord Mayor's aviary. The forest of the king."

His stomach dropped again when he heard her treasonous tone. "What do you mean?"

"Apparently, the Empire's shipments aren't enough for him, so after he closed the zoo, he made it his personal food reserve."

A duck waddled past Elliot's feet, and he stopped and turned around. Iris's eyes were glowing like liquid sunlight in the darkness. "You eat these birds as well," she said. "Most nights, I imagine."

Elliot blinked and then stupidly lowered his gaze to his polished shoes. Never once had he stopped to think about where his food came from. How hard must it be for people like Iris to come by decent meat, something he'd been taking for granted almost all his life. Ashamed, he ran his hand through his hair, only dimly realizing he'd lost his hat somewhere in the graveyard.

"There are sheep here, too, on the northern grounds," she went on. "Some cows and goats as well. And the Lion House was converted into a giant chicken coop. Those rumors about killer bats and snakes are meant to scare people off. The Lord Mayor wants to keep his private farm private."

Elliot furrowed his brow. "How did you find out about it?"

"I knew the man who ran the Reptile House before the zoo closed. My mother... well, circumstances had left her unable to work, and he would pay me to bring him rats to feed to the lizards and snakes."

Elliot's eyes widened. "You mean you... *caught* rats in the street?"

She met his gaze as directly as Cam's when he'd asked about her father. "I'm not ashamed. We needed the money. It probably saved our lives."

"No," he said, shaking his head. "That's not what I meant. That's... that's one of the bravest things I have ever heard."

Her lips parted, betraying the shock that broke across her chest. "What?"

"You risked your life by doing that, and you were only a child. Iris— I mean, Miss Faye," he said, cursing his face as it burned. "You are the single bravest person I have ever met."

The moonlight revealed no blush in her cheeks, but Elliot sensed a sudden pulse of heat inside her heart, and it quickened his blood and emboldened him to take a step toward her.

"You saved my life tonight, Miss Faye. You *killed an active Hyde.* I've never seen a woman or man attack one the way you did."

She stared at him for a moment and then looked off into the trees. "My mother made sure I knew how to defend myself—not only from Hydes. She said it was the most important thing a girl could learn. Soon after we moved here, she paid this retired boxer to teach me how to fight. Back then, well... for the first few years we lived here we had money."

"But where did you learn how to use a gun?"

"My mother grew up on the prairie; she knew how to use a gun. I haven't shot one in years, however. They're much too expensive now."

Elliot furrowed his brow. "Are you telling me you've never killed a Hyde before tonight?"

She turned back and nodded, her lips curling up into a smile, and Elliot shook his head.

"It looked like you'd done it a hundred times. And the way you picked up that marble wing... how did you manage that?"

"You'd be surprised what a little bit of adrenaline can do." A small laugh escaped her. "Well, *a lot* of it actually."

Elliot shook his head in wonder. "But why did you do it at all? You hardly even know me, and you felt such anger toward—" He shut his mouth, his throat going dry as he realized his mistake.

"What do you mean?" she asked, uneasiness gripping her stomach. "I never felt any anger. We had a pleasant conversation."

"No, no. I'm sorry. That—that wasn't what I meant. It's just that most people wouldn't have risked their lives for a total stranger."

"You were going to die. How could I possibly stand by and do nothing?"

He smiled and shook his head again. "Most people would have done that. But you, Miss Faye... you're different. You are absolutely fearless."

She opened her mouth to reply, but then a quail flew across the path, squawking and nearly smacking her in the face as it flapped by. Caught off guard, she screamed and ducked, cowering on the ground, and once it was gone, she looked back up, and they both exploded with laughter.

"Clearly, I'm not fearless," she said, straightening up again.

"Well, quail can be rather terrifying." He laughed. "Those little beaks."

She smiled and smoothed down her dress. "You know, I am afraid sometimes. I just don't let my fears get in the way of what I want."

"And what is that?" he asked, beaming. "What is it you want?"

The remnants of her laughter died like a breeze in a sealed-off room, replaced by a longing that swelled in her chest and spread through the air between them. Its grip was magnetic, like how he imagined the pull of the ocean tide, and he found himself holding his breath, caught in the groundswell of her wanting. After a moment, she glanced behind her, staring at something beyond the trees, and when she turned around, she searched his face with uncertain eyes. Finally, she took a breath and said, "I can show you."

She started to move, but then she glanced back down at the gun in her hand. After another pause, she raised her arm and held it out. "Here," she said. "We may not be safe from quails, but we're safe from Hydes."

Elliot stared at the gun, his breath still caught inside his throat. The gesture was one of great trust, even if she could probably still cut his throat in a matter of seconds. He reached out and gently took the pistol from her hand, but as he did, his finger brushed the inside of her palm. Fire shot through his veins, and he jerked his hand away, shoving the gun in the holster strapped across his pounding chest. He stared at the ground, grateful she couldn't feel what *he* was feeling, but when he looked back up, he saw the trace of a blush in her cheeks. It was gone in a moment, however, wiped away like a trick of the light, and he scolded himself for thinking the fire was anything but his own.

"The head of the Reptile House was discharged as soon as the zoo was closed," she said, stepping off the path and beckoning Elliot to follow. "He was a kind man, and he knew about my interests, so he left me the only key to his office, back behind these trees."

Elliot hurried after her, dodging bushes and birds until they reached the far right wall. There, in a heavy shadow, was the outline of a door.

"The people who tend the birds have never bothered to break inside," she continued, shoving a branch aside and pulling a key from her coat pocket. "I come here sometimes when... well, when I need to get away."

She turned the key, opened the door, climbed the single step that led to the threshold, and walked inside. Elliot followed, shivering as he entered the dark room, which seemed utterly frigid after the warmth of the aviary. Light bloomed as Iris struck a match and lit a lamp, revealing a small, windowless office much like the first one they entered. This one, however, was not bare but covered with framed pictures—charts, maps, and scientific illustrations of birds. The desk that contained the lamp was smooth, clean, and free of dust, and three worn, leather-bound books were stacked upon its surface.

"The zoo had a real aviary once. Do you remember?" she asked.

"Yes. But it was outside. And it was only a handful of cages."

"Exactly," she said, tossing the match in a bin. "A small collection.

Not nearly enough for a long-term, sustainable food supply." She gestured toward the walls. "These belonged to the man who ran it. He was a scientist who traveled the world studying birds. Well, I suppose he still is," she added. "He was lucky. When the quarantine was enacted, he was somewhere in Africa."

Her gaze drifted up to the maps, and her wave of longing returned, but then an enormous gander waddled aggressively into the room, honking, charging Elliot, and snapping at his legs. He yelped, shooed the bird back out, and then slammed and latched the door, but then he realized how inappropriate such an action was. He and Iris had clearly been unchaperoned in the aviary, but being alone in a dim, closed room seemed much more improper. He turned around to see if she was frightened or offended, but she was nearly falling over the desk with wild laughter.

"Well," he said, attempting to hide his blush, "you must admit, that gander was much larger than the quail that accosted you."

She straightened up and took a few deep breaths. "That's true, he was. And in spite of what you may have gathered from the quail encounter, I actually adore birds. That's what I wanted to show you."

She seated herself at the desk and gestured for him to sit as well, so he picked up a wooden stool from beside the door and pulled up beside her.

"Before he left, the reptile master gave me everything the ornithologist left behind. That's where I got the maps and illustrations, as well as these." She picked up the stack of leather-bound books as if she were lifting a child and placed them on her lap, running her fingers over the surface. "These are his journals—all the research and findings from his travels. The top one is from Antarctica; he studied a group of penguins there before he came to the zoo." Delicately, she held out the stack and placed it in Elliot's hands. "The other two are from Rio de Janeiro and India."

Elliot tried to be gentle as he opened the first book's cover, but Iris's pulsing excitement made it hard to steady his hand, and he wondered if she'd ever shared these treasures with anyone else. It occurred to him then how isolated and lonely her life must be. No other girl in the city could have half her education, not even the somewhat cultured ladies of the upper class. How frustrating must it be to have a full and brilliant mind but no one in your life to understand or stimulate it?

"This is written in Latin," he said, frowning down at the page.

"It is," she beamed. "The reptile master couldn't believe I could read it."

"But why would the ornithologist bother to write his journal in Latin?"

Iris didn't blush, and her breathing didn't quicken, but Elliot felt a sudden surge of embarrassment within her. "The other two are written in English—they're his original journals—but the one from Antarctica is a copy he transcribed. It was going to be published just before the quarantine, and I think he only wanted scientists to be able to read it."

Elliot nearly laughed. "Why? What could be so shocking and top-secret about penguins?"

Her discomfort grew, but her hands were calm as she reached out and took the books back. "I couldn't say. And I've read them all at least a dozen times."

She placed the stack on the desk, and Elliot shook his head in wonder. When it came to hiding feelings, Cam had nothing on this girl.

"I'm showing you these because you asked what it is I want," she continued, her sea of yearning rising up and swallowing him again. "This is it. I want to be an ornithologist. I want to travel the world observing and finding new species of birds."

"That's wonderful," Elliot murmured. "That is absolutely brilliant."

She raised a skeptical eyebrow. "You don't... think the idea's mad?"

"Why would it be mad? It couldn't be more perfect. Who better to brave the jungle and make new discoveries than someone who's as fearless and intelligent as you?"

She stared at him for a long time and then quickly looked away, feeling too many conflicting emotions for him to discern them clearly. "Of course," she said, masking her turbulent storm with a steady voice. "In order for that to happen, my other dream must come true first."

Elliot nodded. She didn't need to say what the other dream was: a cure and an end to quarantine. "That's everybody's dream."

A cold wind of bitterness blew through her storm and she started to laugh. "Please," she scoffed. "Of course that isn't everybody's dream."

"What?" he asked, certain he couldn't have heard her right.

"Why would Harlan Branch ever want the quarantine lifted? Before the Hydes, he was just a mayor, and now he's the undisputed king of his own personal kingdom." She sat up straight and met his gaze, her eyes beginning to burn. "And what of the knights and baronets? A decade ago they barely ranked above the middle class, but now that all the dukes and earls are gone, they're London's peerage, and those in Branch's inner circle are practically royalty." Her bitterness sharpened, and this time she made no attempt to hide it. "Like you, for example. You would have been just the son of another doctor, but now you're a virtual prince, complete with a palace full of servants."

Elliot's mouth went dry. "You don't know anything about me."

"I know enough to know you're better off without a cure."

He gaped at her, anger spreading like venom through his veins. "Look, I know more than you can imagine about how hard others have it. No one deserves to be trapped inside this hellhole of a city, and even if you were right about me, I'd still want a cure for *them*." He took a breath and shoved a trembling hand through his tangled hair. "Yes, it's true—I'm fortunate. But if you think that London's not a nightmare for me as well, you're wrong. I want to escape as much as you, and I'd give up a hundred palaces to have my mother back."

Iris blinked. "Your... your mother was killed by a Hyde?"

"Of course she was. Just like everyone else's mother."

He spit the words cruelly, parroting what she'd said at the music hall. His pain and anger were so overwhelming he simply couldn't help it, and he found himself staring at her in a sort of heated challenge. But the bitterness was gone from both her eyes and heart by then, replaced by a sad and stunned remorse.

As well as pity.

"Don't," he muttered, rising from the stool and walking away.

"Don't what?"

He turned his back and closed his eyes. "Don't... pity me."

"I don't. I mean, well, of course I do a bit—I can't help being sorry—but more than anything I'm surprised. I thought women like that were safe."

He released a ragged breath. "She would have been. But she ran out of white."

"What do you mean she 'ran out of white?'"

Elliot turned back around, swallowing hard before he spoke. "My mother was an artist—a painter—and after the quarantine it was hard for her to obtain supplies. The Lord Mayor only requested a small amount each month, and he only did that because of his relationship with my father. One day, when I was twelve, my mother was frantic for white paint. It's impossible to paint without it—white not only softens colors but adds the illusion of light. She'd been without it for over a week, and well..."

He sighed and took a step closer, struggling to explain. "For my mother, painting wasn't merely a hobby. It was like... breathing. When she couldn't paint, she felt suffocated. It nearly drove her mad. Normally, our servants brought her supplies when the shipments came in, but the next slated import day was at least two weeks away. Before the quarantine, she bought her supplies at a shop in the Strand, and even though it had likely closed, she was desperate enough to try. She didn't trust anyone else to find the place or get just what she wanted, and since it was broad daylight, she decided to go on her own."

The memory sharpened, twisting like a dagger in Elliot's stomach, but he found himself unable to stop the story from pouring out. "Hours later, she hadn't returned, so Cam and I went out to find her; my father was at work and I remembered the shop's location. We found her in an alley near the church of St. Mary-le-Strand. A small crowd had already gathered and someone had covered her chest and face with a rough scrap of canvas, but I knew it was her as soon as I saw the tube of paint, crushed flat and staining her hand and the street beneath it white."

He took a breath and sat back down on the stool, rubbing his brow. "My father blamed her death on art. He called her passion a malady and locked the room she'd used as her studio at the palace. I knew where he kept the key, however, and for a while I snuck inside to paint when he was out; I'd found two tubes of white unharmed inside her reticule."

Iris searched him silently, and for once, he was glad for the pain that came with his mother's memory. It muffled the pity he knew she must have been feeling for him then.

"So, you're a painter as well?" she finally asked, her voice grown soft.

"No. I mean, I was... once. Or rather, I wanted to be. My mother used to say she would take me to Paris when London was free, so I could study painting in the capital of art." He ran a hand through his hair again, swallowing a hunger he hadn't felt in years. "But I couldn't paint for very long after she was killed. I tried, but I suppose the memories made it all too painful."

He glanced back up and looked at her through the dim and flickering light. Their eyes locked, and something strange stirred inside his chest, something sharp but also sweet, like the clang of the bells at St. Paul's. It was so unfamiliar and overwhelming he wasn't even sure to whom the feeling really belonged, and he rose to his feet and walked away, shoving his hands in his pockets.

"It was for the best, however," he said, pacing before the door. "Medicine was the practical profession to undertake. Although," he added, nearly, laughing. "I can't even do that now."

"Why not?"

He froze where he stood and cleared his throat. "It's a long story."

"I don't mind long stories. You've been listening to me all night."

"Yes, but the things you have to say are actually interesting. You're hopeful and bright and alive, and I wish..." He swallowed and turned away. "I wish I could be more like you."

In spite of the heat of his feelings, he shivered, chilled to the bone in the frigid room, and Iris rose from her chair and took a hesitant step toward him. "Maybe we should go into the aviary. It's warmer."

Elliot turned to look at her. The coat she wore was thinner than his, and her petal-pink dress was sleeveless. "It's strange," he said, furrowing his brow. "You don't seem cold."

Panic shot through her body like the snap of someone's fingers, and she rubbed her hands together, shivering just as fiercely as him. "Of course I'm cold. It's freezing in here. Come on, let's go back out."

"Wait," he said, raising his hand as she moved toward the door. "I haven't been much of a gentlemen tonight. Please, allow me."

He opened the door and stepped out into the warmth of the aviary, descending the single stair and turning to offer her his hand. She looked at him for a moment and then slowly extended her own, and he held his breath, preparing for the jolt of physical contact. But then the hostile gander from before flapped onto the stair and snapped at Iris's skirt, sending her stumbling into the doorframe. She reached for the open door in an attempt to regain her balance, but her hand slipped from the jagged edge and she fell.

Into Elliot's arms.

She crashed against him, her arms flying up around his neck, and his hands slid up beneath her coat as he caught her around the waist and staggered back against a tree. Fire tore through his blood, and he swallowed a guttural cry; their bodies were touching at almost every possible point of contact. Her dress was so thin he could feel the warmth of her thighs against his own, as well as the intricate lacing of her corset in the back. Smoke and beer clung to her hair, but her skin smelled healthy and clean, and her fresh, full lips were slightly parted in a gasp. He stared at her mouth, a heavy ache spreading through his chest, and when he looked up, he saw that she was staring at him as well. Their hearts beat together, creating a tangible heat between them, and this time he was certain that it wasn't all his own.

But then a bolt of pain shot up his leg, and he stumbled away. The blasted gander was back on the ground and nipping at his trousers. "Bloody hell!" he cried, smacking his head on a nearby branch. "Get the hell away from us, you bloody disgusting bird!" He shooed it away, kicking a wild foot in the creature's direction, but Iris stopped him, grabbing his wrist and pulling him up the stair.

"Let's go back inside. There is no escaping that beast."

She hauled him into the office, released his wrist, and closed the door, and Elliot rubbed the place where she'd touched him, confusion cooling his blood. Her heart had been pounding as violently as his a moment ago, but when she seized his wrist, his fingers had closed around hers as well, and even though her feelings hadn't changed, her pulse had steadied.

"I suppose adoring birds does not ensure they'll adore me back," she said, turning around to face him. "Although, I must admit, I detest that sort of goose. It's nothing like the wild geese I remember from back home. People call them Canada geese, but they live in America, too, and every summer they filled the lake just north of my family's farm." She strolled to the desk, her wistful voice masking her nervous tension. "They're elegant birds with long, black necks and a splash of white on their heads, and I used to love watching them take off from the water and fly through the air, forming a perfect arrow as they soared above our pecan grove." She brushed her hair back over her shoulder, and something caught Elliot's eye.

"Iris—I mean, Miss Faye—look at your hand. I think you're hurt."

He took a step toward her, and she opened her left hand. A dark streak of blood smeared the center of her palm.

"Did you cut it when you—" he began, but then his voice dissolved. The blood was new—fresh and wet.

But there was no wound beneath.

She jerked her hand away and wiped it off inside her pocket. "I think it's only dirt. From when I tried to grab the door." She turned around and crossed to the opposite side of the room. "We should get some sleep before the birds' caretakers arrive. They'll be here in the morning, which is just a few hours away, and I don't want to be miserable and exhausted at work tomorrow."

Elliot's stomach turned; he had to work tomorrow, too. When his father refused to continue his education, he gave him a job—a grim, disgusting business he tried not to think about.

"You're right," he said. "We should get some rest." He approached her, removing his overcoat. "Please, take my coat."

"There's no need. Really, I'm fine."

"I insist," he said, holding it out. "You'll freeze in that."

She let out a breath and took the coat. "Thank you, Mr. Morrissey."

"Please, call me Elliot."

She looked at him, her eyes burning embers in the darkness, but then she turned away and wrapped the coat around her shoulders, murmuring "thank you," again and crouching down against the wall.

Elliot rubbed his arms and crossed to the other side of the office. The floor creaked as he lowered himself against the opposite wall, but other than that, the dim, frigid room was utterly silent. He closed his eyes and took a breath, wondering how in the world he could sleep with Iris a few feet away, but then her bright, sparkling voice rang out across the room.

"Elliot?"

It was as if he'd heard his name for the first time in his life. "Yes?"

For a moment, she didn't speak, and her face was lost in the shadows, but then she finally said, "If you want, you can call me Iris."

A smile spread across his face. "Goodnight, Iris. Sleep well."

Eventually, exhaustion overpowered his excitement, and he curled up against the wooden floor and drifted off. At first, his dreams were as empty and cold as the freezing boards beneath him, but then a heavy warmth began to creep inside his brain. He saw Iris standing in a grove of golden trees, watching a flock of wild geese soaring above the branches. She turned to him, smiled, and reached out to take his hand, and when he clasped her fingers, he could have sworn the touch was real.

The next thing he knew, however, he was waking up in the cold, feeling as though he'd slept beside a fire that had died. His overcoat was draped over his body like a blanket, and when he sat up and rubbed his eyes, he saw that she was gone.

CHAPTER FOUR

ris plowed through the ankle-deep snow as she crossed the
Waterloo Bridge. A bleak, grey sun was rising over the Thames, but
even though the sky had cleared, a frigid wind was blowing. Her foot
slipped, but she righted herself and hurried even faster. She should
have been home six hours ago, and her mother would be frantic.

Of course, she knew that would be the case as soon as the sons of
Harlan Branch and his doctor fell into her lap. She'd planned to follow
Cambrian back to the palace when he left, hoping to either sneak in or
find out how to get past the guards, but instead of heading north, his
carriage had set off toward the docks. When Elliot stumbled out, she
thought she'd gotten her second chance, but then he lost his way and
got attacked.

And everything changed.

Although, if she was honest, things had already changed before
that. The two princes were nothing at all like she'd imagined they'd be.
She'd always assumed they were spoiled brats like the aptly named
Charlie Hands, who believed that being the son of a judge entitled him
to deflower any "flower" he wanted at *La Maison Des Fleurs*. Iris was
used to fending off advances from boys like Charlie, but Cambrian
Branch, the most important and—as she had heard—most handsome
young man in all of London, had not only been respectful but had

nearly burst with excitement when she talked of the outside world. And as for Elliot Morrissey...

She stopped at the edge of the bridge, clenching her fists and taking a breath. It was better not to think too much about Elliot Morrissey.

As she hurried down Waterloo Road and into the lower marsh, however, she realized there were some things even she could not control. His messy hair and boyish grin were emblazoned on her mind, as were his eyes, which were not only lush and green as the aviary, but also wide and clear, as if incapable of pretense. His voice was the same way—raw, emotional, and exposed—and perhaps that was why she'd shared the things she'd shared with him last night, why she'd felt entranced when he talked about his mother and his painting, and why she'd believed him when he told her he thought her dreams were "brilliant."

Her skin warmed as the wind picked up, but not of her own volition. If only she could control her feelings as well as she could hide them.

The lower marsh market was already filling with merchants, wagons, and carts, and Iris picked up her pace, returning her focus to her mother. The Empire's monthly supplies must have come in the day before, as Mr. McKenna's fruit stand on Roberts was actually stocked with fruit. She paused as she passed it, eyeing a box of decent-looking pears. Her mother loved pears, and a gift might help to soften a bit of her anger, but their rent was due tomorrow, and they simply couldn't afford it.

She let out a breath and turned the corner, cursing herself for refusing Cambrian's money the night before. Only a fool would pass up the offer of coins for a conversation, but after getting to know and even like him, it had seemed wrong. Clearly, neither he nor Elliot knew what their fathers were doing, but they were still a part the system she'd sworn to herself to bring down. If she couldn't change the way she felt, she'd find a way to ignore it. Nothing and no one could stand in the way of her only chance at freedom. Even a boy who had looked at her as if he could see her soul.

And smiled as if he'd never seen anything so beautiful.

She shook the thought away as she approached her tenement

building, which stood in the shadow of the old Southwestern Railway Station. As she climbed the steps to their flat on the second floor, she slowed her breathing, hoping to calm her mother with a cool, serene appearance. But even before she'd closed the door behind her, she heard her voice.

"Iris Faye!" she hissed. "Where in God's name have you been?"

She shot up out of her makeshift desk and barreled across the room. Dark circles ringed her eyes, and her face was pale as death. She clearly hadn't slept all night.

And it was all Iris's fault.

"Mama, I'm so sorry—"

"Iris, you answer my question now."

She looked up into her mother's eyes, eyes that had been frightened ever since she could remember. Even before Lady Cullum was killed and the two of them went into hiding—in fact, even before they left the farm and came to London—her mother had been afraid, insecure, and somehow broken. Iris had never understood how a woman so strong and brave could believe she was neither, but mystery was another part of living with her mother, who stored as many secrets in her heart as she did fears.

Still, until that moment, she had thought she would tell her the truth, but now that she was staring into her eyes, the idea seemed crazy. *Well, mother, I tried to follow the son of one of your greatest enemies into Buckingham Palace, even though you expressly forbid me to ever go near the place. Then I attacked a Hyde that was about to kill the boy, even though I wasn't sure he would have a gun I could use. Then I went to the zoo, where—once again—you told me never to go, and spent the night beside him, holding his hand to keep him warm.*

"One of the other girls lost the key to her flat," she said instead. "She was scared to walk to her cousin's place in Limehouse, so I went with her."

A groan of relief escaped her mother's lips, and Iris felt sick. Her ability to conceal any physical "tells" made her an excellent liar, but it didn't stop a wave of guilt from rising in her throat.

Choke it down, she told herself. *You did it for her own good. Besides, with all the secrets she keeps, it's only fair for you to have your own every once in a while.*

"But why are you only getting home now?" her mother asked, rubbing her brow. "Limehouse is only an hour away."

"I stayed with her at her cousin's place until the storm had passed."

Her mother raised an eyebrow. They both knew Iris was hardly at risk of freezing to death in a storm.

"To avoid suspicions," she added quickly. "I couldn't very well walk into a blizzard in front of her."

"I suppose you're right," her mother said, exhaling. "And what you did was kind, but it was also dangerous, Iris. You mustn't do it again."

"Mama, you know I'm not in danger. The Hydes can't hurt—"

"Yes, they can. You have a strong defense mechanism, but you are not immune. Besides…" Her grey eyes darkened like the sky before a storm. "Hydes are not the only danger out there. You understand?"

Iris sighed. "I understand. I won't let it happen again."

"Good." She let out another breath and ran a hand through Iris's hair, which was just as dark and thick as her own. "So you haven't slept at all?"

"No," she replied, and this time she was actually telling the truth. She'd planned to sleep while holding Elliot's hand to keep him warm, but once their bodies were close again, she found she didn't want to. His heartbeat was hypnotic, and his breathing was like a spell, and she only barely stopped herself from curling up in his arms, which had felt so firm and strong when he caught her…

Iris, stop it now.

"We should probably get some sleep before our shifts," her mother said. "At least a couple of hours."

Iris nodded, removing her coat as her guilt rose once again. Both of them worked the same hours—from noon to ten each night—but her mother didn't have her strength, and her job was much more demanding. Iris had to deal with loud-mouth drunks and wandering hands, but her mother, who was a piece of paper away from being a doctor, spent ten hours a day in the cellar of a pub, washing mugs and dishes in the dim, foul-smelling air.

She'd wanted Iris to do the same, as she felt the safest jobs were those where they would never be seen, but Iris knew her youth and beauty could make her twice as much as a waitress in a restaurant. The prospect had worried her mother, of course, but the money was just too tempting. Neither of them wanted to relive that terrible year after Lady Cullum's death, when it was still too dangerous for her mother to show her face, and Iris had to catch rats in order to keep them both alive.

"Here, let me help you undress," her mother said, unlacing her dress, and Iris groaned, hating the fact that her mother had to undress her. Dishwashers could wear practical dresses and corsets that fastened in front, allowing them the ability to change without assistance. The waitresses at *La Maison Des Fleurs*, however, had to wear back-lacing corsets, as customers enjoyed the smaller waists that they created.

When Iris was finally free of all her clothing but her chemise and drawers, her mother walked to the desk and returned with three copper pennies. "Make sure you eat before work," she said, placing the coins in her palm. "The pie shop on James Street should have fresh meat since the shipments came in yesterday. Don't worry, we'll still have enough for Mrs. Granby's rent."

"You can have it. I'm not hungry."

"That doesn't mean you don't need to eat. I'll buy some oysters on my break tonight. Now go to sleep."

There was no arguing with her, so Iris placed the coins in the pocket of her coat and crawled onto the mattress the two of them called a bed. Her mother, however, did not undress, but returned to her seat at the desk.

"What are you doing?" Iris asked. "Aren't you coming to bed?"

"I just need to go over a few more figures." She smoothed down a piece of paper covered in scribbles and dipped a quill in ink. "It wouldn't be so difficult if I had some actual lab equipment. Or at least a book or study written in this century."

Iris's muscles stiffened. Her mother's life consisted of working and looking for a cure, which no one in London but Dr. Morrissey was allowed to do. The breach of the rules didn't worry her—if her mother were found, she'd be dead no matter what laws she'd disobeyed. What she couldn't stand was watching her sacrifice sleep and sanity for something that was not the real solution to their problems.

"Mama," she began, smoothing and softening her voice. "I overheard a few of the other waitress at work last night, and they said the palace is looking to hire more parlor maids for the season."

The scratching of her mother's pen came to a halt. Then, without looking up, she took a breath and resumed her writing. "Iris, we've discussed this. The palace is out of the question."

"I'm pretty enough to be a parlor maid, and Mr. Dorset likes me. I'm sure he would give me a good reference—"

"Iris, the subject is closed."

"But Mama, it would change everything if I could get inside. I could prove what the Lord Mayor is doing—"

"Iris, it *isn't safe.*"

"Not for you, but none of them even know that I exist! The only person who knew you had a daughter was Lady Cullum and she—"

"Is *dead!*" her mother exclaimed, bolting up out of her chair. "And if they find out who you really are, we will be, too."

Silence filled the room, swelling and thinning the air between them. Iris's fingers curled around the patchwork quilt beneath her. The grandmother she'd barely known had sewn it back in Kansas, but Lady Cullum had draped it over Iris's body in bed at night, singing her to sleep when her mother was working late at the lab. Tears stung her eyes, and she quickly fought them back. Crying wouldn't help her cause or avenge Lady Cullum's death.

"Iris, please understand," her mother said, rubbing her temples. "I'm trying to protect you. You don't know what the Lord Mayor is like, the things he is capable of."

Iris clenched her jaw and looked away. Of course she knew.

"I'll make things right. I promise," she continued, sitting beside her.

"Look at me, Iris. I mean it. I am going to find a cure."

Iris raised her head and stared directly into her eyes. "A cure won't do any good as long as the Lord Mayor is in power."

Her mother swallowed, rose to her feet, and returned to her place at the desk. "That isn't our concern. We're hardly equipped to bring down a government, Iris. A cure is the answer."

She sat back down and picked up her pen, ending the conversation, and Iris glared at her back, burning with questions she couldn't ask.

Why can't you see how strong I am—how strong we both could be? Why do you refuse to face the truth of what must be done? Why do you tell me everything about the world's evils but nothing about what's on your mind?

Or who my father was?

Iris had given up asking her mother about him years ago, as the only response she'd ever received was that the man was dead, and because of that, no other information was necessary. Her mother's replies to her musings about her abilities were the same:

"When God gives you a gift, Iris, you don't ask why it was given. All you need to worry about is keeping your secret safe."

And Iris had; even Lady Cullum never knew. Last night, however, she'd almost made the mistake of letting Elliot see, and as she crawled beneath the quilt, she promised herself she would never be so careless about it again.

She curled up on her side, but when she did, she saw Elliot's face—beautiful, peaceful, and inches away from her own, as it was last night. No matter how hard she tried, she couldn't wipe the image away, so she blocked it out by escaping into a sea of unconsciousness.

CHAPTER FIVE

After making his way past the iron fence and the Yeomen of the Guard, Elliot entered the palace through the Privy Purse door as always. He looked dirty and disheveled after sleeping in his clothes on the dusty wooden floor, but none of the servants felt any curiosity as he passed them. Over the last two weeks, he'd learned that most people were too focused on themselves to notice the people around them, but if anyone could have seen into his heart, they would have been utterly blinded by the fire that burned within it.

He should have been worried and panicked; he'd slept too long and missed his job—the only thing that made him remotely useful to his father—but there wasn't enough space left in his mind to worry about it. His thoughts were wrapped in the green of the aviary and gold of Iris's eyes, and all he could feel was the strange sensation that he had just been born.

The fierce, giddy brightness in his chest increased as he turned the corner, coming to a head as he collided with Cam and Andrew. The two of them were emerging from the door to the butler's pantry, where Cam hid the majority of his contraband imports. They were laughing together, Cam's hand resting on Andrew's shoulder, but their glee dissolved when Elliot stumbled directly into them. Cam jerked his hand away from Andrew's shoulder and steadied Elliot's arm, revealing a sudden bolt of nervous tension in his veins. Elliot blinked, unsure as to why Cam would suddenly feel so anxious, but then he remembered how worried he had been about him lately.

"I'm fine," he said quickly. "I know I look like a wreck, but I'm fine, really."

Cam quirked his lips up into a grin, masking a rush of relief. "You always look like a wreck," he said, drawing back his hand. "But now you look like a wreck that spent the night on the floor of a bawd-house."

Elliot's face reddened at the mention of such a place, or perhaps at the memory of how he'd felt when Iris was pressed against him.

"Bloody hell," Cam said, his eyes going wide. "You actually *did*?"

"What? No, of course not!" he stammered.

Cam's grin broadened. "You know, when I told you to get out and live your life, that's not what I meant."

"Cam—"

"Don't get me wrong. I'm rather impressed. Though I don't think I'd like you to come near my bedclothes again—"

"Cambrian."

Andrew's voice was soft, just like everything else about him, but there was a sort of purity and strength about his softness. His light brown eyes were gentle, but they also never wavered, and he carried his slight, boyish body with quiet confidence. Before meeting Andrew, Cam had often mocked boys with ginger hair, but it was hard to criticize someone so warm and self-possessed. He was also the only person with the power to shut Cam up, something Elliot had never accomplished in his life.

"Elliot," Andrew said. "Are you sure that you're all right?"

Elliot took a breath and raised his head to meet his gaze. Andrew's feelings flowed nearly as freely as his own, and looking into his eyes could often be as powerful and painful as physical contact. Now, as always, he saw and felt his genuine affection, as well as the utter forgiveness that he knew he didn't deserve.

"Yes, I'm fine. It's just... it's a long story," he finally answered.

"We have a story as well," Cam said in a hushed, conspiratorial tone. "My sailor came through with those new, twelve-inch records I told you about, and Andrew thinks he can have the Victor repaired by tomorrow night."

"If I can get a part I need," Andrew interjected. "I'm going to look at a pawnbroker's shop in the Strand this afternoon."

Cam's excitement swelled as he leaned a little closer. "But the best part is what's on the records. It's a *new* kind of music."

Elliot's lips parted. "New?"

"Danny—my sailor—he left me a note that said it's a genre called 'Ragtime.' Apparently, it's the most popular thing in America right now. He brought two songs—*The Pine Apple Rag* and *The Weeping Willow Rag.*"

"I wonder what it sounds like," Elliot murmured, as breathless as Cam. The Lord Mayor had a private orchestra for balls and parties, but they played songs that were popular in Queen Victoria's day. As Cam had observed at the music hall, nothing new had been written inside London for nearly a decade. With the symphonies disbanded, and people struggling to survive, it wasn't a very fertile place for new artistic creations.

"I don't know," Cam said, his eyes alight. "But we'll find out tomorrow."

"*If* I can get that part and fix the Victor," Andrew reminded him.

"You will," he replied. "I have no doubts. You're a technological genius."

They looked at each other, creating a sudden tug of warmth between them, and Elliot turned away, biting back his jealousy. He knew he shouldn't begrudge their friendship; Andrew had been a better friend to Cam than he had lately, and it was only natural that the two of them had grown close. Still, he couldn't help the feeling that Cam belonged to him.

"Jennie!" Cam cried.

A parlor maid who'd been passing them stopped in her tracks.

Unlike Cam, who was interested in everything and everyone, Elliot had never paid much attention to the staff, but even he had noticed this particular parlor maid. She had the kind of beauty girls possessed in fairy tales—pale skin, rosebud lips, and shining golden hair. At the moment, she was carrying a basket of freshly cut flowers, and when Cam called out, she nearly spilled them all onto the floor.

"Yes, sir," she said, dipping her head and dropping into a curtsy.

Elliot turned away and shoved his hands inside his pockets. Before his botched experiment, he'd noticed Jennie's beauty, but now she compelled his attention for an entirely different reason: She wanted Cam with every single fiber of her being.

"I found something in yesterday's shipments that made me think of you," Cam said, reaching into his pocket and removing a small glass jar. "It's a hand salve from Scotland that's supposed to repair dry skin. I remembered you telling me once that your hands get chapped in the winter months."

Jennie jerked her head back up, her porcelain face on fire. Her gaze darted from Cam over to Elliot and Andrew, betraying the horror she felt at their knowing she'd dared to have such an intimate conversation with her employer.

"I can't accept that," she said. "I'm sorry, sir. It wouldn't be proper."

"Please," Cam insisted, taking her white-gloved hand and placing the jar in her palm. "I know you work hard, and things like this are difficult to come by."

Her heart bloomed with adoration so fierce her discomfort dissolved, and Elliot swallowed and studied the Persian rug beneath his feet. In his peripheral vision, he saw Andrew doing the same. Her feelings must have been clear even to people who couldn't feel them—at least, to people who weren't Cam, who was not only smiling obliviously but feeling nothing at all for her but friendly admiration.

"Thank you, sir," she said, falling into a curtsy again. Then she cleared her throat and placed the jar in her apron pocket, murmuring, "You're very kind," before taking off down the corridor.

Elliot let out a breath as soon as her feelings were out of range, removing his hands from his pockets and then wiping his brow with the sleeve of his coat.

Andrew turned to Cam, hesitating before he spoke. "Cambrian, I know you meant well, but you shouldn't give gifts to that girl."

Cam raised an eyebrow. "Why not? She'd never get a hold of something like that all on her own."

"I know but, well, she fancies you, and such gestures might... lead her on."

"Lead her on?" Cam laughed. "I was only being kind—"

"I know, but she might see another meaning in your kindness. And if your father found out—"

"Andrew..." Elliot's voice caught in his throat, because it was too late. That cold, metallic, strangely shameful fear had crept inside Cam's blood, so sharp and pervasive, Elliot could feel it in his teeth.

The Lord Mayor detested Cam's affection for the help, claiming it made him look "common," "servile," and "spineless as a woman." At a dinner party when he was fourteen, Cam left his seat to help a maid clean up the tray of china she'd dropped, and in response, his father dragged him out into the hall, calling him an embarrassment and smacking him across the face so hard the whole room could hear it. Now, Elliot felt him shutting down like a waterlogged clock, and though Andrew couldn't feel it, he could sense what he'd done wrong.

"I'm sorry," he said. "It's not my place to tell you what to do."

"Don't worry about it," Cam replied, adjusting the cuffs of his sleeves and flashing them both a brilliant smile. "The two of you worry too much. That's why you need me so desperately."

Elliot tried to force a reciprocal grin, and Andrew nodded. "Well, I'd better go," he said. "I'm late enough as it is."

He started down the hall, and Elliot squinted in confusion. Andrew worked primarily on the second floor of the palace, where the only telegraph in all of London was located, but he was heading toward the garden exit, not the stairs.

"Are you working outside the palace this morning?" Elliot called after him. Besides being the Lord Mayor's personal telegraph operator, Andrew often acted as a second secretary, which sometimes required errands off the grounds, but only rarely.

Andrew stopped and turned around, guilt pricking his chest. "The Lord Mayor has business elsewhere and doesn't need me today. He gave me the day off, but I... I need to tend to my mother."

Elliot's own chest flooded with shame, and he stared down at the floor. When Robert Heron was killed, and the Lord Mayor gave his job to Andrew, he also offered to let him and his mother live at the palace. Anyone else would have gladly accepted, but Andrew's mother refused to live on the grounds where her husband was murdered. According to Andrew, she'd been rather fragile before his death, and afterward, she became reclusive and "somewhat hysterical." When he wasn't working, he cared for her as if she were an ailing child, and all because of Elliot and his act of cowardice.

But why did *Andrew* feel guilty about mentioning his mother? Because he knew that doing so would make Elliot feel ashamed? Elliot sighed and ran a weary hand through his tangled hair. Why the hell did Andrew have to be so bloody selfless?

"I'll see you both at dinner," Andrew said, and he went on his way.

After a moment, Elliot turned to Cam and cleared his throat. "So, formal dinner tonight?" he asked.

"Yes, by the Lord Mayor's decree."

Aside from the nearly two hundred bedrooms for live-in servants and staff, Buckingham Palace had more than fifty royal living quarters, which were not only occupied by Cam and Elliot and their fathers, but also by the current families in the Lord Mayor's favor. As Iris had said, there really was a sort of royal court—a household of people akin to the courtiers of King Henry XIII. Often, they ate and socialized in self-made, shifting groups, but when Cam's father declared a formal dinner, they all attended.

"That's the second one this week," Elliot said, though he'd missed the first, feigning illness and drinking a bottle of wine in his room instead.

"He probably wants to discuss the upcoming season," Cam replied, sliding his hands in his pockets and strolling toward the northern stairs. "It may have snowed last night, but it will be April first on Monday."

Elliot fell into step beside him. "What's there to discuss?"

"I wouldn't be surprised if he wants to lower the age of debut again."

The London season used to begin when Parliament adjourned shortly after Easter Sunday, but now that there was no Parliament, it started around the first of April and ended around July. With no more opera, theatre, or annual art exhibitions, the season consisted entirely of private balls and parties, which Elliot found to be tedious, and Cam found extremely outdated. The season was, at heart, a marriage market for the wealthy—a chance for well-bred girls to make good matches with well-bred boys. Because of that, the girls could not attend until they "came out," a transition that meant they were part of society and ready for marriage. Traditionally, a girl came out at seventeen or eighteen, but in recent years, the Lord Mayor had lowered the age to sixteen.

"The idea is ancient," Cam went on as they walked down the hall together. "Did you know that outside London, there are these women called 'Bachelor Girls' who leave their parents without getting married? They live on their own and support themselves. The sailors told me about it."

"But wait," Elliot said, confused. "Why would he lower the age *again*?"

Cam didn't slow his pace, but something cold ran through his veins, like an aftershock of the fear he felt before. "You've heard his speeches. He's obsessed with getting the whole world married off and reproducing."

It was true; the Lord Mayor often spoke about the importance of replenishing London's dwindling population. Elliot had never understood the logic behind it, as there didn't seem to be enough resources as it was. But then, he hadn't known about the royal food reserve.

"Cam, did you know the rumors about the zoo being filled with dangerous, mutated animals aren't true?

Cam stopped and furrowed his brow. As Elliot had guessed, he hadn't known about it, either. He went on to explain everything he'd learned last night, and when Cam asked how he'd found it out, he told him about Iris—how she'd saved him in the cemetery and taken him to the zoo, but not the way he felt about her or the dreams she'd shared with him. His memory of the night felt closed and sacred to him now, like a folded piece of paper that belonged to them alone.

"Bloody hell," Cam murmured, sitting down on the nearby stairs. "She jumped on a Hyde, slit its throat, and shot it with your gun?"

"And hit it over the head with a chunk of marble," Elliot added, lowering onto the velvet step beside him.

Cam shook his head, his eyes still wide. "If we ever go back to *La Maison Des Fleurs*, remind me not to provoke her."

Elliot laughed and a pocket of warmth broke open in his chest, calming his mind and alleviating his over-burdened heart. That was the power of laughter, he realized, and also the power of Cam. He possessed the rare capacity to create joy out of nothing, a quality as precious as it was miraculous.

And one of the many reasons Elliot couldn't bear to lose him, which he knew he would if he ever found out he'd been spying on his feelings.

"But seriously," Cam said. "When are you going to see her again?"

Elliot's cheeks burned beneath his penetrating gaze. As he should have known, not mentioning his feelings didn't mean they hadn't shown up on his face. During his walk to the palace, he'd thought of nothing but seeing Iris again, but now that he was back, things seemed much more complicated.

"I don't know if she'd want to see me," he answered honestly. "There were times when I thought she might, but she..." *She hates everything and everyone that has to do with the palace, and I'm a pathetic coward with no future and nothing to offer.* "I wouldn't know what to say," he said, staring down at his shoes.

"Why don't you give her a gift?"

Elliot lifted his head. "A gift?"

"Yes. I've been told that ladies can often see gifts as a sign of romantic intent."

He smiled wryly, and Elliot couldn't help but smile back. "What do you think I should give her?"

"Well, what is she interested in?"

Exotic birds. Seeing the world. Making new discoveries.

"I think I have an idea," he said as one occurred to him. "Maybe I'll go to *La Maison Des Fleurs* sometime this afternoon."

"That's my boy," Cam replied, slapping him on the shoulder and sending a rush of affection through him. Then he pushed himself back onto his feet. "I'm going to get some rest. I was too excited about those records to sleep a wink last night."

Elliot rose as well. "Have a good rest. I'll see you at dinner."

Cam began his ascent but turned around near the top of the stairs. "Do you remember what she said her last name was?" he asked.

"Of course," Elliot answered. "Faye."

Cam nodded, a crooked grin spreading across his face. "*Elle est un peu comme une fée, n'est-ce pas? D'un autre monde.*"

Elliot's jaw nearly dropped. "Faye" sounded exactly like the French word for fairy—*fée*—and Cam had said, "She's a bit like a fairy, no? Of another world." But his insight wasn't the only part of the statement that had stunned him. They'd both been tutored in French as children, as well as Latin and Greek, but as interested as he was in the world, Cam had never possessed the patience to learn another language. While Elliot was paying close attention and dreaming of Paris, Cam was drawing caricatures of their tutor's mouse-like ears.

"I never thought you listened," Elliot said. "You hated French."

Cam smiled, turned around, and headed up the stairs. "*Je peux être très surprenant.*"

I can be very surprising.

Elliot grinned and turned to head in the opposite direction. He wasn't tired, but his stomach was growling and sour from last night's gin, and his fingernails were caked with dirt and grime from the cemetery. Before he could eat and bathe, however, he needed to find his father. It was Friday, which meant he would be in his lab instead of at St. Thomas's, and though he wasn't sure how, Elliot had to explain where he'd been.

One thing every school of medicine needed was fresh cadavers—bodies for students to study, dissect, and practice surgery on. Though London was certainly filled with corpses, they weren't necessarily available for use. When graveyards became overcrowded shortly after the Hyde outbreak, citizens took to burning their dead as quickly as possible. It had been the fate of Elliot's mother, whose body was now as absent from the earth as her spirit. But as bleak and harsh as their lives had become, Londoners still recoiled at the idea of medical students slicing open their loved one's remains, so the only way to get whole, fresh cadavers was to steal them.

Once it became apparent that his son's condition would not allow a career in medicine, Elliot's father decided to make him St. Thomas's body snatcher. In the early morning hours, after most of the Hydes were gone and the rest of the city had yet to emerge, he went out with Milo—the stable hand who had been Will's older brother—and the two of them searched for bodies to transport to St. Thomas's. Most of the time they found Hyde victims, less useful because of their missing hearts, but sometimes they got "lucky" and found a person who'd starved, frozen to death, or been killed by human hands.

Elliot detested the work, not only because of its gruesomeness but also because of the fact that it deprived people of their loved ones, but corpses didn't feel, and he could usually handle Milo's grief, and as wrong as it was, he was glad there was at least one thing he could do that didn't disappoint his father.

Except for today, of course, when he was certain he'd done just that.

At the top of the southern stairs that led to his father's basement lab, Elliot paused, as he often did, by his mother's old studio. He brushed the knob with his fingertips and ran his thumb over the keyhole. The key was in a ceramic bowl on a shelf in his father's room, which—unlike the lab since Elliot's intrusion—he never locked. Elliot thought of his mother's things collecting dust inside, and he longed to open the door, pick up a brush, and unravel a canvas. He knew exactly what he would paint: the vision he'd had of Iris as he fell asleep last night, her regal frame in a golden grove, watching wild geese fly overhead.

But then he shook his head and jerked his hand away from the door, swallowing the yearning that had risen in his throat. The few times he'd painted since his mother's death had torn him in two, filling him with joy he knew she'd never feel again and making him feel alive while emphasizing she wasn't.

The longing burned too fiercely, and the sorrow cut too deep, so he blocked them out by continuing down the stairs, as he always did.

A damp chill pervaded the air in the basement and Elliot shivered, but when he approached the door to the laboratory, he started to sweat. He didn't want to feel his father's anger and disappointment, but he knew he'd have to face him eventually, so he opened the door. As soon as he stepped inside, however, he froze with his hand on the doorknob.

He'd expected to find his father reading a journal or scribbling notes, feeling a bit of anxiety or some distant aggravation. Instead, he was pacing along the wall and staring up through the windows, his whole being drenched in glacial, stomach-churning fear. Elliot wondered what on earth his father could be so afraid of, but then he turned and saw him there and the fear evaporated, replaced by a flood of warm, elated relief.

It had been... for *him*?

"Elliot," he snapped, marching over to the doorway. "When Milo said you never showed up this morning, I thought..." He looked away and cleared his throat, rubbing his sandy, grey beard. "I thought I could count on you," he said, "to do this one simple task."

His discomfort swelled and Elliot stared, still stunned that he had been more afraid than angry about his absence. "I'm sorry," he finally said. "I didn't mean to frighten—"

"You didn't." He turned his back, strode over to his desk, and sat down behind it. "I was merely concerned that the students wouldn't have a cadaver today. And they won't, thanks to you and your thoughtless actions. What do you have to say?"

Elliot stared at the floor, but not out of shame for what he'd done. His father was the only one in the world who knew his secret, but instead of bringing them closer, it had pushed them further apart.

Knowing his father's feelings hadn't helped Elliot understand him. If anything, it had made him even more of a mystery. He'd always assumed he was just as cold inside as he was out, but now he knew he was filled with warmth, longing, and even love. But he didn't want to be, and what's more, didn't want anyone to know, and as a result, he avoided Elliot more than ever before. It used to hurt to think his father didn't care about him, but knowing he did but didn't *want* to was somehow even worse.

"I'm sorry," Elliot said. "I promise it won't happen again."

"Good." He picked up a pen and dipped it in ink. "Now go and take a bath. Your clothes are mess, and you smell like gin. It's absolutely repulsive."

But he wasn't repulsed. Even from where he stood, Elliot felt his affection, so why was he pretending that he couldn't stand to be near him, especially when he knew he'd be able to see through the blatant lie? Then he remembered that *was* the reason—he didn't want him to know. So he turned and walked out the door, leaving his father alone with his feelings.

Elliot did bathe, and after he was clean and in new clothes, he grabbed a bacon sandwich from the kitchen and started off. While talking to Cam, he'd thought of the perfect gift to give to Iris, but in order to get it, he had to walk two miles to Mansion House.

The redundant name belonged to the former residence of the Lord Mayor. Back when Buckingham Palace housed the actual royal family, the mayor lived in a building in the old financial district, and during the year before the quarantine, Elliot lived there, too. The three-story mansion contained a façade with six Corinthian columns, a vast collection of famous art, and even a dungeon-like basement complete with eleven holding cells, as the residence had once served as an official court of law. It also possessed a small but quite prolific library, and Elliot hoped the gift he had in mind could still be found there.

Even though he lived at the palace, Cam's father still conducted some business at Mansion House, which was why a handful of guards were always patrolling the grounds around it. Since most of them knew who Elliot was, he got past them easily, saying his father had sent him there on business for the Lord Mayor. Once inside, he climbed the winding stairs to the second floor, breathing a sigh of relief when he found the library unlocked.

The wide, oaken room looked just as it did thirteen years ago, so much so Elliot wondered if it had even been touched since then, though the absence of dust suggested the staff still cleaned it regularly. He closed the door and made his way across the polished floor, his pulse leaping every time a board creaked beneath his feet. It wasn't as though he'd ever been *forbidden* to visit Mansion House, and he wasn't certain anyone else was even in the building, but he was about to take—and not return—a piece of property, and he wasn't sure just how he would explain his thievery.

But his worries subsided as soon as he reached the farthest northern wall. When he and Cam found out they would be moving to Buckingham Palace, Cam decided the two of them should leave their mark on the house. They'd carved their initials into the outer rim of the lowest shelf, and there, above an etched *E. M.* and *C. B.,* was the book he had come for.

He'd remembered it because of the vivid gold of its lettering, which stood out even more brilliantly against its ebony spine. His heart pounding, he pulled it out and slid his hand over the cover, smiling as he read the words: *An Anthology of Birds*. When he flipped it open he saw the vibrant pages he remembered—hundreds of descriptions of both common and exotic birds, accompanied by brilliant, detailed, color illustrations. Even though the book was thick, it was also short and compact, so he snapped it shut and tucked it away in the pocket of his coat.

She was going to love it.

His feet felt lighter as he hurried out into the hall, but then he heard the sound of someone ascending the eastern stairs. He turned around and sprinted in the opposite direction, making it to the western steps just before the person emerged. Sweating, he stumbled down the flight and into a corridor, heading toward a door that led to the gardens in the back. He reached it, but the moment he gripped the knob a hunger rose in his throat, searing his veins and closing his lungs.

The hunger of a Hyde.

He spun around and reached for his gun, but no one else was there; both the hallway and the rooms beyond it were utterly silent. His lungs began to expand, but the hunger didn't abate, so he pressed his ear to the door and listened for movement in the garden. Hydes possessed no stealth or cunning—they hunted like wild dogs—but he heard no pounding feet, snapping branches, or shouting guards. Could he possibly be imagining the fire in his chest?

But now that he thought about it, the feeling wasn't quite the same. Last night, he'd felt as if the flames would rip right through his skin, but even though the heat seemed just as close, the sensation felt muffled. After a moment, he lowered himself down onto the marble floor. Was it coming from *beneath* him?

"Elliot, what are you doing?"

He shot back up, panic flooding his veins and drowning the hunger. Harlan Branch, the Lord Mayor of London, was slowly strolling toward him.

"I—I thought I dropped something, sir," he choked. "But I was wrong."

Branch stepped closer, and Elliot's stomach crawled up into his throat. He'd always been afraid of Cam's father, even though he'd never seen him touch anyone other than Cam. They shared the same piercing, ice blue eyes, but only on Branch's face did the color seem hard and cold. He scratched the side of his silvery jet-black beard as he approached, and Elliot knit his brow, because he wasn't feeling angry. A cool breeze of pleasant satisfaction was flowing from him, as if he were not only confident and content but... entertained.

"I meant, what are you doing here," he said. "At Mansion House. The guards informed me you'd come here on some business of the palace."

Elliot swallowed. "I'm sorry, sir. I lied to them," he admitted, knowing Branch would see the truth on his face if he tried to hide it. "I wanted to go to the library. To find a book."

He raised an eyebrow. "A book? You couldn't find one at the palace?"

"Not this particular book," he said, pulling it from his coat. "I remembered it from when we used to lived here, and I just... I really wanted to read it again."

Branch took the book from his hands and read the title with disdain.

"*An Anthology of Birds.*" He raised his head. "You *wanted* to read this?"

"Sure," he answered, wishing he could melt into the marble. "Birds are... fascinating."

Branch studied his face, and though he didn't seem to believe a word, he tossed the book into his hands. "Dinner's at eight o'clock."

The statement was a dismissal, and Elliot took advantage of it, murmuring "Thank you, sir," and hurrying out the garden door.

CHAPTER SIX

The noonday sun was unusually bright outside *La Maison Des Fleurs*, which made the smoky darkness inside more jarring when Elliot entered. He was grateful to find the hall less packed with people than the night before, but his heart still thumped against his ribs, as he hadn't been wholly sober near a crowd since before his affliction. After leaving Mansion House, he'd considered buying a bottle of gin, but he didn't want to be slow and slovenly in front of Iris. Besides, he *wanted* to feel her spirit. The pain of the others was worth it.

A flash of petal-pink and tension flew by him, but it wasn't her. He squinted through the smoke and caught sight of the manager named Eddie, who was doling out coins to a cluster of dancers down by the edge of the stage. Elliot waited until the girls had dispersed and then approached him.

"Hello," he began, clearing his throat as the man's anxiety stung his chest. "My name is Elliot Morrissey. I was here last night with—"

"Yes, I know. What can I do for you, sir?"

"I was wondering if Iris was here and if I could speak to her."

His anxiety grew. "Why? Was she discourteous to you or to the Lord Mayor's—"

"No, not at all! I just wanted to speak with her. It will only take a moment."

Mildly suspicious, Eddie rubbed his whiskered chin. "She's probably still in the kitchen. She just got here a minute ago."

"Thank you very much."

Elliot turned and walked away even though he wasn't entirely sure where the kitchen was. Soon, however, he spotted a young boy carrying mugs and plates and followed him through a narrow doorway just beside the bar. They traveled down a short corridor and arrived at a second door. The boy went in, but Elliot paused and peeked his head inside.

A middle-aged woman was kneading dough beside a cluttered sink, where the boy dropped off his dishes and then rushed back out the door, too lost in a cloud of yearning to notice Elliot standing there. After a moment, the woman who must have been the cook stopped kneading, and Elliot sucked in a breath and clenched his fists against his legs. Grief flowed from her soul like surging blood from an open wound, so fresh and relentless that when she turned and walked out the door as well, Elliot had to close his eyes and fight tears as she passed him. At first, she didn't notice him any more than the young boy had, but just before she reached the end of the hall, she glanced back around. Elliot opened his eyes, and when the two of them looked at each other, her grief sharpened and sank into his heart like jagged claws. Finally, she looked away and walked through the second doorway, and Elliot clutched his chest and let out an agonizing breath.

"Psst! Iris! Is she gone?"

The whisper came from within the kitchen, spoken by an unknown voice, and Elliot turned around and craned his head back through the doorway. He saw no one, so he edged inside and peeked around the corner, his heart leaping when Iris's figure finally came into view. She was standing before a dusty mirror hanging on the wall, pulling her charcoal curls back from her face with the requisite ribbon.

"Yes, she's gone," she replied to the voice. "But I wouldn't chance it, Mae. She probably went to get a drink. She'll be back any minute."

A note of sadness rose in her, and Elliot guessed she knew why the cook was carrying such grief.

"I got time. She won't even know the two of us was here." Another petal-pink waitress scurried into Elliot's view, cradling a small, grimy dog in her arms like a child. The sand-colored mutt, which looked to be a dachshund and terrier mix, whined until the girl, Mae, scratched its matted chin. "Poor little Boots," she cooed. "It's cold out there today, ain't it, girl?"

"She'll notice it's gone," Iris warned, turning around to face her. "That dog isn't worth getting sacked for."

"Nonsense," Mae said, shoving Boots—who'd apparently been named for her white front paws—into Iris's arms. "Now where is that blasted ham?" She walked to the counter and seized two slices of boiled ham from a tray, then returned to Iris and fed the meat to the salivating dog. "Poor little Boots," she murmured again. "You was hungry, huh?"

She grinned at Iris, and Iris smiled pleasantly in return, masking her disgust and irritation flawlessly. But then she looked up and caught sight of Elliot standing in the doorway, and every other feeling drowned in the wake of her disbelief.

"Elliot?" she choked.

Mae turned and saw him there as well, jerking upright and nearly dropping the ham on the floor.

"Lordamercy," she squeaked. "I'm sorry, sir. How can we help you?" But then she knit her brow and turned to Iris. "Wait, what did you call him?"

"I'm so sorry," Elliot said, taking a step toward them. "I didn't mean to frighten you. I just wanted to speak to Iris."

Mae's eyes bulged, and though Iris's face remained impassive, her pulse leapt with a sudden electric thrill that charged his heart. He gripped the wall and tried to keep from grinning like a git.

"I spoke with your manager. He told me it would be all right."

"All right," she echoed, blinking and then glancing over at Mae. "I'll take her back outside," she said, nodding at the dog. Then she turned to Elliot. "Come on. We can go out here."

She carried Boots toward a door a few feet to her left, and Mae stared, drinking Elliot in from head to toe, envy and hunger twisting inside her stomach like a corkscrew. He hurried past her and followed Iris into an empty alley, rubbing his hands as she closed the door and released the mangy dog, which scurried off as soon as it realized its source of food was gone. The snow on the ground had melted, but a bitter wind was blowing. Elliot started to take off his overcoat, but Iris stopped him.

"Keep it. Really, I'm fine."

He almost argued with her, but he knew she would be insistent, so he pulled the coat back on, stepped toward her, and opened his mouth. At that moment, however, he realized he didn't know what to say. *Hello, Iris. I've brought you a gift. Here it is—enjoy.* He stared at the ground, cleared his throat, and then finally murmured, "How are you?"

Thankfully, she didn't laugh or walk back into the kitchen, and when he lifted his head, he saw her smiling. "Well. And you?"

"Very well." Bolstered by the warmth both on her face and in her heart, he reached inside his coat and took out the book. "I brought something for you."

He held it out, and she took a step toward him and looked at the cover, but when she did, the book nearly slipped from between his fingers. A well of awe sprang up inside her heart and spread through her chest, drowning her lungs as she slowly took the book from his trembling hands. She lifted the cover and combed through the colorful pages with reverence, her throat swelling with joy as grateful tears stung the backs of her eyes. Elliot swallowed and shifted his weight, gesturing down at her hands.

"The Canada goose you told me about is on page twenty-one. You were right. It's beautiful."

She raised her head and met his gaze, and the alley fell away. Nothing existed for either of them but the wonderment in her heart, the warmth and understanding flowing between and all around them.

"This is really... for me?"

"Yes, of course. It's yours. Do you like it?"

She smiled and Elliot's blood sang, his head airy and light. He took a step toward her, and she parted her lips to speak, but then a bolt of panic tore through her body and shattered the spell. Her smile dissolved, and Elliot opened his mouth to ask what was wrong, but she turned away.

"That's very kind of you, but I can't take it."

"What do you mean? Why not?"

She closed the book, turned around, and pushed it against his chest. "Just go back to the palace, Elliot. Don't come here again."

He clutched the book, which suddenly felt like lead in his frozen hands. "I... I don't understand. Iris—"

"Elliot, please. Just go."

She walked away, panic and guilt still swimming in her veins, and Elliot raced to the wall and placed his body in front of the door.

"Iris, please. I don't understand what's happened. What did I do?"

She stared at the ground. Her chest was cracking and splintering with the pain, as if her heart were literally breaking.

"Iris... please."

The pain sharpened, but when she raised her head, her face was stone, and her eyes were empty spheres of golden ice. "What did you do? Nothing, I suppose. Except pick a girl who isn't stupid."

The air in his lungs dissolved. "What—what do you mean?"

"What were you expecting in return for your little book?"

"Nothing. It's a gift. After what you said last night—"

"Boys like you don't give *gifts* to girls like me without some payment, and I am sorry to tell you that this girl is not for sale."

Elliot's face burned, and his pulse began to race. "You're saying you think I brought you this book to... take advantage of you?"

She clenched her jaw and turned her back, but her chest continued to fracture.

"Iris, I don't understand. You trusted me last night. You gave me my gun. You showed me those journals. You slept just a few feet away from me—"

"I know," she said, her voice beginning to break. "It was a mistake."

"Why? I don't understand what's changed."

She took a breath and spun around to face him. "I woke up. So go back to your castle, Elliot. I know why you came here."

"I came here because I've never met anyone like you in my life. I came here because I *owe* you my life, and even more than that. When I walked out of this hall last night, before that Hyde attacked, I'd stopped truly caring if I lived or if I died."

Her heart stopped, and the whistling wind around them seemed to still. Elliot's voice was shaking, but he found himself going on.

"You did more than save my life; you made me want to live it. I'd forgotten what it was to hope or dream until I met you. You're filled with more strength and courage and daring than anyone I know, and being around you makes me feel like I can be that way, too."

She stared at him, an aching warmth rising in her throat. "What are you planning to do, then?" she choked, attempting to harden her voice again. "Marry an orphaned waitress and bring her to live with you at the palace? No girl with half a brain would believe such a bold, disgusting lie." She clutched her skirt and dashed to the side, but he blocked her way again.

"I'm telling you the truth—"

"Like hell you are! I know the truth." She twisted her beautiful features into a hideous mask of anger, but Elliot felt her heart pounding in protest against her words. "The world may say I'm beneath you, but I know the world is wrong. I am worth one hundred of those cronies at the palace, and I refuse to be used and thrown away like a piece of trash."

In one swift movement, she grabbed his shoulder and shoved him out of the way, clearing her path to the door and nearly crippling him with her pain. He stumbled against an overturned box and steadied himself with the wall, his stomach nearly bursting with her grief and self-disgust. Then he raised his head and saw her reaching for the doorknob, and the words came out of his mouth before he could stop them.

"I know you're lying."

She froze with her hand in the air. "What?"

"I know you're lying. You know that's not what I think of you, and you aren't angry with me. Saying what you said just now made you sick. You didn't mean it."

"You don't know what I feel."

"I'm sorry, Iris, but I do." He let out a ragged breath and shoved a hand back through his hair. "I know exactly what everyone who ever comes near me feels."

She lowered her hand and turned to face him. "What are you talking about?"

Elliot closed his eyes and fought the urge to laugh like a madman. He was about to tell a girl he'd known for less than twenty-four hours his deepest, darkest secret—the shameful truth he hadn't even been able to tell his best friend.

"I'm an empath," he finally said, his chest collapsing beneath the weight of both disgrace and relief. "I feel the feelings of people around me as if they were my own."

She stared at him for a moment, then turned her head and laughed, but the sound was thin and uncertain. "Please. That's impossible."

"When you first found out who Cam and I were, you felt such rage toward us that your heart nearly exploded."

Her laughter died and her blood ran cold. "I don't know what you mean."

"I felt it, Iris, so strongly I could barely contain myself, but Cam had no idea, nor did anyone else around us. I think you know how perfectly you're able to hide your feelings. There's no way I could know the truth unless I felt it myself."

"That's ridiculous," she breathed, but her face was pale as death.

"When you showed me that ornithologist's journal about Antarctica, you felt horribly embarrassed when I asked why it was in Latin. And just now, when you held that dog while that other waitress fed it, you smiled at her but really felt repulsed and aggravated."

She shook her head. "You could have guessed that."

"Then how about your cook? She recently lost a loved one, right? A son, around my age?"

"How—how did you know it was her?"

"I could feel her grief, and when she looked at me it grew worse. That happens sometimes when people see someone who looks like the person they've lost."

She searched his face, her body as still as a statue in the breeze. Then she murmured, almost to herself, "You're telling the truth."

Elliot nodded and braced himself for her horror and revulsion, but instead of turning cold, her heart ignited with fascination.

"Were you... born this way?" she asked, her pulse racing.

Elliot shook his head. "It happened because of a grave mistake I made two weeks ago."

Something inside her deflated a bit, but she remained transfixed. "How?"

He explained the experiment briefly, omitting the reason he'd performed it. Thankfully, she didn't ask, though her curiosity grew.

"So, no one knows but you and your father?"

"No one. Except for you."

She furrowed her brow. "Not Cambrian? I thought you two were close."

"He's practically my brother but... it's complicated."

Once again, she didn't pry, and Elliot was grateful. For a moment, they stood in silence, but then she took a step toward him.

"So, how does it work exactly?" she asked, still keeping a careful distance. "Do you feel the emotions more strongly the closer you are to someone?"

"Yes. And physical contact is worse. Then the sensation is so acute it's like being inside their skin."

Her face froze as a sudden wave of embarrassment shot through her veins, and Elliot knew she was thinking about the fire she'd felt when they touched.

"Don't be embarrassed," he said, raising his hands, but it was the wrong thing to say. She turned away and covered her face, her humiliation swelling. "I'm sorry," he cried, rubbing his brow. "I'm sorry—I can't help it. But Iris, you should know, I felt the same."

"Please, just stop." She let out a breath, lowered her hands, and turned back around to face him, her embarrassment giving way to a mixture of fear and bewilderment. "If you've known what I felt this whole time, then you must have known—like you did just now—when I wasn't being honest."

Elliot swallowed. "I can't read minds. I don't know why people feel what they do. But yes, there were times when I knew what you said didn't match the way you felt."

"I don't understand," she said, her confusion growing. "You knew I'd been hiding things, and yet, you not only trusted me, but wanted to see me again?"

It was Elliot's turn to feel confused. "Of course. Everyone hides things. They should—feelings are intimate and privacy is sacred. I respect you and your choice to share or not share whatever you feel."

She stared at him, something inside her stirring, and Elliot knit his brow, but then he realized how blatantly hypocritical he must seem, as he'd invaded her "sacred privacy" just a moment ago.

"I shouldn't have done what I did today—confronted you like that," he said. "It's no excuse, but when I thought I might never see you again... I'm sorry, Iris. I lost control. It was selfish and I'm sorry."

He let out a breath and stared at the scattered debris around his feet, but when he raised his head again, he saw her walking toward him, stopping so close he could smell the smoke still clinging to her hair. Her eyes were wide and shining with warmth that had bloomed inside her chest, and his breath hitched at the unexpected and naked display of emotion.

"Don't apologize," she said. "What you did was tell me the truth. It wasn't selfish but *selfless* of you to open up like that. You gave me something precious and hard to find. You gave me *honesty*, and I am just... I am so incredibly grateful."

"Grateful?" he repeated. "You mean to tell me you're not repulsed?"

She nearly laughed. "No. Why on earth would I be repulsed?"

His chest began to tighten. "Iris, because of this affliction, I am the epitome of helplessness and frailty. I can barely function in the presence of other people. The feelings are unrelenting and can be incapacitating."

"You're wrong," she said. "It's not a curse, and it doesn't make you frail. It's a wonderful, powerful gift."

"What? How can you possibly say—"

"What could be weak about being able to see behind people's masks? If they're carrying secret pain, you'll be able to comfort them. If they're acting with malice or greed, you'll be able to foil their plans. If they're hiding truths that might just mean the difference between life and death..." She let out a breath, frustration and envy curling around her heart. "I promise you, Elliot, it's a gift. A gift I wish I had."

"You mean to say you truly don't find it—"

"Stop." She shook her head and laughed. "You of all people should know. Can't you feel it? I'm not repulsed."

"Iris, what the devil—"

The two of them jumped as Eddie's voice rang out from the kitchen doorway. He stepped outside, his face red with anger, but then he saw Elliot. Immediately, he stopped, cleared his throat, and lowered his voice.

"My apologies, sir," he said. "I didn't know you were still here. I'm sorry, but Iris is needed on the floor, if you don't mind."

"Not at all. I'll be on my way in a moment," Elliot said. "I'm sorry to have taken so much of her time. I appreciate it."

Eddie cleared his throat again and hurried back inside, and Iris turned to Elliot and grinned.

"So, what was he feeling?"

He shook his head and smiled, fighting the terrible urge to laugh. "He felt how he looked: angry. You should probably go back inside."

"You're right," she said, emitting a sigh, but she didn't turn and go. Instead, she looked up into his eyes and said, "So when will I see you again?"

His lips parted. "See me again? But earlier you—"

"Told you lies, exactly as you said. I was trying to do what I thought was right, what I thought someone else would want me to do. But now…" She paused and took a breath. "I'm doing what I want instead."

Elliot didn't understand, but he was too happy to care. "How about tonight when you get off work? At the aviary?"

"Perfect," she said. "I'll see you there around eleven o'clock."

She started to head for the door, but Elliot held out the book in his hand. "Wait—here. Since… you know. I mean, if you still want it."

She smiled and took the book, but instead of walking away, she pressed it to her chest and said, "I should have said this the first time."

Elliot waited, confused, as she didn't say anything more, but then she let out a breath, glanced at the ground…

And took his hand.

He nearly cried out as joy and gratitude shot through his arm like fire, searing his veins, igniting his heart, and bringing tears to his eyes. She lifted her head to meet his gaze, and the world ground to a halt. He swallowed hard and murmured, "You're welcome."

She nodded, released his hand, and then hurried back to the kitchen. Just as she opened the door, however, he stopped her one more time.

"Are you ever going to tell me what's so embarrassing about penguins?"

A burst of laughter escaped her as she stepped over the threshold. "Perhaps," she said, grinning back at him. "We'll just have to see how I feel."

CHAPTER SEVEN

Cam's rooms were the second finest of Buckingham Palace's living quarters; they'd belonged to King Edward back when he was a young man and Prince of Wales. The Lord Mayor lived in the former apartments of the late Queen, and Elliot and his father resided in separate rooms below them on the first floor of the north wing. Eager to tell Cam that Iris had liked the gift and wanted to see him again, Elliot rushed to the second floor as soon as he arrived, but Cam was out, so he trudged to his own room and tried to pass the time by reading *David Copperfield*. Thoughts of Iris were much more appealing, however, so he tossed it aside and spent the afternoon gazing up at his ceiling instead.

Around six o'clock, he figured Cam must be back and changing for dinner, so he climbed the stairs again and approached his private chambers. The sitting room was unlocked, so he stepped inside and navigated his way through the evening darkness, following the lamplight streaming from Cam's open bedroom door. He started to call out to him, but his voice died in his throat, because another voice rang out from the bedroom.

The Lord Mayor's.

"Explain this to me, Cambrian. And don't waste your breath with a lie."

Elliot froze and gripped the arm of the sofa just beside him. He couldn't see the figures of Cam or his father from where he stood, but he could feel Cam's fear and hear the ice in the Lord Mayor's voice.

"I don't know what you're talking about," Cam replied, but his voice was unsteady.

"I told you not to lie!"

A clatter followed the outburst, and Cam stumbled into Elliot's view, staggering backward against the bedroom wall and raising his hands. Slowly, the Lord Mayor approached him, clutching an object in his palm, and Elliot's chest tightened.

It was the salve Cam had given to Jennie.

"All right, I'm sorry," Cam said, his fear growing sharper and more metallic. "I gave that to one of the parlor maids. She told me her hands got chapped in the winter, and I felt sorry for her. I was only being kind. There's nothing going on between us."

"That's precisely the problem, you little shit," the Lord Mayor cried, hurling the salve against the wall and shattering the jar. Cam jumped and Elliot winced, his stomach lurching with fear and loathing so potent he thought he would vomit. He knew he should leave, that Cam would never want him to witness this, but he felt as if his feet were glued to the Persian rug beneath him.

"Kindness isn't what you give to parlor maids," the Lord Mayor spat. "Bits of skirt like that exist for one reason: blowing off steam. You should be having it off with half the sluts on the staff, Cambrian, but instead, you're chatting with them about skin conditions and buying them hand crèmes."

Cam attempted to rise from the wall, but the Lord Mayor shoved him back.

"What were you planning to do with her next? Gossip and share embroidery patterns? Help her dust the drawing rooms and empty the chamber pots?"

"Father, I'm sorry—"

A *crack* split the air as the Lord Mayor snapped the back of his hand across his face.

"I don't need you to be sorry!" he roared. "I need you to be a man!"

Cam blinked and tried to right himself, but the Lord Mayor seized his throat and slammed the back of his head against the wall, pinning him there.

"The son of the Lord Mayor of London will not be a goddamned nancy-boy."

His grip tightened, and Elliot bit his cheek until he tasted blood. He wanted to run inside and tackle the Lord Mayor to the ground, but the flood of terror, rage, disgust, and shame was paralyzing.

"I need to see some changes," he growled in Cam's face. "And I need to see them now."

With a violent jerk, he released his throat and turned to leave the room, and Elliot's sudden panic finally gave him the strength to move. He scrambled behind the sofa just before the Lord Mayor walked by, but when he passed, Elliot wrinkled his forehead in confusion. He'd assume the fear he'd felt from the bedroom belonged to Cam alone, but besides being sickened and full of rage, the Lord Mayor was also strangely, bone-chillingly afraid.

The bewilderment didn't last long, however; as soon as the Lord Mayor left the chamber, Cam began to cry. The sound of his sobbing was bad enough, but the shame that bloomed inside him nearly bought Elliot to his knees. It was worse than the shame he'd felt earlier, worse than anything Elliot had felt in his whole life. His soul writhed as if it were disgusted with itself, churning with hatred that clogged his veins, choked his heart, and blackened his vision. Elliot couldn't breathe beneath the weight of it, let alone cry. The only thing he wanted was to crawl out of his skin.

Finally, he forced himself up and dashed out of the room, running until he reached the clear, free air of the northern stairway. His heart thrashed against his ribs as the feeling began to fade, but part of him still wanted to run back inside and comfort Cam. He knew that if he did, however, he'd only be as vulnerable and useless as before, and Cam would feel even worse if he knew his shame had been exposed.

Iris had been wrong about his empathy being a gift. It didn't give him power or allow him to help anyone. All it did was show him things he wished he'd never seen.

The State Dining Room was one of the loveliest places in the palace. The gold and rose-colored southern wall was covered with oil paintings of the Hanoverian sovereigns, and the northern wall was made up of a panel of tall French windows, leading to a spacious balcony overlooking the garden. The windows were open when Elliot arrived at eight o'clock, and the scents of flowers and freshly mown grass were drifting in on the breeze, but he couldn't see or smell a thing. All he could think of was Cam.

Even though the hall was only the second largest dining space—the first being the Ball Supper Room, which wouldn't be needed until the season began and the nobles who didn't live at the palace attended as well—it was grand enough to hold the eighty or so courtiers who were strolling about the room and greeting each other with drinks in their hands. After surviving the crowd at *La Maison Des Fleurs* without a drink, Elliot had thought he could do the same at the Lord Mayor's dinner, but as soon as he entered, he seized a glass of champagne from a footman's tray—not out of dread of the crowd, but out of fear and concern for Cam. Once he had the glass in his hand, he moved to the back of the room, scanning the crowd for him and taking long, nervous drinks.

"Started the party without me once again," a voice behind him sighed.

Elliot jumped and covered his mouth, nearly spitting out the champagne. He turned around to see Cam standing only inches behind him, his hair sleek, his suit immaculate, and his smile gleaming. If he hadn't been able to feel the pain and anxiety in his chest, Elliot would have thought the afternoon had been a dream.

"You're a bit jumpy," Cam observed. "Here, have another drink. It's truly the only way to get through these arduous formal dinners."

Elliot looked down and saw that Cam was holding two fresh glasses, and also that the one in his own hand was now nearly empty. He drained the rest of the first and accepted the second from Cam.

"Thanks," he said, handing his empty flute to a passing footman. "So... was Andrew able to find that part and fix the Victor?"

He'd hoped that mentioning something exciting to Cam would lift his mood, but instead, his anxiety thickened at the mention of Andrew's name.

"He did find the part," he said, glancing down at the red velvet carpet. "But he hasn't been able to bring it back to the palace and work on the Victor. He won't be coming tonight, either. His mother... well, it's not one of her better days."

Elliot stared at the floor as well, guilt churning inside his stomach along with the champagne. Then, suddenly, Cam slapped his shoulder and filled him with jarring glee.

"I'm a prat!" he exclaimed. "I didn't ask you about Iris! What happened this afternoon? Did you go to *La Maison Des Fleurs*?"

Elliot let out a breath and smiled. "Yes. I gave her this book I thought she'd like from Mansion House. She accepted it and even agreed to meet me again tonight."

Cam beamed, his happiness genuine and rejuvenating. "Best of luck to you, mate," he said. Then he gestured toward his hair. "You'd better comb that mop of yours before you go and meet her."

Elliot had combed his hair—twice—it just didn't make any difference, a fact that Cam knew well. "I'll still be a better sight than you."

He smiled and Elliot's chest relaxed as he took another drink, but then he nearly spit it out again as a young girl approached them.

Her name was Philomena Blackwell, the daughter of the only living Earl who remained in London, and one of the few courtiers whose feelings hadn't been a surprise to Elliot once he was able to feel them, because they were exactly the same as the ones she displayed on her face. While Elliot often felt inept at hiding his emotions, Philomena was perfectly capable of it—she just didn't want to.

Elliot liked her, even more so after his affliction. While he admired how Cam and Iris could mask and control their feelings, there was something exciting and brave about someone who didn't try. Her energy was frenetic and her spirit was nearly wild, and she carried some of the fiercest longings he'd ever come across. To most people, such qualities were out of place in any girl, not to mention the most refined and highborn in all of London, but the thing that made her explosive spirit more striking was its container.

Philomena had turned fifteen a little over a month ago—a week or so after Cam enjoyed his eighteenth "St. Cambrian's Day"—but if anyone were to look at her, they'd guess she was twelve years old. She was only barely five feet tall, and her frame was slight and elfin, though there was nothing small about the way she carried herself, and her smooth, dimpled face was fresh and as sweet as a china doll's. She had bright hazel eyes and shining hair the color of caramel, but Elliot found it hard to think of someone who looked so much like a little girl as *beautiful*.

As she barreled across the dining room toward him and Cam, however, her heart was more alive than any doll's could ever be, which was why he nearly spit out his champagne when she approached.

"Cambrian, is Andrew here?" she asked the moment she reached them.

Cam grinned and raised an eyebrow. "Good evening to you as well, Miss Blackwell."

She groaned and rolled her eyes. "Don't play with me. I'm serious."

He raised his glass to his lips, his grin widening. "Unfortunately, Andrew will not be joining us tonight."

"Blast!" she exclaimed, glaring down at the floor.

Cam chortled into his glass. Elliot smiled as well, in spite of the weight of her disappointment. The daughter of an Earl shouldn't know a word like that existed, let alone shout it out in front of two gentlemen at a party.

"He promised he would play for me tonight," she explained miserably. "The Lord Mayor said I could sing for the guests at the next formal dinner."

"I'll play for you," Cam offered, but she rolled her eyes again.

"I've heard your *attempts* at the piano, Cambrian. You're terrible."

Cam clutched his chest and groaned as if her words were a physical blow. "My dreams have been crushed, Elliot. I'll never play before the king."

"Oh, stop it!" she said, smacking the side of his arm, but she was smiling. "I suppose I'll simply have to wait until the next formal dinner."

"I truly am sorry," Cam said, holding out the drink in his hand. "Would you like a sip of champagne as compensation for your loss?"

Philomena's eyes lit up. "My mother would kill me," she said, but then she seized the drink and drained the whole thing in one gulp. After wiping her mouth and handing the empty glass back to Cam, she flashed a wicked grin and said, "I hope the old bat saw that."

She turned and bounced away, and Cam looked down at his empty glass. "Well," he said. "I suppose that's what I get for being charitable."

Dinner that night was extravagant, as the formal ones always were. The five courses included, among other things: fresh salad, asparagus, peas, sweet bread, lamb cutlets, lobster tail, and the night's main entrée—goose. When Elliot took his first bite of the goose, he couldn't help but think of the hostile gander that had attacked him. Could he be eating that goose right now? Or its brother or its cousin?

He set down his fork and glanced around the table, noticing something strange. At each formal dinner, the seats were assigned and very rarely changed, but tonight the arrangement was different. The Lord Mayor sat at the head of the table with Cam on his right and Earl Blackwell, Philomena's father, on his left. As usual, Lady Blackwell sat in the seat beside her husband, but instead of sitting beside her mother, Philomena was seated across the table, next to Cam. Elliot, who was sitting next to the Blackwells with his father, furrowed his brow and wondered at the odd and sudden change, but then the Lord Mayor stood and gave his customary speech.

As Cam had guessed, the Lord Mayor announced that he had decided to lower the age of debut from sixteen to fifteen. The moment he made the proclamation, however, his gaze landed on Cam, and when it then immediately shifted to Philomena, Elliot sucked in a breath. That morning Cam had felt strangely afraid when he mentioned his father's obsession with getting the world "married off and reproducing," and now Elliot understood why.

The Lord Mayor wanted Cam to marry Philomena, and soon.

It made sense that the Lord Mayor would want the only daughter of the city's last and greatest aristocrat as a match for his son, but why was he in such a hurry to make it happen now? Years ago, it would have been unheard of for a boy of eighteen to marry anyone, let alone a girl who'd only recently turned fifteen. Elliot liked Philomena, and he knew that Cam did, too, but she wouldn't even *look* like a fifteen-year-old girl until she was twenty. The thought of marrying and *having children* with her now... even before meeting Iris, Elliot would have found the idea as disconcerting as Cam.

After dinner, Elliot's father—who'd avoided him as much as he could while sitting right beside him—announced that he was headed back to his lab to do some research. The Lord Mayor escorted him out, and the women departed for coffee, tea, and cakes in the Blue Drawing Room. The rest of the men then filed into the West Gallery, where they would spend the rest of the evening drinking port and brandy. Elliot and Cam sat down on an empty leather sofa, and Cam pulled out his cigarette case as if it were a flask of water and he was dying of thirst.

"It's ridiculous that we can smoke in front of women at places like music halls but not at dinner," he muttered, placing a cigarette between his teeth and then hastily striking a match.

"That's because the two places don't contain the same kind of woman."

Cam and Elliot both looked up to see Charlie Hands, a dough-faced boy about their age and whom they both detested, sitting across from them, crossing his legs and swishing a snifter of brandy in his hand.

"Good evening, Charlie," Cam replied, quickly returning his focus to the business of lighting his cigarette.

Elliot shifted and took a drink from his own snifter of brandy, already feeling sickened and overwhelmed by Charlie's feelings, which as usual were made up entirely of scorn and conceit.

"Speaking of music halls," Charlie said, clearly oblivious to their aversion to his presence. "I think I saw you two at *La Maison Des Fleurs* the other night."

Cam leaned back, took a long, satisfied drag, and blew smoke at the ceiling, so Elliot nodded and said, "Yes. We were there the other night."

"I've got my eye on a pretty piece who works there," Charlie continued. "I don't know her name, but she's got dark hair and these maddening golden eyes."

Elliot stiffened, tightening his grip on the delicate snifter, and Cam sat up and slowly removed the cigarette from his mouth.

"We know her," he said, his voice even and cool. "Her name is Iris."

Charlie snorted. "You mean you actually got her to talk to you? I can't even get the chit to give me the time of day. She's pretty hoity-toity for a common bit of skirt, but I have a feeling I know just how to take her down a peg."

Elliot didn't realize he was about to lunge out of the sofa until Cam put his hand on his leg and pressed him back into his seat. His veins bulged, and his blood screamed as Cam's rage compounded his own, but the physical grip of his hand did keep him from tearing out Charlie's throat.

"Charlie," Cam said smoothly. "Do you happen to speak French?"

Charlie wrinkled his brow. "No. I mean, I know *La Maison Des Fleurs* means 'Flower House' or something like that, but my father said it was useless to learn a language I'd never need."

Cam removed his hand from Elliot's leg and took another drag. "Charlie, *tu es un être humain putride*," he said as he exhaled. "*Honnêtement, je ne sais pas comment ta mère peut être autour de vous.*"

Laughter erupted in Elliot's throat, so he stifled it with a drink. Cam had just said, "Charlie, you are a putrid human being. I honestly don't know how your own mother can even stand to be near you."

"What?" Charlie demanded, turning to Elliot. "What did he say?"

"I think," Elliot said, clearing his throat. "It was something along the lines of 'I do believe there's a spotted cat inside your fountain of cheese.'"

Cam sighed. "He's probably right. My French is terrible."

"Not as terrible as your manners."

The room seemed to still as Cam and Elliot raised their heads. The Lord Mayor was standing beside them, lighting a cigar and leaning back against the wall. Once he'd taken a puff, he bent down between them and hissed in Cam's ear.

"Au moins Charlie est un jeune homme qui sait ce que son pénis est utilisé."

At least Charlie's a young man who knows what his pecker is for.

Elliot's throat closed as the Lord Mayor straightened up, and Cam stared at the ground, ice sliding through his veins. After a moment, he managed to raise his cigarette to his lips, but his face was white as ash and his hand was trembling.

"What going on?" a gruff voice asked.

Elliot looked up to see Charlie's father, Judge Hands, beside the Lord Mayor. In fact, now that he glanced around, he saw a sort of group had started to form around the sofa.

"Like all young men," the Lord Mayor replied, "Our boys are discussing girls. Particularly the better looking ones they've noticed lately."

"I saw one today that took my breath away," Judge Hands exclaimed. "A little parlor maid with rosy lips and golden hair."

"You're joking, right?" Charlie scoffed at his father. "You've never noticed that one? Her name is Jennie, and she is one of the finest bits in the palace."

"I know which one you're talking about," another boy named Paul agreed. "She's the one who's always giving Cambrian the eye."

Cam snuffed out his cigarette and immediately lit a new one, and Elliot drained the rest of his brandy, but it didn't help. The fear in Cam's blood had grown so thick no drink could penetrate it.

"That's her." Charlie laughed, and so did a few of the other men in the group. "How about it, Cambrian? Get your end away with her yet?"

Elliot stared at his empty snifter, wishing he could crawl inside.

Cam avoided his father's gaze and murmured, "No, not yet."

"Damn," Charlie breathed. "If that little jade looked at me the way she looks at you..." He let out a sigh that bordered on a groan, and Elliot gritted his teeth. "I can't believe she didn't catch your eye until tonight, Father. You'd have to be a mandrake not to notice a girl like that."

Most of the other men laughed again, but Elliot cringed at the word. A mandrake was one of the worst things you could call another man, since it meant a man who didn't like women at all, but... other men.

"Or a mandrake to notice and do nothing about it," the Lord Mayor said.

Elliot nearly dropped his snifter to the floor.

The soul-churning, suffocating shame Cam felt in the bedroom was back, curling around his veins and wrapping its tendrils around his heart. He raised his head to meet his father's gaze, and the coils tightened, cutting off circulation to anything but fear and pain. Elliot stared, paralyzed, unable to even think, but then—as if the universe were playing some kind of a cruel joke—Jennie appeared outside the door, carrying a fresh carafe of coffee for the women.

"Oh, Jennie," Cam called in a hollow voice. "Would you come in here, please?"

She was trained to stop for any voice that commanded her to do so, but Elliot knew she wouldn't have jumped like she did had the voice not been Cam's. Both obediently and hesitantly, she stepped inside the smoky room, glancing around at the sea of staring men as she approached. Once she was standing a few feet away from Cam, she dropped into a curtsy.

"Yes, sir?" she said, her voice unsteady.

"I have a question for you."

She straightened back up and gripped the carafe in her hands, her pulse quickening, and Cam leaned back and casually crossed his ankle over his knee, resting one arm on the sofa and raising his cigarette with the other. He placed it between his lips and took a long, languorous drag, masking the terror and shame in his heart with masterful precision. After exhaling a cloud of smoke, he said, "Do you find me attractive?"

Jennie's blood froze. "I—I'm sorry, sir?"

"Do you fancy me? Am I featured in your parlor maid fantasies? Do you dream of wearing fine clothes and dancing with me at a royal ball?" The men snickered, and Cam curled his lip and flicked some ash on the carpet. "These men seem to think you do. So is it true? Am I your fondest wish?"

Jennie's face paled, and her stomach rose into her throat. Sweat broke out on Elliot's brow, but he couldn't raise his arm to wipe it. Between Cam's fear, Jennie's shame, and the cruel delight of the men around them, he wasn't only paralyzed—he was trapped in the depths of hell. Jennie turned to the Lord Mayor with desperate, pleading eyes, but he wasn't looking at her—he was looking at Cam.

And beaming with pride.

After what felt like eternity, she swallowed and turned back to Cam, dropping her head and murmuring, "I only wish to please you."

Cam's grin was razor sharp, and it sliced through his own heart. He took another drag and ran his tongue along the edge of his teeth. "I'm glad to hear that," he said, looking her over as he exhaled. "I'll be sure to seek you out next time I'm in need of being pleased."

Something inside Jennie died, snuffed out like flame deprived of air, but she fell into an obedient curtsy and left when the Lord Mayor dismissed her. As soon as she was gone, the men erupted with raucous laughter, with Charlie actually leaning over and slapping Cam on the shoulder. Elliot placed his glass on the stand beside him, rose from the sofa, and then stumbled through the crowd and toward the door as fast as he could. His first thought was to find an empty room where he could vomit, but once he was in the hall, he found himself running after Jennie.

She was already on the other side of the State Dining Room, which was empty now except for the moonlight streaming in from the windows. Elliot dashed through the darkness and caught up to her in the eastern hallway, but when he called her name, she jumped and spun around in fear. He raised his hands and approached her slowly, taking a few deep breaths.

"I'm sorry I scared you," he said. "I just wanted to tell you that Cam… he didn't want to do what he did just now. He didn't mean it."

She glanced at the floor, trying to blink back the tears swarming her eyes. "He's the son of the Lord Mayor, sir. He can say and do what he likes."

"No," Elliot said, stepping closer. "What he did to you was wrong. But there was a reason he did it. He didn't *want* to treat you cruelly."

She swallowed and murmured, almost to herself, "I thought he was different. That he wasn't..." She sucked in a breath and closed her eyes. "Like his father."

Shame welled up in her stomach, as black and suffocating as Cam's, and suddenly, Elliot thought of something the Lord Mayor said in Cam's room—the part about a real man "having it off" with the female servants.

"Jennie," he said, his throat going dry. "How did the Lord Mayor find out about the hand salve Cam gave to you?"

Her head jerked up and the shame rose into her throat, and Elliot knew.

"He found it in your room, didn't he? He came into your room and—"

"He's the Lord Mayor. He can go where he likes."

She turned and hurried away from him without waiting to be dismissed, leaving her panic and shame inside his chest like a stinging barb. He ran a hand through his hair and wandered back through the State Dining Room, but then he saw a figure standing alone on the balcony, holding a cigarette and looking out over the garden. The figure's back was turned, but Elliot knew it was Cam, so he stepped through the doors and out into the cold and silent night.

"How is she?" Cam asked without turning around, his voice as thin and ghostlike as the smoke curling up through the air.

Elliot glanced at his feet and bit his lip. "She'll be all right."

A hollow laugh escaped Cam's throat. "Oh, El. When will you learn what a terrible liar you are?" He raised his hand and blew a cloud of smoke out over the garden. "She'll hate me forever now. She should. You probably should as well."

"Of course I don't hate you," he said, stepping toward him. "I never could."

"You could. And you would, if you knew..." He paused, rubbed his brow, and threw his cigarette over the ledge. "It doesn't matter," he said, turning around. "What's done is done."

He walked away, his stomach churning with pain and self-disgust, and Elliot turned and followed him through the darkened dining room.

"Where are you going?"

"Anywhere but here."

"I'll go with you."

"No." Cam stopped and then turned around. "Go meet with Iris. You deserve to be happy, El. Please. Just... go and be with her." He tightened his jaw, his chest aching with both affection and envy, and then he turned around and started off toward the hallway.

"Cam, wait," Elliot called. "I don't think you should be alone. Why don't you go and see Andrew and—"

"No!" He spun back around, and Elliot nearly stumbled off his feet, stunned by the pain that sprouted like a geyser from his heart. "I don't need to go see Andrew! I don't need to see anyone right now. I just..." He shook his head and pressed his fingers against his eyes. "I'm sorry, El. I really am. I just need to be alone."

"That's fine," he murmured. "I... I'll see you tomorrow then."

Cam let out a breath and lowered his hands. "Yes, tomorrow." He opened his eyes and gave Elliot the best smile he could muster. "I'm sorry again. Give Iris my regards." Then he turned and left.

Three hours later, at one in the morning, Elliot was sitting in the aviary alone. He'd waited, circled the zoo, crept through all its darkened offices, and then returned to the aviary and waited there some more. He even went back to *La Maison Des Fleurs*, but he didn't find Iris there, either, so finally, at three in the morning, he gave up and trudged back home.

CHAPTER EIGHT

At dawn, the entire city was still and washed in a wet, grey light. Elliot's body jostled against the passenger seat at the front of the carriage, his head aching as Milo guided the horse through the empty streets. He'd barely slept since going to bed at four and rising at six. All he could think of was Iris and why she hadn't shown up last night.

Although, that wasn't entirely true. He'd also been preoccupied with thoughts of Cam's wellbeing. He'd crept up into his room when he got back from the aviary and thankfully found him safe and sleeping soundly in his bed, but while the sight had been a relief, it hadn't erased the memory of his terror, pain, and shame. On his way back down to his room, he had also thought of Jennie, wondering if she ever slept soundly and wishing he didn't know terrible things that he could do nothing about.

Now, as he and Milo slogged through the streets in search of bodies, he found himself thinking about the serum that started it all in the first place. Elliot had created it because he'd heard the Lord Mayor ask his father for a drug to remove compassion, but now that he really thought about it, Elliot couldn't imagine why the Lord Mayor would *need* such a potion. There didn't seem to be a compassionate bone in his whole body.

"You feeling all right, sir?" Milo asked.

Elliot rubbed his brow. "Milo, I've told you a hundred times. You can call me Elliot."

"Sorry, sir," he said, a surge of embarrassment heating his blood.

Elliot glanced at his reddened face and scrawny, awkward frame. "Don't be sorry." He sighed. "I'm the one who should apologize. I didn't mean to be short with you, Milo. I didn't get enough sleep."

"No worries, sir. Only another hour or so and people will be coming out of their houses. Then we'll either be heading home or, hopefully, to St. Thomas's."

Elliot nodded, rubbed his brow again, and looked back out at the road. He had a job to do, and he needed to pay attention. They'd begun to enter Somers Town, a central district of London a few miles west of the old King's Cross, and soon, they'd be nearing Regents Park, where he had spent the early morning hours waiting for Iris.

"We're too far west," he said. "Let's head back along the river. In the East End, we're more likely to find..." *A poor person who's starved or died of some illness.* "Something intact."

"I'd like to check out this area first, sir—that is, if you don't mind. A lot of dodgy establishments have been springing up here lately. We might find a bloke that's been killed in a pub fight instead of by a Hyde."

"All right," Elliot acquiesced. "Let's get out and go on foot."

They dismounted, tied up the horse, and set off in opposite directions. Elliot shivered and turned up his collar, dodging puddles of vomit and piss that convinced him that Milo was right about the abundance of pubs in the area. His heart leapt when he spotted a man curled up beside a pushcart, but then he heard the rattling sound of his heavy, drunken snore. He let out a breath and crept past him, but before he could turn the corner, Milo's screeching voice rang out from the other side of the street.

"Sir—Elliot—here! I think I found us a right fresh one."

Both disgusted and grateful, Elliot followed Milo's voice. After a moment, he found him in a narrow, unpaved alley. Milo waved him over and gestured toward a spot on the ground, where a girl lay sprawled on her stomach.

Wearing a dress of petal-pink.

"I haven't turned her over yet, but I bet she's got her heart. There ain't no blood on the ground, see?"

Something was buzzing in Elliot's ears, causing Milo's voice to sound like a thin and distant hum. Slowly, he stumbled closer.

The girl had dark and curly hair.

"Come on," Milo said, crouching beside her. "Let's get us a look."

Elliot didn't move—the alley was tilting beneath his feet—so Milo turned her over himself.

And the world came to an end.

"See? I was right! She wasn't killed by a Hyde—she's got her heart."

"No. She isn't dead," he said, his voice as distant as Milo's.

"What are you saying? Of course she is." He reached toward her, perhaps to check for reactions or feel a pulse, but Elliot flew to the ground and shoved him back against the wall.

"Get back! I told you she isn't dead!" He couldn't feel the earth beneath him, couldn't see anything but Iris. The knife she always kept in her boot was lying beside her hand, and her eyes were closed, and her face was smeared with dirt, but there was no blood. "Look," he said. "There's no wound—not a mark on her body. It's something else."

"Sir, I already touched her. She's cold."

"That doesn't mean she's dead!"

He gripped his head in his hands. The world was spinning and nothing made sense.

"Sir, just touch her. Feel her pulse. I'm telling you she's gone."

Elliot squeezed his eyes shut and sucked in a stabbing breath. His stomach lurched into his throat, but he forced himself to reach out and take her wrist between his fingers. Her skin was cold but supple, as if she had fallen asleep in a chilly room, but no matter how firmly he pressed or how hard he searched, he couldn't find a pulse. He shook his head and couldn't stop; his body started to rock.

"Sir, do you... did you know her?" Milo asked, his breath quickening.

Elliot doubled over, pain erupting inside his chest. He clutched her hand and pressed it against his forehead, willing her eyes to open.

"Wake up," he moaned. "Come on, Iris. Wake up and talk to me."

"Sir..." Milo said tentatively, rising to his feet. "Sir, we've got to go. We've got to get her to St. Thomas's."

Elliot's pulse roared inside his ears. "No one's going to touch her."

"Sir, we have to take her. A whole, fresh body without any wounds—"

"She's not a body!" He dropped her hand and scrambled up onto his feet. "No one's going to touch her."

"I'm sorry for your loss, sir, but there ain't nothing else to be done—"

Elliot gripped the front of Milo's coat and slammed him against the wall. "We're not taking her to St. Thomas's. I will tear my own heart out before I let them lay a hand on her."

Milo swallowed, his throat swelling with panic. "Then where will you take her?"

Elliot closed his eyes and tightened his grip. He wanted her somewhere safe and warm and clean. "We'll go to the palace."

"The palace! Have you gone barmy? We can't—"

"I'm taking her to the palace, Milo. You can help me or try to stop me, but either way, that's where I'm going."

Milo looked around as if for help, his face starting to sweat. Finally, he nodded and said, "All right. I'll help you take her."

A strange and eerie calm came over Elliot as they lifted Iris and carried her back to the carriage. His eyes were open, but he didn't see. His muscles strained, but he didn't feel them. Once they'd placed her inside, he automatically started to climb in beside her, but then he realized Milo might change his mind and drive to St. Thomas's, so he closed the door and hoisted himself up into the passenger seat. They didn't speak on the way to the palace, and—for once—Elliot didn't know what Milo was feeling, because he couldn't feel anything at all. Not even himself.

They pulled up next to the stables in the rear, beside the garden, and before Milo could stop him, Elliot leapt from his seat, opened the carriage door, and picked up Iris.

"Where are you taking her?" Milo called, his voice shrill and unsteady.

Elliot answered without looking back. "I don't know."

He didn't. All he knew was he wanted her somewhere peaceful and quiet. With numb arms, he carried her through a side door and into a hallway. Halfway through the cramped passage, he passed a room of garden supplies, including a wicker settee with a dusty but unstained cushion. He stepped inside and gently laid her down on the settee, but when he did, the numbness dissolved and the pain behind it rushed back, breaking over his body like a wave and flooding his lungs. Tears erupted from deep in his throat, and he crumbled to his knees, curling one fist against the settee and jamming the other against his teeth so hard he tasted blood.

"Elliot? Elliot! What in God's name are you doing?"

He knew it was his father's voice, that Milo had probably gone to him the moment they got back, but he couldn't stop sobbing or pry his knees from the freezing concrete floor.

"Have you lost your mind?" his father cried, barreling toward him, his panic remote and inconsequential. "You brought a body *here*?"

"She's not a body!" Elliot cried again.

His father misunderstood. He moved around him and bent over Iris, checking the pulse in her wrist and throat and pressing his ear to her chest.

"She's not in *rigor mortis* yet, but Elliot, she's dead. What is wrong with you? Why on earth did you bring her here?"

Elliot couldn't raise his head. Hearing the word "dead" on his father's lips was the final blow.

"I'm going to get a footman to help Milo take her back to the carriage," his father said, his voice stern, but his fear as sharp as a knife. "Pull yourself together."

His footsteps faded away, and Elliot sucked in a rattling breath, pressing the base of his palms against his eyes to clear the blur. Milo might have been easy to fight, but he didn't stand a chance against his father and the footmen. He rose up onto his knees and looked down at Iris's face, which was still smeared with dirt from the unpaved alley where Milo found her. His chest cracking, he reached out and wiped the streaks away, clenching his jaw as his fingertips brushed her soft, cloudlike skin.

He thought of the first time they met, how the beauty of her spirit had stolen his breath before he saw her. The absence of that spirit was more than painful—it was a tragedy. There wasn't just a gaping hole in his heart, but in the world. He lifted her hand and pressed his moistened lips against her palm, feeling so much that his excess emotion seemed to flow into her, leaving his body for one that would never feel anything again. His brain screamed for him to get up, that his father would be back soon, but he closed his eyes and gripped her hand tighter, sliding her palm to his cheek. Her smooth, pale wrist was resting just beneath his lips.

And then, in the tomblike silence, he felt something jump beneath them.

He opened his eyes and raised his lips with a single thought: *a pulse*. But that wasn't possible; his own father had just examined and pronounced her dead. He leaned forward and stared at her face, but it looked exactly the same—until a frantic gasp tore through the air.

And she sat up.

Elliot scrambled backward along the floor, his heart in his throat. He'd lost his mind—his grief had caused his brain to detach from reality. She opened her mouth and another desperate inhale shattered the silence, and then her golden eyes flew open and darted about the room. Wild confusion erupted from her chest as she looked around, checking her body, her clothes, and the settee she was sitting on. She shook her head, as if to clear it, and then caught sight of Elliot, and the two of them stared at each other through the dusty beams of sunlight.

"Elliot," she breathed, and then she coughed, her voice rusty and raw. "What is going on? How did I get here? Where am I?"

Elliot shook his head. "No. This isn't real. You're dead."

Her eyes widened as fear—and strangely, guilt—washed through her veins. "Oh God, you must have found me. You found me unconscious in Somers Town."

"No," he cried, still shaking his head. "Not unconscious—*dead*."

"I wasn't dead," she insisted, raising her hands and swinging her legs to the floor. "I know I seemed that way, but I was alive, and I can explain." She sucked in a breath and rubbed the palms of her hands against her eyes. "Oh God. I let it go too far. I went out for too long."

Her words didn't make any sense, but Elliot didn't really hear them. The only sound that existed was the beat of his own heart, which pulsed with the same two words again and again: *She's alive, she's alive.*

She lowered her hands and exhaled. "What time is it now? Where did you bring me?"

Alive, alive, alive, alive.

"Elliot, where are we?"

He blinked and swallowed, his brain on fire. "I brought you to the palace."

Her lips parted, and Elliot felt her lungs freeze.

"I'm in Buckingham Palace?"

"Yes," he said, chilled by her sudden fear. "Iris, what's wrong?"

"I—I can't be here. I thought—before, I used to want—but now—" She clutched her skirt, her chest filling with panic. "What if she's right?"

"What do you mean? What if who's right?"

"I have to go. It might not be safe—"

"Holy mother of God."

Iris raised her head, the whites of her eyes expanding with terror, and Elliot leapt to his feet and turned around to see his father. He was standing in the doorway with a footman just behind him, his eyes wide, and his face as pale as a corpse.

"It's not possible."

Elliot opened his mouth and tried to think of what to say, but before he had the chance, Iris bolted from the settee. She flew past him and charged through the doorway, nearly knocking his father and the footman off their feet. Once she was gone, what was left of Elliot's reason dissolved, and he dashed through the doorway as well and tore after her down the hall.

"Iris, wait. You don't know where you're going!" he called.

But she didn't stop. She turned and ran down the corridor that would have led to the garden, but instead of turning left she turned right and into the palace proper. Elliot scrambled after her and into the Marble Hall, which was not only filled with priceless statues and art but busy servants. They stumbled against the walls and screamed in fright as Iris shot past them, but no amount of shouting or barriers could slow her down. Not until she reached the archway that led to the Grand Hall, where a sleepy, oblivious Cam strolled out and walked into her path.

The collision knocked them both off their feet and onto the marble floor, creating a thunderous *crash* that nearly stopped Elliot in his tracks. Cam sat up and gripped his head, releasing a string of expletives, but the words died in his throat when he saw Iris sprawled before him.

"Iris! Are you hurt? What are you doing—" he began, but she crawled back onto her feet and darted past him without a word.

"Cam!" Elliot yelled as he neared him. "She's trying to get out! But she's going the wrong way! We have to help her—"

"Stop that girl!"

Elliot turned around to see his father and the footman running through the Marble Hall. He and Cam looked at each other, and then the two of them dashed after Iris beneath the Grand Hall archway, screaming for her to stop and turn down a different corridor. But she didn't listen and didn't stop, and soon she was headed straight toward the palace's Grand Staircase, which led to the second floor and even fewer places to flee. Elliot's father was only a few steps behind him. In desperation, he shouted over his shoulder, "Let her go! She means no harm!"

"Elliot, that girl just *rose from the dead*!" his father cried.

Then everything stopped, because Iris collided with someone at the foot of the stairs. She stumbled backward and fell to the ground, just as she had with Cam, but this time, when she looked up, she remained frozen where she sat. Standing above her was Andrew and, beside him, the Lord Mayor, whose burning gaze roamed over her as if she were made of gold.

"What is this I hear about a girl who can rise from the dead?"

CHAPTER NINE

T he private space closest to the Grand Staircase was the
Green Drawing Room. It was as much gold as it was green, with
gilt mirrors and picture frames and buttery yellow fringe lining
the silken emerald curtains. The furniture was also green with delicate
gold accents, and Iris was curled in one of the chairs against the southern
wall. The Lord Mayor had ordered a maid to fetch her a warm blanket.
She didn't look cold, as usual, but it seemed the proper thing to do for a
girl in a dirt-stained dress, and the thick, blue flannel was currently
wrapped around her shoulders. The blanket made her look like a weary
guest being comforted, but everything else about the scene made her
seem more like a criminal being watched and interrogated.

She was the only person sitting. Elliot's father and the Lord Mayor
were standing a few feet in front of her, the Lord Mayor leaning back
against the fireplace mantle. Cam and Andrew were standing beside
a desk to the Lord Mayor's left, Andrew with his secretarial quill and
notebook ready. Elliot hung back away from everyone, near the
room's closed door, watching Iris and trying to slow the breathing her
fear had quickened.

"Now," the Lord Mayor said, straightening up from his place at the
mantel, concealing his excitement with a cool and even tone. "Who
would like to begin? How did this girl come to be here today?"

Elliot swallowed and looked at his father, who glanced at the Lord Mayor.

"Elliot was helping me with a job for the hospital," he said. "He and Milo went out this morning to look for potential cadavers."

Cam and Andrew raised their heads and stared at Elliot, and even Iris's frightened gaze flitted in his direction.

"You were out... looking for bodies?" Cam asked, not bothering to mask his horror.

Elliot's throat grew dry as he searched for what to say.

"Yes," his father said calmly. "Just for today. As a favor to me."

Elliot looked at his father, gratitude swelling inside his chest, but then he remembered the reason he was lying for him now. He didn't want the Lord Mayor to know the mistake his son had made, what a weak, repulsive creature he'd become as a result.

"He and Milo found this girl," he continued to the Lord Mayor. "But instead of taking her to St. Thomas's, they brought her here. Because..."

He glanced over at Elliot and then quickly looked away. Back in the garden supply room, Elliot had been too distraught to wonder what his father thought of his actions and his tears. Now, however, he felt the knife twisting inside his heart. He didn't know Iris, but he knew she meant something to Elliot—that he'd brought her there in the madness of grief he understood himself. Grief he'd been trying to hide, deny, and forget for the last five years.

"I suppose he wasn't certain she was dead," he quickly recovered. "So he brought her here to me, and I examined her myself." He turned back to Iris, a resurgence of disbelief transcending his pain. "She had no breath and no pulse, Harlan. I swear on my life she was dead."

"I wasn't dead."

Iris's voice rang out like a bell, and everyone turned to her. Her fear was giving way to the rage she'd felt in the music hall, and just as she had then, she masked the feeling with sheer perfection, glancing down and murmuring, "If you would pardon me, sir."

"My dear," the Lord Mayor said. "It is you who must pardon us." He stepped toward her, his fierce delight and fascination swelling.

"We've been terribly rude, I fear. Won't you please tell us your name?"

"My name is Iris Faye."

"And you're an American it seems."

"Yes, sir."

She went on to tell him the same story she'd told Cam and Elliot, how her late mother had come to London to work with English suffragettes, though this time she left out the crack about absolute monarchies. The Lord Mayor listened with interest, but Elliot's father seemed not to hear her. Instead, he stared at her face with a heavily furrowed brow, feeling a peculiar blend of confusion and recognition.

"Your eyes," the Lord Mayor said when she finished. "They're quite remarkable. And I think I've seen those dresses on the girls at *La Maison Des Fleurs*." He turned to Cam with an eyebrow raised. "Is this the waitress I heard you and Charlie Hands discussing the other night?"

Elliot's blood burned as he remembered Charlie's words, but Cam's ran cold with fear, which he hid with a crooked smile. "Yes. She waited on us when we were there a few nights ago."

"What a coincidence," the Lord Mayor replied, turning back to Iris, whose rage had only increased at the mention of Charlie's name. "So you say you weren't dead, my dear," he began, looking her over again, and Elliot sank his fingernails into his palms inside his pockets. The Lord Mayor's sense of power had inflated with the news that she was the "chit" Charlie wanted to "take down a peg," and now he was intrigued by more than her possible resurrection.

"My friend, Dr. Morrissey, is the most renowned and accomplished physician in London," the Lord Mayor continued. "And he swears on his life that you were dead when he saw you this morning. And yet, here you sit—alive and claiming you always have been. So, if you please, explain to me why Dr. Morrissey's wrong."

Iris looked into his eyes, her demeanor smooth and cool, but Elliot felt the storm of emotion building beneath her skin. It was not only made up of rage and terror, but also exhilaration, as if she'd been handed a gift she both dreaded and desired. After a long pause, something locked into place inside her, and although the fear remained, a quiet confidence took over. She straightened her shoulders and let out a breath.

"Dr. Morrissey believed I was dead because I had *almost* no pulse. I'd slowed my heart and breathing as far as I could without actually dying. My heart was still beating, just too slowly for anyone to detect."

The Lord Mayor's mirth dissolved. "What do you mean you *slowed your heart*?" he asked, stepping toward her.

"Exactly what I said. I slowed it the way other people close their fists or open their hands. It's something I've been able to do ever since I can remember. If I tell my body to do something, it does it. I have complete control."

Silence swelled in the room, and Elliot's father shook his head. "I don't understand. Your body does whatever you *tell* it to do?"

"Yes. Well, anything the body is capable of. I couldn't tell it to fly, for instance. The body doesn't do that. But hearts speed up and slow down, flesh heals, temperatures rise and fall, so I can make my body do all those things, and do them faster."

"You're saying you can change your heart rate and temperature at will?"

"More than that. I can give myself bursts of adrenalin to make myself faster or stronger. I can hold my breath under water longer than most people if I have to. I can stop myself from feeling pain by deadening my nerves, and even though I still need to eat, drink, and sleep to stay alive, I don't have to feel hungry, thirsty, or tired if I don't want to. I can make my body fight infection before a virus takes hold, and I can heal a flesh wound within a matter of seconds."

For a moment, the Lord Mayor simply stared at her, his eyes on fire. Then, abruptly, he turned around and charged toward the desk, leaving Cam and Andrew just enough time to leap out of the way. He rifled through a drawer, closed it, and then returned to Iris, holding out a silver letter opener. "Show me."

Iris stood, removed the blanket, and took the opener from him. Then, without hesitation, she dragged the blade across her palm, not even flinching as blood erupted along her smooth, white skin. Once she was done, she dropped the hand with the blade and held out the other, and Elliot's mouth grew dry as he watched the wound instantly close, leaving her palm a little bloodstained but whole and good as new.

He thought of the night in the aviary, how he'd seen a streak of blood on her hand but no injury beneath it. That night she'd also claimed adrenalin helped her to lift the marble wing, and when he'd mentioned how cold it was, she'd shivered as if on cue. Now he understood how she could feel shame without sweating or blushing, how rage could roar inside her while her pulse stayed slow and even. He shook his head, and in spite of the frightful and dire situation, an astonished smile crept across his face.

She *was* like a *fée*.

The room was silent, except for a murmured "Jesus Christ" from Cam, but then Andrew—who never spoke out of turn—said, "It's like she's a Hyde."

Perhaps they'd all been thinking it—even Elliot, in the back of his mind—but his father soon reminded them of why that couldn't be.

"Hydes only heal in their monstrous state, not in their human form," he said. "Besides, the drug is fatal to women. She couldn't be a Hyde."

"You're right; I'm not," Iris said, sitting back down and setting the blade on a stand beside her chair. "I've been able to do this my whole life, even back in Kansas."

The Lord Mayor inclined his head and stared down into her face, no longer bothering to hide his fascination. "What of the rest of your family? Could they do these things as well?"

"No. My mother and my grandparents were perfectly ordinary."

"What of your father?"

"I don't know. I never knew who he was."

She said the words without shame, just as she had at the music hall, which seemed to shock the Lord Mayor as much as anything else.

"You say you slowed your heart rate and breathing on purpose the other night," Elliot's father said. "Why would you do such a thing?"

Iris let out a breath and tucked a curl behind her ear. "Adrenalin can make me fast and strong enough to outrun or fight off the average man, but without a gun, I don't stand a chance against a Hyde. I may be able to heal, but I can't regrow a heart, so the only way to protect myself from them is to play dead. They hunt by sensing heartbeats—that's why they don't attack the dead—so if I slow mine down enough, they miss it and pass me by. Last night, however, I must have gone too far and lost consciousness."

"How did you manage to finally regain it?" Elliot's father asked.

Iris glanced at Elliot, and he knew she hadn't meant to, because her throat began to close and she quickly looked back at her lap. "I don't know. I've never had that happen to me before. But if I hadn't, or if your people hadn't found me first..."

A genuine shudder ran through her, and Elliot shook as well, imagining her burned or buried alive, or something worse.

"I think it's safe to say what happened was fortunate for all of us," the Lord Mayor said, squatting down before her so the two of them were eye to eye and speaking gently, as if she were a lost and frightened child. "You are a unique and fascinating young woman, Miss Faye, and I'd like for you to stay with us and let Dr. Morrissey study you. Surely, there is much we can learn from you and your special gifts."

It wasn't a request, because the Lord Mayor didn't make them, and once again, Iris was filled with both fear and elation. The Lord Mayor smiled, and everything inside her recoiled from him, but she blinked and parted her lips as if flattered.

"I'd be honored, sir."

"Excellent," he said, straightening up. "I'll send word to *La Maison Des Fleurs* that Iris Faye will not be returning to work for quite some time. While you're here, everything you need will be taken care of. We'll even have a formal dinner tonight to introduce you. I'm sure one of the ladies will have a suitable dress you can wear, at least until we're able to have some new ones made for you."

"But Harlan," Elliot's father interjected. "How will we explain... I mean, surely you don't want the others to know—"

"I've already thought of that, Frank. We'll tell everyone that Iris is Andrew's long-lost American cousin. She and her family came here before the quarantine, but her parents have died, and since Andrew's mother can't care for her, we've taken her under our wing. Everyone knows Lorraine's been out of her mind since Robert's death."

Shame and even a rare burst of anger erupted in Andrew's chest, but only Cam and Elliot glanced in his direction.

"I'll have the servants prepare a room," the Lord Mayor said to Iris. "I hope I can trust you won't attempt to run from us again."

Iris blushed, but her blood was cold as ice. "Of course not, sir. I only ran this morning because I was frightened and in a strange place. What girl in her right mind wouldn't jump at the chance to live in a palace?"

Everything was cream in the room the Lord Mayor gave to Iris. After the footman who'd led her there left and closed the door behind him, she stood in awe, surveying the chamber's gold and ivory draping. The bed in the center was tall, sturdy, and carved from smooth, pale oak, and when she ran her fingers over the bedspread, she found it was silk. She hadn't been in the presence of such nice things since Lady Cullum's death, and for a moment, she felt like a carefree little girl again.

It was only a moment, however, because she wasn't at Lady Cullum's. She was at Buckingham Palace, the place her mother had absolutely forbidden her to go, having just told the Lord Mayor of London the secret she'd promised her never to tell.

But it's all right, she told herself. *Just as you said, no one here knows who you really are. They never knew Virginia had a daughter; your mother is safe.*

She closed her eyes and fought the wave of guilt that rose in her stomach. Her mother might be safe, but she was certainly wild with panic. Knowing what Iris had done would make her livid, but knowing nothing was worse. Somehow, she had to find a way to let her know what happened.

Exhausted, and still not entirely sure she hadn't lost her mind, Iris sat down on the bed, but then she felt something poking at her thigh through the skirt of her dress. Realization dawned as she reached into her pocket and drew out *An Anthology of Birds*. With reverence, she started to place the book on a nearby nightstand, but then a knock at the door caused her to jump and nearly drop it. She slowed her breathing, sat the book down, and went to answer the door, but when she pulled it open, her heart leapt into her throat again.

Elliot stood before her, filled with so much emotion it seemed to be coming off him in waves, his wide green eyes so urgent and intense it made her breath hitch. She pushed back the blood that had rushed to her cheeks, but then she remembered that there was no point, which was simultaneously thrilling, liberating, and terrifying.

"I know it's improper," he said. "But may I come in?"

"Yes, of course."

He looked both ways down the hallway and then quickly stepped inside, and Iris closed the door and turned to face him. "I'm so glad you're here. I wanted to thank you earlier but—"

"Thank me?" He spun around. "For what? For bringing you into the lion's den? For making you a captive?"

Iris blinked. "Elliot, if anyone else had found me lying unconscious in that alley—"

"Iris, I came here to tell you I can still help you get out. The Lord Mayor doesn't care about anyone but himself. He's perfectly willing to hurt other people to get the things he wants. And he wants something from you, badly, though I'm not sure what."

"I know," she said. "Trust me, I... I know what kind of man he is. But it's my choice to stay here—that's why I chose to tell him the truth. I knew he would be intrigued, that he would want to keep me close." She exhaled and took a step toward him. "I'm sorry I didn't tell you the truth myself before today, especially after you were honest with me about your gift."

He shook his head and laughed, though she wasn't exactly sure why. "You don't have to apologize for anything," he said. "I told you before, your feelings are yours to do with as you wish." He shoved his hands in his pockets as if to somehow contain himself. "So you really want to stay here? Even though it might not be safe?"

"Yes. I really do."

"Why?"

She took a breath and clenched her jaw. "A lot of reasons."

Elliot bit his lip and lowered his gaze to the ivory carpet, and she couldn't help but ask, "Do you... not *want* me here?"

He laughed again, removed his hands from his pockets, and shoved them back through his hair. "I want you safe, and I want you free—not some kind of prisoner for the Lord Mayor to dissect. But, of course, the thought of always having you near..." He paused and met her gaze, and the naked longing inside his eyes stole the dwindling breath from her lungs. "Of course I want that."

Iris moved her mouth but, for a moment, no sound came out. "I—I suppose I thought that maybe you'd be... repulsed."

She'd intended the comment to be a joke, poking fun at his reaction to *her* discovery, but once the words had passed her lips, she realized they were true. The thought of him being repelled by her was nothing less than crushing, and until that moment, she hadn't realized how much she truly feared it.

"Iris," he said. "This morning, when I thought that you were dead..."

His jaw twitched, and Iris quit breathing, lost in the storm of his eyes. She wanted to tell him that he was one of the reasons she wanted to stay, that he shouldn't be, that she'd tried to make him not be, but he was. She could slow her heart or speed it up, but she couldn't stop it from wanting this boy who saw inside her soul, this boy who, with or without his gift, was filled with audacious compassion, who was brave enough and strong enough to trust her and tell her the truth. She trusted him, too, with abandon that was insane and electrifying, and suddenly, she found herself reaching up to touch his face. The moment she did, however, he sucked in breath and clenched his fists, and she dropped her hand and backed away.

"I'm sorry," she stammered. "I didn't mean to feel... I mean, to try and touch... I know it's hard for you to—"

But she didn't get to finish, because Elliot threw his arms around her and pulled her against his chest, so tightly she could feel the strain of his muscles beneath his coat. A startled breath escaped her, and she collapsed and melted against him, clinging to him and burying her face against his neck. His breath hitched, and he shuddered against her but didn't let up or let go, and she trembled, too, as if she were both on fire and under water, aching with heat but also strangely soothed and satiated. She lifted her head and looked up at his face, but the moment their eyes locked, something even stranger happened. A feeling shot through her veins, another bolt of fire and water, but there was something *other* about it.

As if it weren't her own.

She gasped and backed away, and Elliot's face burst into flames.

"I'm sorry," he said. "I shouldn't have done that—"

"No! No, that's not it!" She paused and pressed her hands to her mouth, staring up at him. "Elliot, since becoming an empath, have you ever... shared *your* feelings with someone else?"

"What do you mean?"

"Have you ever tried to see if you can not only feel the feelings of others, but *give* your feelings to them?"

He furrowed his brow. "Of course not. Why?"

"Because," she said, lowering her hands. "I think you just did."

"What?"

"Just now, when we looked at each other, I felt something that wasn't *mine*. It was like a copy of what I was feeling myself, but not the same thing. It was... foreign somehow."

Elliot's lips parted. "That's a bit what it feels like for me. When I feel the feelings of others."

She nodded, her breath growing shallow. "And what's more, I think I've felt it before. This morning, in the moments just before I woke up at the palace, I remember feeling something bracing and powerful." She took a step toward him. "Elliot, I think it was you. I think you gave your feelings to me, and they were what revived me."

"What? That's impossible! I wasn't even trying—"

"Some of the things I can do I discovered without really trying, either. Here—take my hand and see if you can do it now."

He laughed and backed away. "Do what? *Give* my feelings to you?"

"Yes."

"I wouldn't have the first idea how to—"

"Here. I'll guide you through it." She took his hand, and he flinched at the touch but didn't pull away. "Maybe you can do it the same way I talk to my body. Close your eyes and calm your mind—imagine something peaceful."

He shook his head and laughed again as if she had lost her mind, but eventually he relented, closed his eyes, and took a breath. They stood together in silence, and for a while, nothing happened, but then, gradually, she felt his breathing begin to deepen. Soon, his face was smooth and relaxed, as if he were falling asleep, and his pulse took on a slow and even beat beneath her fingers.

"What are you thinking of?" she murmured, unable to help herself.

His face flushed, but he swallowed and answered, "Painting with my mother."

Iris swallowed as well and slowed her heart so it wouldn't disturb him. "All right," she said. "Now, imagine letting your feelings leave your body. Think about them flowing out of you and into me."

Elliot took another breath and slowly began to exhale, and when he did, she felt the same invasion of something foreign, but this time the feeling was warm and bright, like a steadily burning candle. It pulsed inside her, filling her body with light and hope and joy, and she gasped and squeezed his hand.

"You did it, Elliot! I felt it!"

Unfortunately, her exclamation jolted his concentration, and he jumped and dropped her hand, causing the feeling to dissolve.

"What did you feel?" he asked, blinking and opening his eyes.

"Peaceful and safe. Confident and alive. Like I was... home." She beamed at him, still glowing from the warmth. "It was beautiful."

"I can't believe it," he said, expelling a disbelieving breath. "I think I felt it, too. I felt something spreading from me to you."

"You see?" she said. "I was right. It was you who brought me back."

"Now wait, we don't necessarily know—"

"It was you. I'm certain." She moved toward him and gripped his hand again. "You saved my life."

His skin warmed beneath hers, and he steadied himself with a breath. "If I were Cam," he said, clearing his throat, "I'd make some kind of joke about how we're even now."

She smiled and reached up to touch his face. "I'm glad you're not."

"Elliot, I never knew you were such a ladies man. A new girl arrives and you're inside her room in less than an hour."

Iris dropped her hand and spun around to face the door, where a girl in a lavish blue and ivory dress stood with her arms folded. She was small and slight, as if barely old enough for the corset she wore, but her eyes were keen as a cat's, and her lips were curled in a knowing grin.

"Philomena?" Elliot cried, stepping away form Iris. "How did you get in here?"

"As much as it might astound you, I'm quite adept at opening doors." She marched to Iris and held out her hand. "I'm Philomena Blackwell."

"Um, hello," she replied, taking her hand. "I'm—"

"Iris Faye. I know." She dropped her hand and turned to Elliot. "Now run along. Iris and I are going to have a chat."

Elliot looked at Philomena as if he wanted to kill her, and Iris couldn't help but feel the same. "All right," he finally said. "I'll see you both at dinner tonight." He glanced at Iris again and then turned and left the room, emitting a heavy sigh as he closed the door behind him.

"Now," Philomena said, taking her hand. "Let's begin." She guided her to the bed, hopped up, and patted the spot beside her, and after a moment of stunned silence, Iris sat as well. "The first thing you should know," Philomena continued, "is I know everything. Who you are, what you can do, and why you're really here."

"What?"

"I was listening outside the door while you were in the Green Drawing Room. I have a footman who's loyal to me and lets me know whenever anything happens in the palace. After you tore through the

Marble Hall this morning, he came and found me. I just thought you should know straight away that I know all about you."

"A-all right," Iris stammered. "So… is that why you're here?"

"You mean because you can heal yourself and all that? I couldn't care less. I'm here because you've lived in the city and worked in a music hall."

Iris blinked, sure she hadn't heard right. "Hold on a minute. You know I have the power to *heal*, and you're here because you're interested in hearing about music halls?"

"Partly," she said, entirely matter-of-fact. "It *is* my dream to perform, but what I really want to know are the basics of city life."

"Why?"

Philomena took a breath and set her dainty jaw. "I know you'll probably think I'm a spoiled, ungrateful brat for saying this, but I want more than anything to leave the palace forever."

Iris didn't say anything, because Philomena was right: The statement sounded not only spoiled and thankless but also insane.

"Let me ask you this," Philomena said, reading her face. "I've lived in this palace since I was two—that's thirteen years now—in all that time, how often do you think I've left the grounds?"

Iris shrugged, so Philomena answered.

"Zero times. I haven't left this palace once since I was two years old."

This gave Iris pause. As grand and safe as the palace was, the thought of spending her whole life trapped inside it was suffocating.

"I will escape," Philomena continued. "And if the quarantine's ever lifted, I'll leave London, too. But as it stands, I need to make a plan to live in the city. That's why I need you—to tell me what I need to know." She took a breath, her fierce, serious face hardening further. "It's truly a gift that you came here now, because I don't have much longer. I need to get out of this palace by the end of the coming season."

"Why?"

She shifted, looking uncomfortable for the first time since she came in. "Because my parents are planning to have me married by the fall."

Iris's eyes widened. "But you're only fifteen years old."

"They've said for years they would marry me off as soon as my courses came, and in early September, they did. I managed to keep it hidden until a few days after Christmas, when my mother discovered a stash of bloody rags I had yet to clean."

A wave of pity swarmed Iris's heart. When her courses came, she and her mother actually celebrated, spending their extra coins on two vanilla and almond meringues. "Why on earth would they want you married so soon?"

"Because they're frightened. They think I'm wild and dangerous, like a rabid dog or an unbroken horse, and only a man and a passel of brats will tame me and save them from shame."

Iris looked at Philomena. She may have begun her courses, but her body was still a child's. If she conceived that year, would she even survive the birth? She raised her head and saw the fear that had sharpened on Philomena's face, and she knew she wasn't the only one of the two of them to think it.

"I won't let it happen," Philomena said. "I will get out."

"How do you plan on escaping?"

"That's actually the easy part. Albert—my footman—has already consented to smuggle me out. The hard part is what happens after, how to stay hidden and make a life for myself out in the city. That's why I need you."

Iris bit her lip as an idea took hold in her mind. "The footman—you trust him completely?"

"With my life. He'll never betray me."

"How can you be sure?"

Philomena sighed. "I suppose it makes me a terrible person for using him like I do, but he had a sister who died last year, and I remind him of her. He's lied for me, spied for me, and looked out for me at night when I've gotten restless and wanted to roam. He's had countless opportunities to betray me and never has."

Iris searched Philomena's face. She'd only just met this girl and didn't know the footman at all, but it might be safer to contact her mother through someone she *didn't* know, someone with no reason to ask any questions or dig any deeper.

"Do you think if I gave you a letter," she asked, "and you gave it to him to deliver, he could be trusted not to read it or tell anyone where he took it?"

Philomena met her gaze with the same fierce and unabashed frankness with which she entered the room. "Alby wouldn't do anything if I told him not to do it."

Iris let out a breath and scooted closer to Philomena. "Then we have a deal," she said. "What would you like me to tell you first?"

CHAPTER TEN

Elliot had been nervous at the previous night's formal dinner, but not nearly as nervous as he was at eight that evening. He'd combed his hair until he thought it might fall out of his head, and even though his eveningwear was clean, he was sweating beneath it. Once again, he was standing against the wall in the State Dining Room, but this time he had refused the glass of champagne a footman offered. He shoved his hands in his pockets and searched the room, looking for Iris, but then he saw Cam walking toward him and wearing a playful grin.

"She'll be here soon," he said, strolling over to his side. "She and Andrew are brushing up on their family history."

Joy and excitement were fizzing inside his chest like champagne bubbles, and when Elliot glanced at his face, he saw it reflected in his eyes.

"What are you grinning about?" he asked, and then it dawned on him. "Did Andrew fix—"

"He did," Cam beamed. "The Victor is now in working condition. We're trying it out tonight, and you are formally invited."

"The pantry at midnight?" Elliot asked, as that was when and where they usually met to test the contraband.

"Yes. And, just so you know, Miss Faye will be in attendance as well. I invited her a moment ago, and she graciously accepted."

Elliot's faced flushed. "You didn't have to—I mean, just because I—"

"I don't know what you're talking about," Cam said, taking a sip of his drink. "I simply thought that, as an American, she'd appreciate hearing some new music from her country."

Elliot smiled, his chest blooming with gratitude and affection. "Well, that was very thoughtful of you. I'm sure she appreciates it."

"Speak of the devil," Cam replied.

Elliot immediately turned to the dining room entrance.

Iris was walking beneath the archway, holding Andrew's arm. Her curls were piled on top of her head for the first time since he'd known her, with a few dark, corkscrew tendrils framing the sides of her face. Elliot didn't know whose dress she was wearing, but it seemed too small, stopping at her ankles and revealing more of her bosom than was currently fashionable. His cheeks burned, and he quickly forced his gaze back up to her face. However small, the dress's purple hue made her eyes stand out even more, and they glowed like pools of liquid gold in the flickering candlelight.

"She's truly beautiful," Cam remarked.

Elliot nodded, beyond the envy he'd felt when Cam said the same thing after they met at the music hall.

"*Et magique,*" Cam continued. "*Juste comme nous le pensions.*"

Elliot smiled. He'd said, "And magic. Just like we thought."

He managed to speak with Iris for a moment before dinner started, just long enough for her to confirm that her dress was indeed too small and that she would join them in the pantry. Before he could ask what Philomena had wanted back in her room, however, the meal was announced, and the guests all took their seats at the dinner table.

As Elliot had expected, Iris was seated next to Andrew, but the two of them were too far away for him to talk to her. He watched her, though, and she handled herself with confidence and grace, pleasantly chatting with those around her and smoothly correcting herself if she picked up the wrong utensil. When the Lord Mayor stood and announced why she'd joined their company, the rest of the courtiers nodded and smiled at her with mild acceptance. Beneath their veneers, however, most of the women felt madly jealous—both of her beauty and of the grand attention she was receiving—except for Philomena, who grinned and gave her a little wink.

Elliot's favorite reaction, however, was that of Charlie Hands. He hadn't noticed Iris at all until the Lord Mayor's speech, and when he realized that she was not only seated at the table but also Andrew Heron's cousin, the rage and frustration he felt burned through the flesh of his doughy face. He couldn't touch her now, couldn't *talk* about her the way he used to. She might still only be working class, but Andrew was one of the Lord Mayor's most valuable assistants, and he couldn't chance offending someone so close to the hand that fed him. Still, a wicked part of Elliot wanted him to try, just to give Iris the chance to hand him his arse on a silver platter.

Once the meal was over, Philomena got her wish; the Lord Mayor moved the crowd to the Music Room to hear her sing. The courtiers settled themselves in the chairs laid out on the hardwood floor, and Andrew took his seat behind the mahogany grand piano. The tall, domed, horseshoe-shaped hall had excellent acoustics, but once Philomena began to sing, it was clear she didn't need them.

The song she had chosen was *Love has Eyes*, an old piece Elliot had heard many times before, but he had never heard anybody sing it like Philomena. Even though the melody was cheerful and upbeat, most girls sang the song in a tone that was smooth, airy, and light. Philomena, however, belted the notes with strength that nearly shook the room, proving her voice as large, fierce, and powerful as her spirit. The sound was piercing but beautiful in a resonant, soul-stirring way, and Elliot preferred it to any other voice he'd heard. As he looked around, however, he found most of the women—especially her mother—felt shocked and uneasy, while the men found her entertaining, like a kitten that thinks it's a lion. Eventually, he closed his eyes and focused on only her feelings, which were so bright and full of joy they wiped out all the others.

At midnight, Elliot crept through the darkened hallways and down to the pantry, his heart pounding so hard he thought it might burst right through his chest. It was true that he was breaking the rules, and also about to hear music no one in London had heard before, but seeing Iris was more exciting than either of those things. Normally, when he and Cam and Andrew had these secret nights, they didn't bother dressing in anything more than their shirtsleeves and braces, but because of Iris, Elliot had decided to wear a suit, complete with a coat, vest, and tie—as was proper in front of a woman. When he tiptoed down the steps and into the darkened pantry, however, he saw that he was the only one of the three of them to do so.

"Out for a night at the opera?" Cam asked, stifling a laugh.

He and Andrew were sitting on a crate of fruit against the wall, their giddy excitement so heady and thick it almost made Elliot dizzy. At Cam's remark, Andrew started to laugh but stopped himself, looking up at Elliot with apologetic eyes.

"Don't listen to him. We should have dressed properly, too, since Iris is coming."

"What about me?"

Elliot spun around to see Iris slipping down the stairs, but once she stepped into view, his pounding heart leapt into his throat. Once again, her hair was down and billowing over her shoulders, but instead of a dress, she was wearing a cream-colored nightgown trimmed with lace. The frock was thick and covered her from her neck down to her slippers, but Elliot flushed as if she were standing in front of him totally naked. The purple gown had been skimpy, and the waitress's dress had been skin-tight. But beneath them both, her body had still been bound by a formal corset, which made it seem contained and distant somehow, as if sealed off. The nightgown, however shapeless, was loose and clearly a single layer, and he'd never been near a woman with so little fabric between them. When she saw him blush, she knit her brow, but then she looked down at herself.

"Oh, I'm sorry," she said, looking back up. "It's just, that purple thing was a nightmare, and my old dress is still so dirty—"

"It's fine," he said, clearing his throat. "You look absolutely lovely."

"What am I—chopped liver?"

Elliot blinked as Philomena materialized next to Iris. She was dressed in a nightgown as well, but hers was a frilly, pale sky blue, and her hair was done up in little rag curls that made her look even more like a little girl than usual. Her presence was a surprise, but Elliot didn't feel truly shocked until a tall, broad-shouldered footman emerged from the shadows just behind her. Cam and Andrew leapt to their feet, equally alarmed, but Iris raised her hands and stepped forward.

"Don't worry. I know it wasn't my place, but I invited Philomena. She already knows the real reason I'm here."

"She *what*?" Elliot gasped.

"That's why she came to see me today. She was listening outside the drawing room when I told the Lord Mayor the truth. We can trust her; she brought Albert along to keep watch for us tonight."

"You're welcome," Philomena added, marching over to Cam. "I can't believe you were going to listen to *brand new music* without me, you prat!"

She smacked him on the arm, and he winced and put up his hands in defense. "My mistake, Miss Blackwell. One I shall never make again."

"You'd better not," she growled, and then she returned to the waiting footman. "Stay near the doorway and warn us if someone's coming, Alby. Thanks." She raised herself onto her toes, and he bent down to allow her to kiss his cheek. Then he turned around and hurried back up the stairs without a word.

"Well," Cam said, after a moment of stunned and awkward silence. "Now that we've got girls..." He crouched beside the crate and produced a cut-glass bottle of bourbon. "And something to drink, it's a party."

In order to ensure no one else would hear the Victor, Cam had decided to try it out in the subterranean kitchens. He handed the bourbon to Andrew, lit a candle, and opened a door in the back, and they followed him out of the pantry and down a set of worn, stone stairs.

"Iris," Andrew murmured as they followed Cam through the dark. "When Cambrian got out the bourbon, it reminded me of a question I had. Do you think your abilities would allow you to consume alcohol without feeling the effects? The thought occurred to me at dinner, and I was curious."

"I don't know," she answered. "I've never really tried. Dealing with drunken men every day has dimmed the appeal of spirits for me. I don't mind if the rest of you drink, however," she added quickly.

"Good," Philomena chirped, seizing the bottle from Andrew, removing the stopper, and taking a swig. Her eyes bulged, but she blinked against the burn and grinned once she got it down. "That was exhilarating. Later, I'll have to have some more."

The stairs opened up to reveal a small space, sort of like an open room, lined with shelves and cabinets and a couple of massive ovens. The air was cool and perfumed with herbs and spices like thyme and rosemary, and their shoes made soft little scraping sounds against the uneven stone. Cam sat his candle on top of a shelf, and then he and Andrew walked to a cabinet in the back, returning with the Victor Talking Machine in both their arms. The palace had an old gramophone that everyone except for Iris had heard at one time or another, but this contraption was newer, sleeker, and apparently, could produce much better and longer lasting sound. Once he and Andrew had placed the machine on the floor, Cam opened a side compartment and pulled out the two new records.

"Which should we play first?"

The rest of them crowded around and took a peek at the records' titles: *The Pine Apple Rag* and *The Weeping Willow Rag*.

"*The Pine Apple Rag*," Philomena suggested. "The other one sounds sad."

"*The Pine Apple Rag* it is." Cam grinned. "The fruit before the tree."

He slid the second record back inside the side compartment, and everyone else spread out and took a seat on the flagstone floor. They formed a sort of reverent semicircle around the machine, with Iris on the left, Elliot beside her, Philomena next to him, and Andrew on the right. The room swelled with silence and electric anticipation as Cam laid out the record, turned the crank, and dropped the needle. At first, there was only static, so he took the moment to lower himself to the ground on Andrew's right. Then, with abruptness that jolted them all, the music began to play.

It was truly unlike anything Elliot had heard. Only a single piano played the foreign melody, but the vigorous, bouncing beat of the song made it seem like an orchestra. The tune was light but pulsing, and the rhythm was strong but erratic, like the wild heartbeat of someone who'd just dashed up a flight of stairs. Elliot found his own heart speeding up as he took it in, so much so that it leapt into his throat when Andrew spoke.

"Now I understand," he said. "I know why they call it 'Ragtime.'"

"Why?" Philomena asked.

"Because it's ragged. It's syncopated."

Cam blinked and furrowed his brow, turning to Andrew. "Sorry?"

"The rhythm," Andrew explained. "The accents on the beats are, well, purposely displaced. The weak ones are strong and the strong ones are weak. It makes the song seem uneven and disjointed. Not smooth, but ragged."

"It's thrilling," Iris murmured.

Elliot turned to look at her. Her breathing had grown as shallow as his, and her heart was singing with joy that quickened the blood in his own veins. Then, out of nowhere, a woman's voice soared out over the piano.

> Hark to that music, it's the Pine Apple Rag
> Lordy goodness how entrancing.
> Who on earth can keep from dancing?
> Tease up to me, ease up to me,
> Set me a reeling, Lord what a feeling,
> Oh, the Pine Apple Rag.

"How cheeky," Philomena exclaimed. "I adore it!"

In no time, she'd completely memorized the "cheeky" lyrics, and was singing along to the tune with her bright and robust voice. Slowly, the bourbon made its way around the semicircle, and at first, Elliot—like Iris—simply passed it along. As before, he didn't want to appear slow or sloppy in front of her, but soon the excitement grew so intense that his hands began to shake, and the next time the bottle came his way, he took a hasty gulp. Iris must have seen the desperation in the gesture, because she leaned over and whispered, "What's wrong?"

Elliot tightened his grip on the bottle and lowered it to his lap, closing his eyes as the alcohol seared his throat and swarmed his stomach. "It's just... too much," he murmured in reply. "Too much feeling."

Iris studied his face and then scooted a little closer. "What if you shared it with me?"

"Shared it with you? You mean share what... *everyone* is feeling?"

"It might lessen the impact for you, make it easier to bear."

"I don't even know if I can."

She smiled, took the bottle, and reached across him to give it to Philomena, causing his breath to hitch as the lace of her nightgown brushed his chest. Once she'd passed it off, she leaned back and offered him her hand. "You won't know until you try."

Elliot set his jaw, closed his eyes, and placed his hand in hers, flinching only slightly when their flesh made contact this time. He took a breath and concentrated just like earlier, imagining the excitement leaving him and flowing to her. After a moment, he felt the sensation slowly begin to drain, and his heart relaxed to a steady pace, and his breathing became more even. Iris sucked in a quiet gasp, and he knew that it was working, that the two of them were sharing the weight of the room's emotional pulse. He blinked, opened his eyes, and withdrew his hand from hers, and even though the feelings came rushing back, they seemed less daunting.

"It worked," he whispered. "Even now, I feel a bit more calm. Like the feelings are still there, but I'm not so overwhelmed."

She turned to him, her cheeks flushed. "How on earth do you do it? How do you handle... feeling so much?"

A small laugh escaped him. "Until I met you, I really didn't."

The song ended and, for a moment, all five of them sat in silence, in awe of the otherworldly thing they'd just experienced. Finally, Cam leapt up and took the record off the Victor, his euphoria so intense his feet seemed to barely touch the ground.

"Now it's time for *The Weeping Willow Rag,*" he announced, switching the discs. "We'll see if it's as sad as the lovely Miss Blackwell surmises."

He dropped the needle and then sat back down, taking a swig of the bourbon, and after another moment of static, the song began to play.

It wasn't sad. The rhythm was much slower than the previous song's had been, but it was just as "ragged" and somehow even more exciting. The melody had a lazy, dragging feel, like a heavy breeze, and it stumbled along with a rough but sweet and almost drunken air. Elliot felt it pull at him the way he imagined the ocean would, tugging him up and down along the waves with its honeyed strains.

"We have to dance," Philomena exclaimed, climbing up onto her feet, her eyes wild and her face flushed from the bourbon and the song, which—unlike the first—seemed to be entirely instrumental. "Who'll dance with me?"

"We don't know how to dance to this kind of music," Andrew said.

"That makes it even better," she replied. "We'll make it up."

She grabbed his hand and jerked him up onto his feet, and he stumbled against her, laughing in a way that implied he'd drunk as much bourbon as she had. With a lavish air, she laid her hand on his shoulder and placed his hand on her waist, and he followed her lead. She leapt and spun them both in graceless circles. Elliot, Cam, and Iris laughed, Cam louder than anyone, and Philomena stopped and attempted to glare at him through her smile.

"If you think you can do better, Cambrian, come and take his place."

"No, thank you," he replied, leaning back against the stone. "This is one of the most entertaining things I've ever seen."

He grinned at Andrew and Andrew grinned back, until Philomena grabbed his arms and swept him back into the dance. Cam laughed again and raised the bottle to his lips, his eyes like pale blue flames as he watched them twirl around the floor. Then, amid the fog of glee, Elliot felt something shift in Cam, something stronger than mere delight or riotous amusement. A longing spread through his body, from his fingertips to his toes, a soul-stirring ache as raw and magnetic as the music. Elliot blinked, furrowed his brow, and looked at Philomena. Could Cam possibly feel more for her than brotherly affection?

At the moment, she was convincing Andrew to lift her off the ground, but once he did, he tripped and stumbled back against a shelf, causing a massive jar of preserves to crash against the stone. They all erupted with laughter, Philomena most of all.

"The problem is that we're the only ones trying," she decided. "Elliot and Iris, you get up here, too."

"And what—dance?" Elliot asked, still laughing.

"No. Recite Shakespeare." She grabbed Iris's hand and seized the collar of Elliot's coat, dragging them onto their feet. "Yes, dance. Come on. I know you want to."

She flashed them both a wicked grin and returned her attention to Andrew, and Elliot stared at Iris in her single-layer nightgown. If he took her waist, as was proper, he'd be practically touching her naked skin. When he looked back up at her face, however, he saw she was smiling at him, so he swallowed, ran a hand back through his hair, and stepped toward her.

"Miss Blackwell!"

The voice sliced through the buzzing, cheerful air like an icy blade, and they stopped and spun around to see Albert rushing down the stairs.

"The Lord Mayor is coming."

The temperature dropped, and Elliot's mouth went dry.

"That's impossible," Cam said, leaping up and stopping the Victor's needle with a *scratch*. "He's asleep."

"No, he's in the Grand Hall. When something crashed, he started this way. He'll be here any minute."

The terror that flooded the room melded Elliot's feet to the floor, and for a moment, every one else seemed equally paralyzed. Then, abruptly, Cam bent down and seized the bottle of bourbon.

"I know what to do," he said, turning to Iris. "Come with me."

He grabbed her wrist without waiting for a response and started toward the stairs. She lurched after him, and Elliot finally pried up his feet and followed, Andrew, Philomena, and Albert stumbling close behind him.

"What are you doing?" he hissed at Cam. "You won't make it out in time!"

"I know," Cam replied. "We're not leaving." He reached the top of the stairs and threw open the door to the pantry, guiding Iris through it and then turning back around. "Stay down here and don't make a sound," he said. "No matter what."

He stepped through the door and closed it behind him, and Elliot, Andrew, Philomena, and Albert froze in the darkness. After a moment, however, Elliot noticed a sliver of light—a gap between the hinges of the door and the pantry wall. He crouched behind it and found that he could see into the room, and soon Andrew and Philomena were ducking close behind him. They watched as Cam steered Iris to a shelf lined with small glass jars, turning her to face him and placing the bourbon on the floor.

"Iris," he whispered, the ice of his terror penetrating the door. "I know you could probably throw me across the room, but please—don't."

"What?"

The floorboards beyond the pantry's outer door began to creak, and Cam reached out and knocked a few of the jars onto the floor. Iris gasped and started to speak, but he gripped her face, slammed her against the shelf, and covered her mouth with his own.

The air in the stairway dissolved, and Elliot's stomach dropped into his feet. He clutched the wall beside him, digging his fingernails into the stone, wanting to close his eyes but unable to look away.

"Cry out," Cam whispered.

Iris released was what likely a genuine yelp, because he clutched the hem of her nightgown and hiked it up her legs, exposing not only her stockings but a flash of smooth, white thigh. He drove his body into hers and crushed her mouth with his own again. Something in Elliot's brain snapped, and he started to leap to his feet. Fortunately, Andrew clasped his shoulder and jerked him back, and Elliot sucked in a startled breath, not only from the realization of what he'd almost done, but also because of the rage and disgust that had swarmed him at Andrew's touch. For whatever reason, the two of them were feeling exactly the same.

"Cambrian?"

The Lord Mayor's voice was stern, but Elliot felt the stunned excitement sizzling beneath it.

"Father!" Cam exclaimed, freeing Iris and backing away, twisting the fear he felt into a mask of alarmed surprise. The Lord Mayor descended the stairs and stepped into the light, glancing at Iris, whose thighs were still exposed by her bunched up skirt. She gasped and smoothed the fabric back over her legs, her cheeks darkening.

"I'm sorry, Father," Cam began, bending down and clumsily scooping the bourbon off the floor. "I came down here for a drink—although I'd probably already had too much—and Iris was here, looking for more of those pastries we had at dinner." He swallowed and glanced at the floor, his guise of shame so masterful Elliot thought he might actually blush. "Like I said, I'd had a bit to drink, and when I saw her here, wearing nothing but that nightgown…" He cleared his throat. "I suppose I lost control."

"And the pantry?" the Lord Mayor asked, nodding toward the shattered jars.

Cam bit his lip. "She wasn't exactly receptive to my advances."

A surge of amusement, and even a bit of pride, swept through the Lord Mayor, but his face was filled with nothing but sympathy as he walked to Iris and guided her away from the cluttered shelf. "Are you hurt, my dear?"

Her stomach lurched at his touch, but she shook her head and murmured, "No, sir."

He brushed her shoulders as if she were a child who'd fallen while playing. "You said that, with your adrenalin, you could muster enough strength to fight off the average man. If you don't mind my asking, why didn't you?"

She looked at him, eyes wide. "I would never do such a thing to the son of the Lord Mayor of London."

His lips curled into a grin, and he shook his head and sighed. "You've lived among women for most of your life, have you not?" he asked her gently. "After your mother passed, you lived in a girl's home or boarding house?"

She nodded, and he sighed again.

"Let this be a lesson to you about living amongst grown men: If you walk around in attire like that, chances are you'll get a response you won't be too pleased about."

Rage seared Iris's veins, but her face remained pale and cool, and the Lord Mayor patted her cheek and turned his attention to Cam.

"I trust you've calmed down enough to allow Miss Faye to return to her room without further interference?"

"Yes, of course," he said sheepishly.

The Lord Mayor smiled, and Elliot thought he would turn and leave, but instead, he walked to Cam and guided him back away from Iris, coming so close to the door Elliot sensed their heat through the boards.

"As tempting as it might be," the Lord Mayor murmured in Cam's ear. "I need you to leave the subject of my research untouched and intact."

Cam's blood froze, but he nodded obediently. Then, after a final grin, the Lord Mayor turned, climbed the stairs, and exited the pantry.

Neither Cam nor Iris moved or spoke for a solid minute. Then, slowly, Cam crept up the stairs and into the hall, returning after a moment and closing the door behind him.

"He's gone."

Elliot rose, opened the kitchen door, and stepped into the pantry, with Andrew, Philomena, and Albert emerging just behind him. The air in the room was warmer than that on the stairs, but it seemed frigid, and the silence that swelled around them only sharpened the bitter chill.

"Are you all right?" Cam asked, approaching Iris, but she stepped away.

"Yes. I'm fine."

"I'm sorry," he said. "It's the only thing I could think of to do—"

"I'm fine."

But she wasn't fine. She felt numb and sick, like she needed to go sit down, and Elliot opened his mouth to suggest it, but then Cam turned to him.

"El, I'm sorry. You understand, don't you?"

"Yes, of course I do."

Cam shifted his gaze to the rest of the group, remorse and self-disgust rising up inside his throat. "All of you—I'm sorry you had to see—"

"Cambrian, relax." Andrew stepped forward, the warmth in his heart reflected in his eyes. "You thought on your feet, and you did what you could to stop him. We're all grateful."

Cam looked at Andrew, his heart aching so badly Elliot thought it would break.

"Well, I *suppose* I'm grateful," Philomena said with a lavish sigh. "Even if you only chose the *second* prettiest girl."

She'd clearly meant the comment to be a joke to lighten the mood, but for Elliot, it actually had the opposite effect. It would have been unthinkable for Cam to choose Philomena, as she was the kind of girl men married to bear their noble children. The Lord Mayor might be set on a marriage between the two of them, but he would never condone Cam taking her virtue in the pantry. Cam had chosen Iris because he knew where she stood in the Lord Mayor's eyes; if it weren't for her abilities, she would be as disposable to him as a parlor maid.

Perhaps the same realization was currently sinking into Iris, because she cleared her throat and said, "I'll see you all tomorrow." Then she turned and climbed the stairs without waiting for a response.

"Iris," Elliot called, but she disappeared through the door, so he scrambled up the stairs as well and followed her into the hall. "Iris, wait," he whispered, and she stopped and turned around.

"Elliot, please. I'm really fine," she said as he approached, but then she paused and breathed a bitter laugh. "Oh, right. I forgot."

"If you want to be alone, I understand, and I'll let you go. But please, just let me tell you something first."

She sighed. "All right."

Elliot walked to a doorway to his right and turned the knob. The door was unlocked, so he pushed it open and beckoned Iris after him, and the two of them stepped inside a dark and silent gallery.

"I know how you feel," he said as he closed the door behind him, but then he realized how obvious and stupid the statement was. "I mean—you know what I mean—and you have every right to feel that way, but I thought it might help if you understood why Cam did what he did."

"Elliot, I understand—"

"I know you understand that he was trying to protect us, but he wasn't just afraid of being caught and reprimanded. The Lord Mayor, if he would have found out the truth... what he would have done..." He paused and swallowed. Cam wouldn't want him to tell her, but she needed to know. "I've never known a father who beat his son like the Lord Mayor beats Cam."

Iris's blood cooled. "I suppose I'm not surprised."

"And it's more than that," he continued. "The way Cam feels about his father... even I had no idea until after my affliction." He paused, suddenly thinking of something. "Here," he said, extending his hand. "I have no idea if this will even work, but may I try something?"

Iris placed her hand in his, and he swallowed against the wave of her apprehension and closed his eyes. He calmed his mind like he'd done before, and then he thought of Cam, dredging up the memories of his crushing fear and shame. The feelings gathered and pooled inside him, poisoning his blood, and then—before he could change his mind—he let them flow to Iris. She sucked in a breath and doubled over, her body going rigid, and he opened his eyes and released her hand.

"I'm sorry," he said. "I didn't want you feel something so terrible, but I thought if you knew, it would help you understand—"

"He feels like that?"

She raised her head, her eyes wide with horror, and Elliot nodded.

"I've never felt fear like that," she said, her breathing sharp and shallow. "And it's not only fear, but shame—murderous shame. Like he... loathes himself."

He nodded again. "I know. And I don't understand it at all."

She tilted her head, her lips parting. "That's why you haven't told him about your empathy," she murmured. "You don't want him to know you know."

Elliot nodded. "He'd feel betrayed. Not to mention even more ashamed than he already feels." Guilt swarmed his stomach. "Perhaps he'd be right; I betrayed him just now."

"No," she said. "You helped me to understand him, to see his heart. Think about how different the world would be if we could all do that." Elliot glanced away, and she craned her head to meet his gaze. "Elliot, I'm telling you—it's a gift, not a curse."

He let out a breath, suddenly much too tired to argue about it. "I'm just glad for Cam's sake that the Lord Mayor didn't catch us."

Iris sighed as well. "I'm glad for Philomena's sake, too. She told me that if her mother discovered she'd snuck out of bed again, she'd hire one of the parlor maids to be her personal guard."

Elliot furrowed his brow. "Her personal guard? What do you mean?"

"Someone to stay in her room with her at night and keep her from leaving."

A strange and hopeful plan began to take shape in Elliot's mind. "Come on," he said. "We need to go and talk to Philomena. If her mother wants someone to guard her, I know exactly who it should be."

CHAPTER ELEVEN

Elliot **persuaded Philomena to agree, but only after** assurances that Jennie wouldn't really prevent her from going wherever she wanted, only stay in her room at night and pretend to be her guard. He didn't tell Philomena or Iris why he wanted to make the ruse; when they asked, he simply said he would be grateful for the favor. As he'd expected, Philomena's mother was overjoyed, and once she'd agreed, he went to find Jennie and tell her the news himself. At first she was stunned, and then she merely curtsied and said, "Yes, sir," but both her heart and eyes were swimming with gratitude and hope. Elliot knew the arrangement wouldn't protect her from harm forever, or make any difference to the other female servants, but it made a difference to Jennie, and that would have to be enough.

For the next few days, Elliot's father suspended his corpse snatching duties, paying a medical student to go out with Milo instead. He wanted him to be present during the study sessions with Iris, which took place in the mornings before the official workday began, down in the secluded privacy of his laboratory. He, Elliot, Cam, Andrew, and— of course—the Lord Mayor, watched her heal from deeper flesh wounds, make her heart rate undetectable, raise and lower her temperature, and even lift sofas and tables off the ground all by herself. As breathtaking as her feats were, and as much as Elliot liked being near her regardless of them, he didn't really understand why his father wanted him there. But then one morning, after the session was over, he found out.

Everyone else had just left the lab—Iris to rest and the Lord Mayor, Andrew, and Cam to go about their day—but just as Elliot stepped out into the hall, his father called him back.

"Elliot, a moment."

He turned back around, his heart stilling. Since his affliction, his father hadn't sought out his company unless he absolutely had to. Even now, as he beckoned him closer, his fear and apprehension were enough to make Elliot shiver.

"I need to know what Iris has been feeling during these sessions."

Elliot's lips parted. Now he understood why his father had wanted him around, but he couldn't imagine why he cared how Iris had been feeling. She was a fascinating subject to him but a subject nonetheless, and during the sessions, all he'd felt toward her was clinical interest.

The answer to the question, however, was equally confusing, and it had been bothering Elliot since the study sessions began. He understood the rage Iris felt toward the Lord Mayor—by now, he felt the same way himself—but he didn't understand why she felt equal rage for his father. She hid it perfectly, of course, and Elliot had respected her privacy and refrained from asking, but over the last few days, it had begun to weigh on his mind. Still, there was no question as to how he would answer his father.

"She feels a bit nervous sometimes, but mostly she feels honored and eager for answers, like everyone else."

His father searched his face, and Elliot's pulse began to race. According to Cam, he held the title of World's Most Terrible Liar, but he held his father's gaze and looked as innocent as he could. Eventually, his father gave a satisfied nod and dismissed him, but Elliot felt the uneasiness that lingered in his chest.

At the top of the stairs that led to the lab, Elliot stopped and paused at his mother's old door like he usually did. With a heavy breath, he reached out and pressed his palm against it, aching with the familiar combination of longing and grief.

"What's in there?" a voice asked, and he gasped and spun around to see Iris walking toward him. She'd been given a gown that fit by then—a simple day dress of checkered grey—and her hair was smoothed back and gathered in a knot at the nape of her neck.

"I'm sorry," she said when she saw him jump. "I didn't mean to scare you."

"No, it's fine. It's just—I thought you had gone to your room to rest."

"I tried, but I couldn't. I suppose I'm feeling restless."

She was, as well as curious, and he knew she'd seen the reverent way he'd pressed his palm to the door.

"This was my mother's room," he confessed. "The one I told you about, where she painted and kept her supplies."

"The one you used to sneak inside and paint in. I remember." She paused and took a step closer. "Are her paintings still inside?"

"Some. At least I think they are. I haven't been in there in years."

She looked at him, her interest swelling, and Elliot stared at the floor.

"I'm sorry," she said. "You don't have to show me. I know it's painful to—"

"No, it's all right." He took a breath and looked back up. For years, he'd been longing to go back inside, but the prospect of the pain had always been too frightening. So far, however, being with Iris made things he'd once considered daunting somehow bearable. If there was ever a time to take the chance, this was it. "Wait right here," he said. "I'll go and get the key."

The first thing that hit him the moment they opened the door to the room was the smell. It was musty, as the place hadn't been cleaned in a number of years, but the sharp, metallic scent of paint still permeated the air, and it shot through Elliot's veins and stirred his blood like nothing else, quickening his heart but also setting his teeth on edge. He swallowed and flipped a dusty switch, filling the room with electric light, and Iris sucked in a breath as she slipped through the doorway behind him.

Except for the dust, the room looked as lived-in and cozy as it used to. Blank squares of canvas were stacked in a pile against the wall, and worn, paint-spattered sheets covered the furniture and the floors. An empty easel stood near a table of brushes and tubes of paint, and hanging on the wall beyond them were Elliot's mother's paintings. Immediately, Iris walked toward the mounted frames, and Elliot closed the door and followed.

There were only three, though Elliot knew she'd painted more than fifty; he had no idea why these were still here or what happened to the others. The largest one, which hung on the left, had intrigued him most as a child, as it was a sweeping landscape of a dark and stormy bay. In thick swirls of grey and blue, the waves rose and crashed against a row of jagged rocks, their arcs so vivid and full of motion that Elliot used to think he could see them rolling across the canvas.

The painting in the center was a still life: a glass of red wine, a dusty pink rose, a piece of paper, and a quill arranged on a white tablecloth. The objects were typical for a still life, but also slightly off. A bit of the wine had spilled and was trickling down the glass, a few of the rose's petals were torn off and strewn across the table, the piece of paper was balled up and crumpled in a wad, and the quill was dripping with ink and staining a spot black on the tablecloth. Still lifes were supposed to be clean, symmetrical, and perfect, but Elliot's mother had called this one "true" and "unflinchingly itself."

To the right of the other two was the smallest painting of all, a framed canvas about the length and width of the average chest. Iris moved toward it as if drawn by a hidden string, and Elliot followed her gaze and stepped beside her, but then his throat closed. Before them was the portrait of a boy.

A portrait of him.

He remembered the picture vividly, though he didn't remember his mother painting it, as he'd only been two. Like the still life, it wasn't exactly a standard child's portrait. Usually, the child would be posed with an object, like a toy or a book, dressed in their best and sitting up straight as they stared out of the frame. In this one, however, Elliot was crawling beneath the sheets of a bed, peeking his head out from under the fabric and laughing up at the ceiling. His mother had told him that some mornings he would slip out of his nursery and crawl up into his parents' bed. According to her, those moments were some of the very best of her life.

"Is this you?" Iris murmured, glancing back.

Elliot nodded.

She blinked and turned back to the painting. "It's brilliant," she said. "All three of them are. I haven't really seen a lot of paintings in my life, but these... they make me *feel* when I look at them. You know what I mean?"

Elliot swallowed and glanced at his feet. His mother had always said the same thing—that art was for feeling, for moving hearts, not decorating walls. Maybe that was part of what added to London's desolation; without art, its people were stifled, their hearts closed off and tucked away like the room he was standing in.

"Are any of yours still here?" she asked, turning to face him again.

"No. I threw them out years ago. Once I realized how much it hurt to paint, I wanted them gone." Pity flooded her chest, and he cleared his throat and went on. "The morning after I met you, however, I passed this room and thought of painting again for the first time in years."

"You did? What were you going to paint?"

"You—sort of," he said, flushing. "I had this vision of you in the pecan grove you told me about, watching a flock of Canada geese flying overhead."

Iris's eyes widened. "You should do it! I'd love to see you paint."

"What—you mean, right now?"

"Yes. You have all the things you need here, right?"

"No, I mean—I do—but Iris..." He backed away, as frightened of her yearning as his own. "I told you—"

"I know you're afraid, that you think it will hurt, and you're right—

147

it probably will. But Elliot—" She stepped closer, staring straight up into his eyes. "I remember the way you talked about painting that night in the aviary. I didn't have to possess your gift to know how you felt about it. I saw the love in your eyes and heard the longing in your voice, and it breaks my heart to think of you denying yourself such joy."

He felt her heart aching, as well his own, and he clenched his fists and closed his eyes. "I'd feel too much. I don't even know if I could hold a brush steady."

"We already know how to fix that," she said, taking another step closer. "If it gets too painful, you can ease the pain by sharing your feelings with me, and I can concentrate on feeling calm and peaceful for you."

He opened his eyes and stared at her. "You... you would do that for me?"

"Of course. You'd do it for me, wouldn't you?"

Elliot parted his lips to speak, but then he closed them again. He couldn't think of anything he *wouldn't* do for Iris. It had probably been true since the moment he first met her, but now there was no denying that his heart was tied to hers in a way that could never be undone.

"Yes," he finally said. "Grab a canvas. I'll mix the paint."

Hours passed, or what seemed like hours, but also only moments. Space and time fell away like he remembered they used to do, and nothing existed but canvas, paint, and the picture in his mind. Sometimes, it did hurt, and sometimes, he had to stop and close his eyes, but Iris was always there beside him, ready to take his hand, ease the pain, and calm his mind. Finally, when his fingers, sleeves, and even his brow, were smeared with paint, he let out a breath, sat down the brush, stepped back, and looked at the painting.

It was his vision, exactly as he'd seen it in his mind. Iris's frame was small, but also the picture's focal point, a simple but powerful silhouette against the golden grove. The trees curled up around her, stretching their fingers toward the sky, which glowed with the orange and purple of a sleepy summer sunset. Above them, a flock of black and ivory geese soared through the air, creating an arch that drew the eye and balanced out the scene. Pride bloomed in Elliot's chest, and he let out a shuttered breath.

He'd captured the hope and wonder of Iris's spirit on the canvas.

"My God," she said, stepping back beside him, her breathing shallow. "It's beautiful, Elliot. So beautiful. I... I can't believe it."

"Does it look anything like the grove you remember?"

"Yes and no. It doesn't look the same but it... *feels* the same somehow." She turned to him, her heart pounding. "You really are an artist."

He turned to her as well and looked down into her eyes, which were nearly overflowing with her joy and admiration. His cheeks flushed, but not as deeply as when she raised her hand and wiped a smear of paint from his forehead. He couldn't help but tremble as her fingers brushed his skin, and her own pulse leapt in response, but she didn't steady it. Instead, she slid her hand down the side of his face and traced his jawline, igniting his veins and causing his heart to thrash against his ribs. He covered her hand with his own and raised the other one to her face, cupping her velvet cheek and staring down at her parted lips.

"You know," she whispered, her voice breathless and raw. "You know what I'm feeling."

Elliot set his teeth and gripped her hand tighter. "Yes, I know."

"And you know what I want," she said, dropping her gaze down to his lips. He wet them, unable to help himself, and she shuddered and looked back up. "If you know what I want, and you feel the same way, then... why don't you do it?"

He swallowed, clutching her face as if it would keep him bound to the earth. "Knowing what you want isn't the same as having permission."

The fire in Iris's blood tore through her veins and seared her skin, and after a ragged breath, she whispered, "Kiss me," and he did.

He'd meant to be gentle, but once his mouth was on hers his brain caught fire, and he seized her by the waist and pulled her body flush against his. Rather than dissolving in shock, her yearning only grew, and he nearly collapsed beneath the collective weight of their desire. He clasped her tighter, and she reached up and raked her hands through his hair, clutching the tangled locks and crying out against his mouth. A savage groan escaped him, and he kissed her even more deeply, sliding his hands to her skirt and gripping the fabric around her hips. She cried out again and dragged her gasping mouth from his lips to his cheek, emitting bursts of hot, flickering breath against his ear. The hair on the back of his neck stood up, and his muscles went rigid with pleasure, and he lowered his head and pressed his burning lips to the base of her throat.

"Elliot," she breathed, and his own breath evaporated. It felt like a miracle to hear her say his name like that. "Elliot, please," she moaned again. "I want to feel what you're feeling."

He kissed her throat more urgently, and her pulse roared under his lips. "It's the same," he murmured against her skin, which tasted like salt and smelled like lavender soap. "Exactly the same."

"Please," she begged, pressing her lips to his forehead. "I want to feel it."

He raised his head and kissed her lips again, sliding his hands up her back, and then he sucked in a breath and focused on gathering his feelings. With more effort than he'd ever needed before, he pushed them to her, but then he cried out, because she sank her fingernails into his neck.

"I'm sorry!" she gasped, dropping her hands. "I suppose I didn't really believe it could actually be the same."

He laughed and drew her close again, pressing their foreheads together, but then her body stiffened and she whispered, "Wait—did you hear that?"

Elliot raised his head and listened, and after a moment, he heard a voice calling, "Mr. Morrissey?" He looked back down at Iris, and she nodded in confirmation; she'd heard the same thing—*Mr.* Morrissey— which meant the voice was looking for Elliot and not his father. With a heavy breath and enormous effort, he removed his hands from Iris's waist and the two of them walked to the door. He pulled it open and peeked out into the hall, seeing no one, but then the figure of Albert materialized, rushing toward him.

"Mr. Morrissey, sir," he said breathlessly. "Miss Blackwell sent me to find you. It's Lord Branch, sir. He needs you."

"Cam?" Elliot asked as he and Iris stepped into the hall, just to clarify that Albert didn't mean the Lord Mayor.

"Yes, sir. He's been injured. Miss Blackwell and Mr. Heron believe he needs medical attention."

"What do you mean, he's been 'injured'?" Elliot asked, his blood running cold.

"With the season starting, Lord Branch decided the butler's pantry was no longer safe for hiding that music machine, what with all the new servants creeping about the place, so he moved it into a wardrobe in his own private chambers. An hour or so ago, however, the Lord Mayor came in and found it."

Fear erupted in Iris's veins, and Elliot's stomach dropped, but he set his jaw and closed the door behind him. "Take me to him."

CHAPTER TWELVE

Cam was apparently still in his room, so Elliot and Iris followed Albert up the stairs and into the north wing of the palace. Elliot's stomach churned as he hurried through the familiar halls; he'd seen Cam bloody, bruised, and even with sprains and broken bones, but not since his affliction, and never when *he* was the one expected to fix him and make it better.

Albert opened the door to Cam's apartments when they arrived, and the moment Elliot stepped through the doorway his blood stilled in his veins. The Victor—or what was left of its splintered remains— was in the corner, and pieces of the broken records were strewn about the floor. A chair was knocked over, as well as the sofa he'd hidden behind a few nights ago. He edged toward the door to Cam's bedroom with Iris close behind, and Albert slid back out into the hallway, keeping watch.

"Elliot? Thank God you're here."

Andrew's voice rang out before Elliot made it through the doorway. He rushed toward him, his fear as heavy and fierce as a wrecking ball, and Elliot gripped the wall to keep from stumbling back into Iris.

"Cambrian says he's fine," Andrew said. "But Philomena and I, well, we think something's really wrong."

"I'm still here, and, astoundingly, I still have the power of speech."

Andrew turned around, and Elliot looked inside the room. Philomena was seated on a chair beside the bed, feeling anxiety he'd never sensed from her before. Cam was propped up beside her, resting back against the headboard, dressed in only his shirtsleeves and rolling his eyes as if annoyed. At first glance, he didn't even seem to be injured at all—his face was clean and clear of bruises, and there was no blood on his clothes. But then he took a breath, perhaps to emit a dramatic sigh, and the effort caused him to wince in pain and clutch the side of the bed.

"Come on," Andrew said. "Let me show you."

He turned around and strode to the bed, but Elliot didn't follow. Andrew's fear and Philomena's anxiety were bad enough, but Cam was feeling grief that fastened his feet to the cluttered floor. It was raw and pervasive, as if a loved one, and not the Victor, were lying broken and lifeless in the next room, and Elliot understood—he'd felt Cam's joy that night in the pantry. The music hadn't only been something new and exciting for him; it had been an escape, a lifeline to hope and the outside world. Iris saw his hesitation and placed her hand on his back.

"Share it with me," she whispered. "It will help. You can do this."

Elliot closed his eyes, sucked in a breath, and slowly released it, along with the excess grief, fear, and anxiety around him. Iris stiffened but didn't remove her hand, and soon he felt strong enough to open his eyes, move away from her, and step into the room.

Andrew walked to the side of the bed across from Philomena, approached Cam, and then reached down to unbutton the front of his shirt.

"I can do it myself," Cam muttered, brushing him away, his chest flooding with shame he quickly hid with a crooked smile. "Although I don't know if these ladies can handle the sight of me undressed."

"You forget I saw it earlier," Philomena quipped from her chair, feigning boredom and disappointment. "Somehow, I'm still standing."

"It looks to me like you're sitting," Cam replied, and she shot him a phony glare. He grinned and raised his hands to his collar, but then he winced again.

"Just let me do it," Andrew said. "Elliot, come here."

Elliot approached as Andrew undid the row of buttons, but once the shirt was open, he sucked in an audible gasp. The sound of it deepened Cam's shame and sharpened everyone else's fear, but Elliot couldn't help it; the sight was truly horrible. Cam's entire torso was a mess of purple bruises, and a strip of fabric covered a bloody gash along his shoulder. Elliot knew it probably stretched the rest of the way down his back; he'd seen that mark on Cam before.

"Gun holster buckle?" he asked.

Cam nodded and looked away.

"There are more in the back," Andrew said. "We've already cleaned them and covered them up."

Elliot swallowed and gestured toward the bruises. "What about these?"

"Boot," Cam murmured, clenching his jaw.

Elliot gripped the headboard to steady himself against the shame.

"It's the bruises we're concerned about," Andrew interjected. "That one there, it's smaller but also darker than the others, and if he moves or breathes too deeply, it causes him terrible pain. I'm worried he's broken a rib, or that something's been punctured inside."

"And if that's the case," Cam said, somehow managing a theatrical tone, "the ladies at the ball tomorrow will surely be disappointed."

"Tomorrow?" Elliot asked. "The season's first ball is set for tomorrow?"

"By the Lord Mayor's decree."

It seemed a minor point, but Elliot had asked because Cam's injuries now made sense. The Lord Mayor hadn't touched his face or neck because of the ball.

"Can you tell?" Andrew asked. "If something's broken or injured internally?"

His fear was so thick that Elliot blinked, nearly blinded by it. "Let me look," he said, and he knelt down over Cam. He'd been watching and helping his father for years, but he'd only just begun officially studying himself, and since his affliction, he hadn't gone near the hospital, an injured person, or even a medical book. Still, he'd seen broken ribs and knew how to tell if a lung had been punctured.

"I need to listen to your chest," he said to Cam. "Is that all right?"

"You know I never refuse a chance to cuddle with you, El."

Elliot steeled himself and crawled up beside him on the bed, terrified to touch him but more scared of not checking the wound. After a breath, he lowered his head to Cam's chest, but then he flinched. The shame wasn't quite the same as when his father berated him, but it was just as painful, like the ache of a frightened child.

"What's wrong?" Philomena asked, rising from her chair.

"Nothing," Elliot said. "I just need quiet for a moment."

He closed his eyes and tried to clear his mind like Iris taught him, concentrating on nothing but the task he had to complete. Soon, his pulse began to slow, and he lowered his head again, pressing his ear to Cam's chest and ignoring the shame and pain. He listened closely, blocking out everything but the sound of his breathing. His lungs were expanding, and air was flowing through them like it should. Elliot opened his eyes and sat up, relief flooding his veins.

"Your lung isn't punctured," he said. "And your rib isn't broken, either."

"How can you tell?" Iris asked, stepping up beside the bed.

"If his lung were punctured, I wouldn't be able to hear the air moving through it." He moved to the side and showed her the bruise. "And if a rib were broken, his ribcage would look a little misshapen, indented by the broken frame. This bruise is bad, but the shape of his torso is perfectly intact."

"My shape is perfect," Cam echoed, raising an eyebrow. "Can't say I'm surprised." He grinned at Philomena, who rolled her eyes at him but smiled.

The relief Elliot felt before spread through the rest of the room, except to Andrew, who still seemed hesitant.

"So what's wrong with him then? Why does it hurt him to breathe?"

"I think the rib is cracked, not broken," Elliot explained. "I just need to splint it—wrap it. If he keeps it bound, it should heal and be good as new in a couple of weeks."

"What do you need to wrap it with?" Iris asked.

"Some strips of clean linen."

Philomena walked to the bedroom door. "I'll send Albert to get some."

Elliot started to rise from the bed, but Cam gripped his hand and pulled him back, nearly stopping his heart with the force of his gratitude.

"Thank you, El," he said, looking up into his eyes.

Elliot covered his hand with his own, wishing he could tell him that he didn't need to say it.

"It's nothing," he replied. "And I'm sorry about the Victor."

Cam released his hand and leaned back, letting out a breath. "At least I convinced him the Victor and records were only a one time thing. I suppose…" He glanced at his lap, his blood going cold. "It could have been worse."

Albert returned with the strips of linen in only a matter of minutes, and Andrew and Elliot helped Cam off the bed and removed his shirt. Carefully, Elliot splinted his torso the way his father had taught him, keeping the wrapping tight and holding the cracked rib in its place. Once he was done, Cam confirmed that his side didn't hurt as badly and that breathing was easier.

"Does anyone know what time it is?" Iris suddenly asked.

Andrew removed a pocket watch from his vest. "Half past four."

Iris and Elliot exchanged stunned glances. They'd walked into his mother's room at around eleven o'clock, and neither would have guessed that over four hours had passed inside.

"I have to go," Iris said, and then to Cam, "I'll be thinking of you."

She turned and hurried out of the bedroom, and Elliot followed her.

"Where are you going?" he asked when he caught up to her in the hall.

Iris paused and sighed. "I was supposed to meet with these seamstresses in my room at four o'clock. They're making alterations on a gown for me, for tomorrow."

"Oh. For the ball, you mean."

"Yes." Her face flushed the slightest bit.

Elliot furrowed his brow.

"What's wrong?" he asked. "And I'm not invading, I mean—I can see on your face that you—"

"I know," she said, sighing again. "It's absolutely ridiculous given everything that's going on, but I... I'm nervous about it." She glanced at the floor. "I don't know how to dance."

Real embarrassment flooded her veins, and Elliot took a step closer.

"You'll be fine," he said. "Maybe after tomorrow's session, Philomena could teach you. I could help, too—be the stand-in man and all that. You'll pick it up."

Iris smiled and took his hand, sharing her gratitude, and Elliot smiled back and let his happiness flow to her. She laughed and dropped his hand.

"You were wonderful back there," she said.

"Only because you helped me."

"I helped at first, but the rest you did yourself, and it was amazing." She stepped a bit closer, looking up into his eyes. "You told me once that your empathy was the reason you would never be able to study medicine, but based on what I just saw in there, you're as much of a doctor as you are a brilliant artist."

Elliot glanced at the floor. "Iris, I didn't do anything—"

"Yes, you did. You not only diagnosed and repaired Cambrian's rib, you calmed him down and eased his mind—all of our minds. Don't you see?" She let out a breath. "Can I ask you something?"

"Of course," he said, looking up.

"Why did you attempt to remove your empathy?"

Elliot's heart stilled. All he'd ever told her about his affliction was that it was the result of an experiment. He'd never said what he'd been trying to do when he performed it.

"How did you—"

"I know you think your empathy is a curse, so it stands to reason you would never have wanted to do what you did. My guess is your experiment was supposed to do the opposite, to remove your empathy. Am I right?"

Elliot nodded, his mouth dry.

"But why?" she asked. "Why would you ever want to be like that? Look at the Lord Mayor, at what he did to his son today. Why would you want to be a man with no kindness or compassion?"

A lump rose in Elliot's throat, as well as a wave of shame. "It's a long story," he said.

Iris took his hand again, startling him with the power of her confidence and trust.

"Those seamstresses have waited this long. They can wait a bit longer."

Over the next few minutes, as they walked to Iris's room, Elliot told her everything: how he'd watched a Hyde turn into Will, and then failed to execute him, how Will then killed Andrew's father and sent his mother over the edge. Iris listened intently and didn't speak until he'd finished. Then, just as they reached her bedroom door, she turned to face him.

"Let me ask you this," she said. "Do you think if Andrew had been in your place, he would have acted differently?"

Elliot blinked; he'd never thought to ask himself that question. "I'm sure he would have done what was right."

"You think he would have actually killed that sobbing, wretched boy? I've only known him for four days, and I don't think he would. I don't think Cambrian would have, either—no decent person could."

"No *decent person*? Iris, he was a monster. The law demands—"

"The Lord Mayor made that law, and it's wrong."

Elliot parted his lips, but for a moment, no sound came out. "The Hydes are deadly, Iris. People have to be protected."

She looked at him, her golden eyes alight with a sudden fire. "There are other ways to protect them—humane ways. The first night I met you, you and Cambrian mentioned Lady Cullum. She found a way to help the infected and still keep London safe."

"But it didn't work; she was killed in one of those shelters, *because* of her mercy."

Iris didn't flinch or blink, but the rage and sorrow that sprouted in her heart nearly knocked him backward. He opened his mouth, but then the door behind her suddenly opened.

"There you are," a woman exclaimed as she burst out of Iris's room. "We thought we heard voices out here. Come along, we have other fittings to do today, Miss Faye."

"I'll be right there," she said. "Please, just give me one more moment."

The woman's exacerbation swelled, but she nodded and stepped back inside.

"I'm sorry," Iris said once she was gone. "I have to go."

"Iris, what you felt just now, that anger and pain—"

"Elliot, I promise I... I'll explain everything eventually. I know it's a lot to ask, but can you let it go for now?"

He let out a breath and nodded. "Of course. You can tell me whenever you're ready."

The door behind her began to open again, so she rushed toward it. "I'm coming!" she called inside, and then she ran back to Elliot and kissed his lips, blinding him with a double dose of bliss. "See?" she whispered, smiling up at him. "It *is* a gift."

She hurried back to the door and stepped inside, and Elliot grinned, turning around and walking away like a giddy little boy. When he passed the stairway, however, thoughts of Cam came rushing back, so he climbed the steps to the second floor to check on him again. He slipped through the door to his sitting room, which was still a terrible mess, but just before he reached the door to the bedroom, he stopped in his tracks.

He was standing exactly where he'd stood the night he watched the Lord Mayor smash the hand crème Cam gave to Jennie, and like that night, he couldn't yet see anyone inside. The emotions beyond the door, however, were so potent and overwhelming they sucked the breath from his lungs. Cam's grief and shame were still present, as well as a touch of someone's fear, but there was also affection so strong his temperature started to climb. Could Philomena still be inside, and could he have been right about Cam having feelings for her? He knew he should back away, that what was inside was none of his business, but curiosity drew him to the edge of the slightly cracked door.

Cam was standing beside the bed, but Philomena was gone. The only other person left inside the room was Andrew, who was guiding Cam's arms through the sleeves of his shirt and pulling it over his shoulders. Once the shirt was on, he reached down and started to button it up, but then he stopped and laid his hand against Cam's splinted torso. Sorrow and shame, but also yearning and tenderness, swelled in the room, so dense and pervasive, Elliot couldn't tell whose feelings were whose. Andrew raised his gaze to Cam's, and Cam swallowed and looked away, his muscles tensing up as if the glance caused him physical pain. But Andrew didn't pull back; instead, he slid his hand to Cam's shoulder, exposing the bandaged gash from the Lord Mayor's gun holster buckle. He paused a moment, and then bent down and placed his lips on the wound. Cam shuddered and closed his eyes, causing a single tear to slip down the side of his rigid face.

"Andrew."

The word came out in a rasp, like a desperate, audible ache, and Andrew lifted his head and placed his hand against Cam's cheek. He brushed the tear away with his thumb, and Cam opened his eyes, which were filled with even more helplessness and longing than his voice. They looked at each other, not breathing

And then Andrew leaned forward and kissed him.

The world ground to a halt. Elliot wanted to blink, to move, to breathe, but he couldn't do anything, and—at first—Cam seemed equally stunned and paralyzed. After a moment, however, a cry erupted from deep in his throat, and he gripped Andrew's face and kissed him back as if he would die if he didn't. The passion and joy that burst in both their hearts stopped Elliot's, and he turned around and dashed out into the hall, unable to breathe.

Once he had gotten a few feet away from the door, he managed to take a breath, but then he started to shake so hard he thought he might collapse. Before that could happen, he bolted down the stairs and toward his room, running as though he could physically escape what he'd just seen.

CHAPTER THIRTEEN

Elliot hid in his room and didn't emerge until the next morning, his mouth dry and his head heavy and aching from lack of sleep. He hadn't been able to get what he'd seen in Cam's room out of his mind, and moments of rest he did manage were only filled with nightmares—graphic, violent images of the Lord Mayor murdering Cam.

Because, if he ever found out, that was surely what he would do.

Terror for Cam was the driving force behind his insomnia, but wild doubt and unsettling confusion plagued him as well. In a way, what he'd seen last night made bizarre yet perfect sense; it explained why Cam felt so much fear and hatred for himself, why he'd ached with longing while watching Philomena and Andrew dance. It also explained why Andrew felt as jealous and full of rage as Elliot when Cam kissed Iris. But that was the most confusing thing of all:

It felt the same.

Elliot had always been told that men like that were deviants, that if they had any feelings at all, they were twisted and depraved. Since his affliction, he'd come across the vilest of human emotions: hatred, arrogance, cruelty, and many other feelings with a sense of *wrongness* about them. But what he'd felt from Cam and Andrew last night was nothing like that. The fire that burned between them wasn't some evil, destructive force; it was pure, selfless, regenerative, and... beautiful.

Exactly like the fire that burned between Iris and him.

After becoming an empath, one of the things that shocked Elliot most was just how wrong many of his childhood teachings were. Women felt as much lust as men, and the lower classes were no less noble or good than anyone else. The things he'd been taught about men like Cam and Andrew may have been equally wrong, but that didn't change the facts of the world in which they lived. Other people wouldn't be able to feel what Elliot felt, wouldn't be able to see inside their hearts and understand. Especially the Lord Mayor, to whom Elliot's mind always inevitably returned.

The more he thought about it, the more Elliot wondered if the Lord Mayor suspected already. It would explain the fear he'd felt the night he smashed the hand crème, the rage that consumed him whenever Cam didn't act like enough of a "man," and the premature rush to have him married to Philomena. Perhaps he had suspicions, but he certainly didn't *know*, because if he did, Cam would be dead.

Of that, Elliot was certain.

During Iris's session in his father's lab the next morning, Elliot stood with his back to the wall, away from the rest of the group. He'd often found himself shivering in the subterranean chamber, but this time it was fear, and not the cold, that shook his bones. Cam and Andrew had placed themselves on opposite ends of the room, both their demeanors cool, reserved, and absolutely normal. Every now and then, however, they'd steal a glance at each other, causing the room to erupt with heat that hammered Elliot's heart.

"Miss Faye," the Lord Mayor said as Iris sat back down in her chair, weak from holding her own breath for over twenty minutes. "Do you know if your abilities would allow you to... stop aging?"

She paused and knit her brow. "I don't know."

"What do you think, Frank?" the Lord Mayor asked, turning to Elliot's father. "Based on what we've seen, could such a thing be possible?"

Elliot's father sat down behind his desk and rubbed his chin. "So far, just as she told us, her ability to control her body only extends to acts the body is naturally capable of; she simply does them faster and in ways that are more extreme. But time erodes all things, including the body. She couldn't stop that."

"But she can heal herself," the Lord Mayor countered, turning back to Iris. "Aging is nothing more than the body breaking down. If she can heal flesh, could she not also strengthen disintegrating joints, fortify exhausted lungs, and repair a weakened heart?"

"I suppose it depends on the brain. Miss Faye's ability seems to lie in the brain—just like the Hydes. As long as her brain was still functioning, she could conceivably tell her body to do what you described. But time erodes the brain as well."

"But if she methodically strengthened and repaired her brain before such erosion, couldn't she prevent it from deteriorating as well?"

"I... I suppose she could." Elliot's father looked at Iris. "Which, in essence, would make her—"

"Immortal."

The Lord Mayor's eyes blazed with the fire in his chest, and even Cam and Andrew stared, forgetting the world around them. Iris's lips parted, and her heart ground to a halt. Clearly, the idea had never occurred to her before.

"The Hydes," Andrew said. "Could they be immortal as well? Even though they spend most of their time in a human state?"

"No one knows," Elliot's father answered. "They've never been studied. All known Hydes are in hiding, and the unknown ones would hardly volunteer themselves for research."

Something started inside the Lord Mayor, almost like a flinch, but since his face remained cool and passive, no one but Elliot noticed. Then, as if he somehow knew that Elliot sensed his reaction, the Lord Mayor turned to look at him, and Elliot glanced away.

"You're a lucky girl," the Lord Mayor said, returning his gaze to Iris. "What do you think of the news that you could possibly live forever?"

Iris glanced at her lap, then, after a moment, looked back up. "I don't know that I'd want to."

The Lord Mayor froze, stunned and even angry. "Why on earth not?"

"I know it sounds strange, considering how—well, *abnormal* I am—but I'd rather live out the normal, natural cycle of my life. Living forever goes against nature, and probably just causes pain. I wouldn't want to watch everyone around me grow old and die." The Lord Mayor continued to stare in disbelief, so she went on. "Besides, like the Hydes, I could, you know... still be killed. So, I'm not immortal."

"True," the Lord Mayor replied. "But you certainly stand a better chance than the rest of us, Miss Faye."

For a moment, no one spoke. Then, abruptly, the Lord Mayor sighed and shoved his hands in his pockets. "Well, I think that's enough for today. I'm sure you'd like to get some rest before the ball tonight."

Elliot's father opened a notebook and got out a quill and ink, lowering his head to record the morning's findings. Cam, Andrew, Elliot, and Iris took the cue, exiting the room and climbing the stairs to the first floor. The moment they reached the hallway, however, Philomena appeared.

"Oh," she exclaimed. "I'm so glad I ran into you just now—"

"There's no need," Iris said. "They're still in the lab. It's just us."

Philomena exhaled with relief. "Oh, thank goodness. I love to perform, but I truly hate pretending. Come on, let's go."

Apparently, Iris, Philomena, and even Cam and Andrew had discussed a plan to teach Iris how to dance the previous night. Squealing with excitement, Philomena grasped her hand, taking off down the hall and leaving the boys to follow behind. Eventually, the five of them reached the palace Music Room, where Philomena had sung for the courtiers a few nights ago. They cleared away the chairs to make some space on the hardwood floor, and Andrew seated himself on the bench behind the piano. Moving slowly, but looking as though he felt better than the night before, Cam sat down beside him, and the two of them grinned at each other. The temperature in the tall, domed room began to climb, and Elliot shuddered, suddenly finding it difficult to breathe.

"I'll show you what to do first," Philomena said to Iris. "Then, after you've watched me, you can try it for yourself."

Without warning, she walked to Elliot and seized his hand, sending a bolt of confidence and excitement through his veins. He jumped, and though Philomena hardly noticed, Iris did.

"How about I try it first, and you guide me through it," she said.

"Trust me," Philomena replied. "It's easier if you watch."

Iris looked at Elliot, asking if he was all right, and he swallowed and nodded, placing his other hand on Philomena's waist.

"Andrew," Philomena called to the piano. "Play a waltz."

Andrew started to play a traditional song in three-four time, and Elliot moved with Philomena across the hardwood floor. His body went through the motions he had learned as a young man, but his mind couldn't focus on anything but Cam and Andrew. As Andrew played, Cam watched his fingers dance across the keys, his heart stirring with warmth that drew beads of sweat from Elliot's brow. Every now and then, Andrew glanced up and met his gaze, and Elliot nearly stumbled against Philomena, his lungs collapsing.

"Remember to keep your shoulders back," Philomena said to Iris. "And keep your eyes on his, not your feet."

After a few more rounds around the floor, she stepped away, releasing Elliot's hand and then guiding Iris toward him. "Now you try," she said. "Step backward first, with your left foot."

Iris took Elliot's hand, jolting his heart with her concern. "Is something wrong?" she whispered as she placed her hand on his shoulder.

"No," he lied, taking her waist. A few nights ago, the prospect of dancing with Iris had kindled his blood, but now that she was in his arms, he barely even felt her. The rising heat between Cam and Andrew filled his veins with ice, creating a violent storm of longing and fear he couldn't cope with.

Philomena straightened Iris's shoulders and lifted her arms. Then she moved away and murmured, "Go," and Iris stepped back. Elliot pushed her around the floor, but he still couldn't concentrate, especially when he glanced at Cam and Andrew over her shoulder.

They'd scooted even closer to each other on the bench, and Andrew was looking at Cam, drinking him up with hungry eyes. Cam grinned, returned the look, and bit his lower lip, and Elliot's fear dissolved, replaced by a sudden, violent rage. Who did they think they were to be so reckless with their lives? So brazenly unconcerned with the deadly consequences?

"Elliot, what's wrong?" Iris whispered.

He dropped her hand.

"I'm sorry," he said. "I —I'm not feeling well. I have to go."

He turned around and walked away before anyone could stop him. At first, his only thought was to simply get out of there, but once he arrived in his room, he headed straight toward his bed, reached beneath the mattress, and retrieved a bottle of gin he had stashed there weeks ago. Without hesitation, he unscrewed the top and gulped down as much as he could, leaning back against the wall as the alcohol seared his throat. His muscles relaxed, and he slid down and collapsed against the floor, drinking until he'd taken at least an inch off the top of the bottle.

"Elliot, what are you doing?"

He nearly choked but somehow managed to get his current gulp down, and when he opened his eyes, he saw Iris standing before him.

"I'm sorry," he said, his face burning. "I needed to get away."

"Why? What's going on?"

Her anxiety was so pervasive he raised the bottle and took another swig without even thinking.

"Elliot, please," she said, crouching before him. "Talk to me."

He swallowed and lowered the bottle, glancing away. "I can't. I'm sorry."

"Is it... is it because of what the Lord Mayor said today? About me being... immortal?"

Panic flooded her veins and Elliot looked back up in shock. She was afraid that he was somehow repulsed by the revelation. "No, no—not at all. It's nothing to do with you."

"Because I meant what I told him. I wouldn't want to live—"

"Iris, I promise, it isn't you." He rubbed his brow and closed his eyes, already feeling dizzy. "It was the feelings of other people. They were just... too much."

"Then share them with me," she said, reaching out. "I'll ease the burden."

"No," he cried, and the sound came out much harsher than he'd intended. Iris flinched, pain splitting her chest, and he covered his face. "I'm sorry," he said. "I'm so sorry, Iris. I can't think straight right now. It's probably better if you just go and leave me alone for a while."

"I'm not leaving you alone like this. There has to be a way for me to help, to make it better."

Elliot crawled to his feet and walked to the other end of the bedroom, terrified of hurting her again. "I'm sorry. You can't."

"Just let me try. Let me feel it, or tell me—"

"Iris, I *can't* tell you." He clenched his jaw and turned away, remembering when she said that immortality "went against nature." What would she say about Andrew and Cam?

"Elliot, you know that you can tell me anything."

A small laugh escaped his throat. "How could I know that, Iris? You don't tell *me* everything."

Her heart froze and he turned around to look at her again, but the movement caused him to sway on his feet. The gin was hitting him—hard.

"I told you," she said, her blood running cold. "I *will* tell you, in time."

"But why don't you trust me now? After everything we've been through?" He gripped the bottle, trying as hard as he could to steady himself, but it was no use; he felt control and composure slipping away.

"I do trust you."

"Sure, you trust me. Just not enough to tell me why you feel so much rage for my father."

Her stomach sank, but he didn't turn away or soften his gaze. His tongue felt thick, and he knew the word "father" had come out a little bit slurred, but he found he didn't care. He was miles off the earth.

"Why did you decide to stay at the palace?" he asked, approaching her. "Why did you feel such rage the first time you met me and Cam?

Why, when you speak of your mother, do you feel no grief at all, but when you speak of Lady Cullum, your heart nearly breaks with it?"

She set her jaw and glared at him, but her chest was full of pain. "Yes, I have secrets," she said, her voice unsteady. "But they aren't mine to tell. It's not just me I'm protecting. It's other people, including you."

Somehow, the last comment angered Elliot more than anything else. "What is that supposed to mean? You think I'm so weak and helpless that I need you to protect me?"

Iris glanced down at her feet. "I think you were right. We shouldn't talk now."

She turned and walked away, heading back toward the door, her pain and revulsion so powerful they penetrated his haze.

"Iris," he called. "I'm sorry! I didn't mean—"

But then she was gone.

"Damn it," he muttered, closing his eyes and rubbing his brow. "God*damn it!*"

He hurled the bottle against the wall before he could stop himself. The glass shattered, causing his room to explode with the smell of gin. Raking his hands through his hair, he slumped back down against the floor, his stomach churning with both the alcohol and self-disgust.

"Elliot?"

His heart stopped, and he opened his eyes; his father was in the doorway. How long had he been standing there? How much had he heard?

"What is going on?" he asked, wrinkling his nose as he stepped inside the room. "I thought I heard something break…" He glanced at the wall and saw the shattered bottle. "Elliot—"

"Everything's fine," he said, climbing up onto his feet. He could barely feel his legs, and his words were quite slurred now.

"You're drunk?" his father murmured. "Christ, Elliot. It's not even noon!"

Even in his stupor, Elliot felt the bite of his fear. "It's not like you really care," he said, then a hollow laugh escaped him. "Oh wait—I forgot. You *do* care. It's just that you don't *want* to."

His father parted his lips. "How dare you—"

"Why don't you just go away and pretend I don't exist? That's what you're good at, and that's what you really want—to not have a son."

Pain erupted inside his father's chest, and he stared at him. Then he glanced at the door, as if he wanted to run after all, but he set his jaw, barreled at Elliot, and gripped his sleeve.

"You will sleep this off and clean yourself up before the ball tonight. I will not lie to your friends for you like I did in the Green Drawing Room."

"Lie to my—" Elliot furrowed his brow. "You mean about the cadavers?"

He'd assumed his father had lied about the body snatching being a one-time thing for selfish reasons—to keep the Lord Mayor from finding out how weak his son had become. Had he actually lied to *protect* Elliot? To keep Cam, Andrew, and Iris from looking down on him?

"I mean it," his father said, releasing his sleeve and turning away. "I'll send a servant to come clean up this mess. Now go to bed."

Elliot blinked, kneaded his temples, and sat down on the bed. Then, after a moment, he fell backward and closed his eyes, too confused and tired to argue with anyone anymore.

CHAPTER FOURTEEN

When Elliot woke, his room was dark and still smelled faintly of gin. He rolled over and squinted at the clock beside his bed. It was half-past eight, which meant the dinner before the ball had begun. His head ached, and his stomach felt sour, but he managed to get up, bathe, and change into his eveningwear. By then, he knew the dinner would be over, so he crept to the kitchen, and after a couple of salmon patties, a hunk of bread, and quite a bit of water, he felt better. Physically, anyway—the fear he'd felt that morning was now joined by shame and regret.

The ballroom was by far the largest space in Buckingham Palace—fourteen meters high, thirty-four long, and eighteen wide—and the massive gold and ivory room was currently filled with people. Still, when Elliot crept through the doors and edged inside the room, he spotted Iris immediately, and his heart stilled.

She must have completed her lesson with Philomena after leaving his room, because she was on the dance floor, waltzing with grace and precision. Her partner was a young man Elliot vaguely recognized, but it didn't really matter who he was—he only saw Iris. The gown that had been made for her not only fit perfectly but seemed to be fashioned out of pure gold. Her hair was pulled up and styled on top of her head with golden pins, her lips and cheeks were flushed, and her golden eyes were glowing.

"*Notre fée ressemble à un ange ce soir. Une vision de l'or et de lumière.*"

Elliot's pulse leapt as he turned to see Cam beside him. He was smiling, holding a glass of champagne, and he'd said, "Our fairy looks like an angel tonight. A vision of gold and light."

"She does," Elliot said, taking a breath and trying to steady himself. He hadn't spoken to Cam one-on-one since discovering his secret, and suddenly, he was terrified of giving his knowledge away. "How are you feeling?" he asked to cover his fear, nodding at Cam's injured rib.

"Fit as a fiddle," he said, taking a sip of his champagne. Then, more seriously, "How about you? You gave us a fright today."

"Oh, yes, I'm feeling much better. It... must have been something I ate."

He flushed—the lie sounded unconvincing even to himself—but strangely, Cam let it go. When Elliot glanced at his face and followed his gaze, however, he figured out why. Andrew was out on the dance floor, waltzing with a girl whose name Elliot couldn't recall. A warm ache flooded Cam's chest as he watched him move across the floor, as well as a feeling Elliot realized he hadn't felt from Cam since the night with the Victor:

Joy.

In that moment, the world seemed to shift, and everything suddenly changed. After his initial shock, Elliot had accepted the way that Cam and Andrew felt; how could he not, when he knew their love was no different from his own? Still, he'd been plagued by fear for them and angered at their recklessness, but now, as Cam's joy washed through his veins, the anger completely dissolved. He was still afraid, of course, and he probably always would be, but the fear seemed inconsequential in the face of such happiness. For once, Cam was full of hope and void of fear and self-hatred, and Elliot simply couldn't wish for anything else for him.

"Cambrian," an annoyed voice rang out from behind them, and they turned around to see Philomena letting out a sigh. Her gown was a deep, emerald green, and her caramel hair had been curled into ringlets and piled on top of her head. She looked lovely, and more like a real, grown woman than ever before, but the angry pout on her face slightly ruined the effect.

"I need you to dance with me," she said. "So my mother will get off my back."

Cam pressed his hand to his heart. "Why, Miss Blackwell, that's the most romantic thing anyone's ever said to me."

"Oh, shut it," she said, swiping his glass and setting it down. "Let's go."

She seized his hand and led him away, and Elliot stifled a laugh. Once they were out on the floor, he returned his gaze to Iris. He needed to get her alone so he could apologize for that morning. As soon as the current song ended, however, another man approached her for a dance, and she accepted. Elliot let out a breath and edged a bit closer to the dance floor, determined to catch her the next time. While he waited, he looked to see if Cam or Andrew were free, but he couldn't find either of them, and Philomena had a new partner.

Finally, the orchestra finished the song and Elliot started for Iris, but the moment her partner released her, she turned around and walked off the floor. Elliot darted after her, weaving his way through the shifting clusters of people and their feelings. She walked to a door in the back, glanced behind her, and then slipped out, and Elliot picked up his pace and followed her into the empty hallway. He started to call out her name, but she was quite a bit ahead of him, and he didn't want to frighten her by crying out from the shadows. So instead, he hurried faster, trailing her into the State Dining Room. The vast space was silent and dark, except for the moonlight streaming in through the glass of the tall French windows, and just as Iris stepped into one of their beams, Elliot spoke.

"Iris," he whispered as softly as he could, but she still jumped. "I'm sorry," he said as she turned around. "I didn't mean to scare you."

"Elliot," she gasped. "I didn't think that you were here."

"I wasn't until a few minutes ago, and I'm sorry again to have frightened you, but I had to apologize. The way I behaved this morning... there's simply no excuse for it."

She let out a breath, and Elliot's caught in his throat when he felt her forgiveness, which was not only immediate but whole and unrestrained. "It's not completely your fault," she said. "You told me to leave you alone; I shouldn't have pushed you like I—"

"No. You were only trying to help me, and I should have been grateful, not rude. If I could, I would take back all of those terrible things I said. You can tell me whatever you want whenever you choose. Your secrets are yours." He paused and took a breath. "Also, you look lovely tonight."

He watched as the blood that burned in his own cheeks rose in Iris's, and she smiled and glanced at the floor. "Thank you," she said. "So do you."

She started to meet his gaze again, but then suddenly she froze, staring out over his shoulder through the glass of the French windows. Her heart stopped, and Elliot spun around to look as well. There, in a shaded corner of the moonlit balcony, were Cam and Andrew—pressed against the wall.

Kissing each other.

Even in the darkness, there was no mistaking the scene. Cam was slowly lacing his fingers through Andrew's ginger hair, and Andrew was parting his lips with his own, drinking him up like water. They clung to each other, absorbing each other, kindling a fire Elliot felt through the panes of glass, but the ice in Iris's veins brought him back to reality.

He seized her hand, fighting the bolt of her fear, and dragged her out of the room. When they reached the doors to the Blue Drawing Room, he flung them open, pulled her inside, and quickly shut them again. The room was filled with sofas and chairs, but Iris sank down to the ground, staring straight ahead as her skirt billowed up around her. Silence swelled as the fabric of her dress slowly deflated, and then, after a moment that felt like forever, she finally spoke.

"You knew, didn't you?" she murmured. "That was what you felt today, what you didn't want to tell me."

Elliot nodded. "Yes, but, Iris..." He sucked in a breath and crouched down beside her. "It's not like what we've been told about... about people like that. They aren't sick—their feelings are just like ours. It isn't *wrong*. I know that's hard to believe and understand but—"

"Elliot, you don't need to explain," she said. "Yes, I'm a little bit shocked, but I agree—I don't think it's wrong."

He furrowed his brow, his mouth going dry. "But yesterday you said that immortality went against nature. If you think that's wrong, then why would you not feel the same?"

"Because it doesn't."

"What?"

"The way that Cam and Andrew feel. I don't think it goes against nature."

"You don't?"

Bizarrely, a wry smile crept across her face. "Do you remember the ornithologist's journal about Antarctica? The one that made me embarrassed when you asked why it was in Latin?"

Elliot blinked, entirely lost. "Yes, of course I do."

"I don't know if you know this," she said. "But penguins are one of only a handful of species that mate for life. They form a pair bond with one bird and stay with them until death. The scientist who wrote that journal confirmed it in his findings, but he also observed that some of the bonds were not between males and females. Sometimes, the males would mate with other males, the females with other females." She paused and shook her head, a bitter laugh escaping her throat. "In his journal, he actually called the penguins' behavior 'depraved.' That's the reason it's written in Latin. He thought the findings were too obscene to reveal to the general public. Can you imagine calling a group of *penguins* obscene and depraved? They're natural creatures doing what comes naturally. It's ridiculous."

"So, you don't think any less of Andrew and Cam?"

"Of course I don't. They're good, kind, and loyal people. There's nothing wrong with *who* they want, and it's not as though they can help it."

"How do you know they can't?"

She looked at him, and his temperature rose, not only because of the sudden ache that pulsed inside her chest, but also because of the fierce, magnetic longing in her eyes. "I can't help wanting you," she finally said, the slightest catch in her voice. "The whole world calling it wrong and unnatural wouldn't change a thing."

Elliot's cheeks burned, and he glanced down at his lap, but Iris reached out and guided his chin back up with her fingertips. He shuddered at her touch but forced himself to look into her eyes.

"Do you..." she began, and then, "I mean, I know how you felt when we kissed, but is it... the same for you? Do you want me, not only in moments like that, but—"

She stopped, because he placed his hand on her cheek and shared his feelings with her. Longing, respect, awe, and admiration flowed between them, as well as the only feeling he had yet to name out loud.

Love.

Her breath hitched, and she covered his hand with her own and closed her eyes, and when she opened them up again, her lashes were wet with tears.

"Elliot," she murmured, leaning closer to his face, but then she froze. "Oh, I'm sorry. Is it... all right if I kiss you?"

He laughed, loudly, and after a moment, Iris laughed as well. Then, with laughter still on her lips, she pressed her mouth to his.

A warm tide rose inside them both as he kissed her back. Unlike the raging fire that consumed them the first time they kissed, this feeling was slow and sweet, like the Weeping Willow Rag. Iris melted against him, slid her hands to his coat lapels, and pulled him down with her as she laid back against the carpet. He raised himself up, pressing his palms on either side of her body, but she ran her hands through his hair and drew his body back down to hers, deepening the kiss and arching her back against the floor. The slow heat became much more urgent then, and Elliot trembled, his muscles going rigid against the softness of her body. He lowered his mouth to her throat, parting his lips to taste her skin, and she rewarded the gesture with a ragged, breathless cry.

"Iris," he murmured, dragging his lips down to the edge of her bodice, causing her heart to explode and hammer wildly beneath his mouth. He shuddered and gripped her waist. "Maybe... maybe we should stop."

Her fingers found his hair again, and she pulled him back up to her face, responding with a kiss that scorched his veins and seared his brain. He kissed her back, parting her lips and tasting the tip of her tongue, and the power of their combined desire obliterated the world. She seized his coat and shoved it back over his shoulders. He shrugged it off and tossed the heavy fabric aside without any hesitation. Once he was free, he bent back down and kissed her mouth again, and she moaned against him, raised her hands, and pulled the pins from her hair, causing her charcoal curls to spill out over the velvet carpet. Elliot reached beneath her skirt and slid his hand up the side of her leg, past her silken stocking, all the way to her naked thigh. She tightened her legs around him, and he groaned and buried his face in her neck.

"Iris," he murmured, his voice raw and low in his throat. "I love you."

He knew she already knew, that he'd shown her just moments ago, but the words felt important and sacred somehow, and saying them suddenly seemed as vital and necessary as air. Her heart swelled, and she clung to him, returning the glorious feeling, but then she froze as a bolt of pain and fear cracked through her chest. The sting spread, joined by a wave of guilt that turned Elliot's stomach, and he pried himself off of her and sat back against the floor.

"Iris, what is it? What's wrong?" he asked, attempting to catch his breath.

After a moment, she raised herself up, and he saw the well of pain and guilt reflected in her eyes. "I love you, too," she said. "I think I have from the first night we met."

"Then what's the matter? Why did you suddenly feel—?"

"This morning I told you I couldn't answer your questions because of your safety. That was true, but there was another reason I didn't tell you. I haven't been completely honest because... I don't want to lose you."

"What? Why would you think—?"

"It was wrong of me," she continued. "And I understand that now. You deserve the truth, and because I love you, I'm going to tell it to you. Even if it hurts or changes the way that you feel about me."

"Iris," he said, edging closer. "There is nothing you could tell me that would change my feelings for you."

Doubt rose in her throat, but she swallowed it back and nodded. "When you stopped me in the State Dining Room, I was headed to the Throne Room."

Elliot furrowed his brow. "The Throne Room? It hasn't been in use since before the quarantine. From what I've heard, the Lord Mayor used the place for storage space."

"Jennie told me the same thing. That's why I was going there." She took a breath and lowered her gaze to her lap. "This morning you asked me why I really decided to stay at the palace. One of the reasons was to find proof—proof of something terrible the Lord Mayor has been doing."

"What?"

She set her jaw and raised her head. "Purposely infecting London's people with the Hyde drug."

The blood drained from Elliot's face. "That's—that's mad."

"It's true. The only reason the drug still exists is because he's continued to make it. He found out how from the man who first synthesized and sold the tablets, before both he and Dr. Jekyll were killed by an angry mob. Go to Limehouse or Whitechapel, and you'll hear stories of people waking up in the streets infected, people with no memory of ever taking the drug."

"Of course I've heard those stories. But they're rumors—fairy tales."

"The Hydes were only a fairy tale until the epidemic. I can't tell you how I know, but I promise you it's true."

He shook his head. "But why? Why would he do such a thing?"

"Because of the reasons I told you that first night in the aviary. If the Hydes are ever cured or the infected all die out, the quarantine will be lifted and the government will come back, and the Lord Mayor will no longer be king of an absolute monarchy."

Elliot's lungs stilled, because he knew that she was right. The Lord Mayor worshiped power and control above all else.

"But why did you think that telling me this would change my feelings for you?"

She shut her eyes for a moment, fear closing around her throat. "Because your father not only knows what he's doing, he's helping him."

Elliot's mouth went dry. "No. You're wrong. He wouldn't do that. My father's entire life consists of looking for a cure."

"He's not," she insisted. "He can't be. The Lord Mayor would never allow him to live if he really were."

"How do you know?"

"Because when Lady Cullum found out the truth, he murdered her."

Ice slid through Elliot's veins. "Lady Cullum was killed by a Hyde."

She shook her head. "The Lord Mayor staged it to look that way. He already hated her, because her shelters were helping the city, and then when she discovered he was making the drug and infecting the public, he killed two birds with one stone by killing her and blaming the Hydes."

Once again, Elliot couldn't deny that the Lord Mayor would do it. But his father?

"I believe you," he said. "But not about my father. You don't know him like I do. After my mother's death... I simply can't believe he'd be content with making more monsters."

Iris glanced at her lap, her skepticism thick, and Elliot knit his brow again.

"What were you planning to do," he asked. "If you found proof tonight?"

"Make it public knowledge somehow," she said, raising her head. "Show the people of London what the Lord Mayor really is. If they knew, they'd rise up against him, and all of this would be over."

"But what if you can't find proof? Or if you do and no one believes you?"

Fear chilled her blood, but at the same time, courage warmed it. "I'll do what I have to do."

"Do what you have to do?" he asked, his own blood going cold. "What do you mean... *kill him*? You would assassinate the Lord Mayor?"

"He's a murderer. He not only killed Lady Cullum, and God knows who else, he's responsible for every Hyde and victim in this city. Think of what he's done to Cam, what he'd do if he knew his secret. Look me in the eye and tell me he doesn't deserve to die."

Elliot clenched his jaw, fighting the panic in his throat. "Maybe he does, but Iris, to plot such a thing is utter madness. If anyone even *heard* what you just said, you'd be executed."

"That's a risk I'm willing to take. Nothing in the world is more important than stopping him."

A sharp pain pierced his heart as he stared at her hardened face. Perhaps it was the height of selfishness and even cowardice, but the most important thing to him was sitting right before him.

"Wait," he said as an idea formed. "What if I remade the serum that gave me my empathy? If I could somehow inject the Lord Mayor and make him an empath as well, then he would no longer be able to do such terrible things to people. It would hurt too much to cause such pain, and maybe it would even help with Cam—"

"Elliot, the answer is not experiments and drugs!" She let out a breath, rose to her feet, and crossed away from him. "That was Jekyll's mistake, what caused this misery in the first place. No concoction of chemicals can right the world's wrongs. Evil and injustice can only be conquered by human action, by people strong and courageous enough to fight for what is right."

"But why does it have to be you?" he demanded, rising to his feet as well. "Who decided that saving the world is your responsibility—that you must be the one to risk your life for everyone else?"

The disappointment that broke across her chest was like a physical blow. "You haven't been listening," she said, walking to the door. "If I know the truth and do nothing, I'm as guilty as the Lord Mayor."

She opened the door and stepped out into the darkness of the hallway, and Elliot bit back a curse and collapsed on a nearby sofa. He wasn't sure how long he sat with his elbows against his knees, staring down at the golden constellation of pins on the floor.

Harlan Branch raised his cigar to his lips in the dim corridor, peering through the door to the ballroom and scanning the crowd for Iris. Somehow, he'd lost track of her, and loss of control—no matter how slight—always set his teeth on edge.

Not that there were many things in the world he *didn't* control. In fact, there were only two, and tonight he would remedy both.

Just thinking about the first one turned his stomach and chilled his bones. He'd been trying to stamp it out for years, and recently, he thought he'd started to see a bit of success. But then, only minutes ago, he'd watched his son creep out of the State Dining Room, his lips and cheeks flushed, followed only moments later by Andrew, his hair askew. The lit cigar crumbled in his fist as he recalled the scene. *No more,* he thought, attempting to calm himself. *Tonight you fix it.*

The second thing that eluded his control would also be remedied soon—at least it would if that little bitch would ever reappear. Gritting his teeth, he tossed the ruined cigar down onto the floor, ground it into the carpet with his foot, and wiped his hands.

Then, finally, he spotted the gleam of her golden dress. She wasn't in the ballroom, however; instead, she was hurrying through the darkened hallway to his right, heading toward the stairs that led to the palace's northern wing. She was going back to her room already? He grinned and let out a satisfied breath.

It couldn't be more perfect.

First, however, he needed to set his other plan in motion, so he straightened his tie and slid back into the ballroom, looking for Andrew.

Tears were pricking Iris's eyes when she finally reached her room, but she fought them back and dried out her tear ducts before they could emerge. She should have continued on to the Throne Room after leaving Elliot, but the only thing she wanted was the solitude of her room. After closing the door, she lit her lamp and laid on her bed, wishing she were able to remove her gown herself. Because of the corset and the design, she'd need a chambermaid's help, but they would all be occupied for at least a few more hours, so she closed her eyes and tried to disappear into the silence.

Moments later, however, the sound of a turning doorknob broke the silence in the room, and she bolted upright and forced her hammering heart to beat evenly. Elliot wouldn't just open her door; he'd knock and ask to come in. No one would simply walk into her room, except—

The Lord Mayor appeared in the doorway, his pale blue eyes alight and his lips curled into a smile. Iris rose from the bed, fear erupting in her chest.

"Sorry to barge in, my dear," he said, closing the door behind him. "I hope I didn't frighten you."

She slowed her breathing, hiding her terror and rage. "Of course not, sir."

"Good," he replied, walking toward her. "I had a question—a theory really—that I've been meaning to pose to you."

His manner was even calmer and more pleasant than usual, as if he weren't bursting into her room in the dead of night. He strolled closer, so near she smelled the tobacco on his clothes.

"First, let me ask you this," he said. "You're a virgin, are you not?"

Her blood froze, and she didn't reply, which he seemed to find amusing.

"You see," he said, stepping closer, and her lungs closed against her will. "I was wondering, if you were, and if a man did take your virtue—if you could not then heal yourself and become a virgin again. If so, then, theoretically, a man could take your maidenhead every time he took you to bed." He paused and looked her over, curling his smile into a leer. "And what man wouldn't want a girl he could endlessly deflower?"

Her stomach lurched into her throat, and she glanced around the room. This could be it. If she had to kill him now, she'd find a way.

"I have to admit," he continued as he slowly looked her over. "I wouldn't mind performing the experiment myself. Unfortunately, I have something much more important I need from you first. Maybe, however, in time..." He glanced at the nightstand beside her bed, which held the lamp she'd lit as well as the book from Elliot.

The lamp! she thought. *Yes, I could break it and use the glass.*

"*An Anthology of Birds,*" the Lord Mayor murmured. Iris started. He turned to her, a knowing and lascivious glint in his eye. "Perhaps our young Mr. Morrissey has tested my theory already."

A blush rose into her cheeks before she could stop it, and he laughed.

"Well, this is simply fascinating," he said, pressing his tongue to his teeth. "So, tell me—was my theory correct? Did you knit yourself back up after Elliot was done?"

With adrenalin coursing through her veins, she drew back her foot and kicked him between the legs as hard as she could. He screamed and doubled over as she seized the lamp beside her and raised her arm to break it over his head and cut his throat. Before she had the chance, however, he reached inside his coat and pulled a pistol from his pocket. Her arm froze as he cocked the gun and pointed it at her face.

"You little bitch," he groaned, clutching his groin with his other hand. "You couldn't have thought I'd really come to your room so unprepared."

She lowered her arm as he straightened up, his face beet-red with pain, but he kept his hand steady, aiming the gun at the spot between her eyes.

"You said yourself this morning, you can be killed like anyone else. So if you want to live, you'll come with me and do as I say."

CHAPTER FIFTEEN

Elliot was knocking on Iris's door for the third time. As soon as he'd woken, he'd dressed and gone to her room to talk to her, but just like the second and third attempt, he'd received no response. He was about to actually open the door and search for her inside when Cam appeared, walking toward him and looking disturbed as well.

"El," he said, chilling the air with the bite of his uneasiness. "You haven't seen Andrew, have you?"

"Not since last night. Why?"

He bit his lip and glanced at the floor. "He disappeared during the ball. I'd assumed he'd gone to tend to some crisis with his mother, but a letter just arrived from her, asking to send him home. Apparently, he hasn't been there since the night before the ball."

Elliot furrowed his brow. "That's strange. I can't find Iris, either. I've been knocking on her door all morning and haven't received an answer."

"Have you gone inside?"

"No. I was thinking about it just now."

"Let's try. I'll go with you."

Elliot nodded, turned, and gripped the doorknob; it was unlocked. Slowly, he and Cam stepped inside the darkened room. Iris wasn't there, but the chamber looked as it should, until the light from the hallway caught the gleam of glass on her carpet. The lamp from her nightstand was lying on its side against the floor.

"Let's go see Philomena," Cam said, his fear compounding Elliot's. "She knows better than anyone what's happening in the palace."

As they walked to Philomena's room, Elliot tried to calm himself with benign scenarios, but he couldn't wipe Iris's hardened face and treasonous words from his mind. What if she had been snooping where she shouldn't and someone caught her? His heart began to race and his hands began to shake, and by the time they reached Philomena's door, he was trembling.

Cam knocked, and when Jennie opened the door, his face grew red, and Elliot's fear was momentarily smothered by Cam's shame. Jennie blushed as well, but she curtsied obediently.

"Is—is Miss Blackwell here?" Cam asked.

"Yes, sir," she murmured, moving aside and dropping her gaze to the floor. "Miss Blackwell, Lord Branch and Mr. Morrissey are here to see you."

They stepped inside the sitting room, and Jennie closed the door behind them and melted against the wall like furniture as she'd been trained. Philomena emerged from her bedroom, dressed but still looking sleepy.

"What do you two want so early?" she asked, rubbing her eyes.

"We were wondering if you'd seen Iris," Elliot said. "We can't find her."

"Andrew, too," Cam added, unable to entirely conceal his anxiety.

Philomena wrinkled her brow. "No. Not since last night."

"If I may, Miss Blackwell..."

The three of them turned to look at Jennie. Her voice was hesitant, and her cheeks were deeply flushed, but she swallowed and went on. "I saw Miss Faye at midnight, climbing into a carriage."

Elliot's lungs stilled. "Where was she going? Who was she with?"

"I don't know, sir. I only noticed at all because her dress caught my eye in the dark. It looked like there was a man with her, but I don't know who it was."

The fear in Elliot's chest spread through the room, and no one spoke.

"Maybe it was Andrew," Cam suggested after a moment, but the hope in his voice was unconvincing. "Maybe they're together."

Philomena walked to the door. "I have an idea. Albert... well, he delivered something for Iris once. I'll send him back to see if anyone there knows where she is."

"Cam and I can go to the stables," Elliot said, following. "Maybe Milo or someone else there knows where the carriage went."

But just as the three of them reached the door, it suddenly opened before them, revealing the figure of Lady Blackwell, Philomena's mother. At first, she looked startled to see two men unchaperoned in her daughter's room, but once she realized that one of them was Cam, her insides melted. She dipped her head as excitement swelled in her breast and colored her cheeks.

"Lord Branch," she murmured. "Good morning, sir."

"Good morning, Lady Blackwell," he replied, forcing a smile.

"If you wouldn't mind, sir, I need a moment to speak with my daughter alone."

Philomena's eyes burned with her anger and frustration. "Mother," she said through gritted teeth. "Can't this wait until later?"

"I'm sorry, my dear," she replied with equal venom. "We must speak now. Jennie," she barked. "Some tea."

Jennie slipped out, and Cam and Elliot turned to Philomena. She gave them a nod and look that said, *Go ahead. I'll find you later.* With a bow to Lady Blackwell, the two of them hurried out the door.

Cam and Elliot could have easily walked to Mansion House, but instead, they rode two horses Milo had fetched them from the stables. Fear had coursed through Elliot's veins when Milo said Iris was there, but when he mentioned that armed guards had accompanied her carriage, panic overtook him, and he'd demanded that they ride. Cam had agreed, feeling nearly as worried as Elliot, but the closer they got to their destination, the more fear cooled his blood.

The guards outside the mansion parted immediately for Cam, and he and Elliot walked inside without so much as a question. The building was dim and silent in the early morning light. They listened for sounds and voices as they crept through the corridors, but nothing reached their ears but the scrapes of their shoes against the floor.

Eventually, they reached the spot where the Lord Mayor discovered Elliot stealing the book he'd given to Iris. Elliot stopped, looking down at the floor and remembering something. That day, before the Lord Mayor appeared, he'd thought he felt the presence of a Hyde somewhere in the building, even though he'd heard nothing and seen no evidence of a commotion. The feeling had seemed blocked off somehow, as if coming from beneath him...

"Cam," he whispered. "Do you remember the basement in this place?"

He almost laughed. "Of course I do. It's a bloody medieval dungeon."

Elliot nodded. Before becoming the residence of the Lord Mayor, Mansion House had been a court of law, complete with a jail.

"Remember how we used to play down there when we were kids?" Cam asked. "Until that time I accidently locked you in one of the cells. I honestly thought your mother was going to murder me for that."

"I have a feeling..." Elliot murmured, looking off toward the stairs. "I know it's strange, but I think we should go down there."

"If you say so. It's not like there's anything going on up here."

They crept to the staircase and carefully made their way down the ancient steps, which changed from wood to stone as they slunk deeper into the earth. Finally, the two of them reached the jail's outer door, which was massive and made of solid oak, as Elliot remembered. Its rusty lock had been replaced by a new one made of iron, but when Elliot turned the knob, he found the entrance to be unlocked. As he pushed it open, Cam lit a match to light their way inside, but only seconds later, they discovered they didn't need it. The formerly murky dungeon had been wired with electric lights, all of which were presently on and buzzing in the silence. Elliot's lips parted as he looked out into the room, and Cam's match slipped from his fingers and onto the concrete floor.

Why had so much money and labor gone into a basement no one knew about, let alone used?

After a moment, the two of them walked down the stairs that stretched before them, down to the room where eleven barred holding cells lined the wall. Elliot's heart stopped as he glanced at the floors of the cells; some were covered in dark red stains he was sure hadn't been there before. He opened his mouth to say something to Cam, but then a flash of terror nearly knocked him off his feet. Before he could even lift his head, he heard Cam's strangled cry.

"*Andrew*?"

Elliot's blood ran cold as he followed Cam's gaze.

Andrew was standing behind the bars of the final holding cell.

Cam bolted down the corridor toward him, and Elliot followed, barely able to feel his own feet in the wake of Cam's alarm. Andrew saw them coming, and for a moment, his face lit up, but once they reached his cell, he backed away against the wall, swallowed by fear that tripled the blinding terror in the room.

"Andrew!" Cam shouted, his chest heaving. "What are you doing here?"

"The Lord Mayor sent me to Mansion House during the ball," Andrew said in a quavering voice. He was pale as death and still wearing his evening wear from the night before, though the seams of his coat were now torn at the shoulders, as if they'd been wrenched apart. "He said he had an errand for me to—No, Cambrian! Don't do that!"

Cam had begun to fiddle with the padlock on the door, and his eyes widened at Andrew's violent protest. "Why the hell not?"

Andrew shook his head, closing his eyes and gritting his teeth, and Elliot gripped the bars to withstand the sudden wave of pain.

"I'm infected," he finally choked through his anguish. "I'm a Hyde."

The blood drained from Cam's face. "No. That's impossible."

"I waited here for your father like he instructed me to do, but when he arrived, he struck me in the head with the butt of his gun."

Elliot looked at Andrew's face. A knotted, purple, and slightly bloody bruise bulged at his temple.

"I fell to the ground, seeing stars," he continued. "And the next thing I knew the Lord Mayor was on top of me, holding me down. He shoved a tablet between my teeth and covered my nose and mouth. I thrashed against him, but it was no use—I couldn't break free or breathe—and eventually my body gave in, and I swallowed against my will." He paused, his voice breaking. "He locked me in this cell, and I transformed immediately. I'm not sure how long I stayed in that state, but eventually I changed back, and ever since then, I've felt this *burn* inside that won't go away."

Cam sucked in a breath, his chest collapsing. "That doesn't make sense!"

"He's been making the drug, Cambrian—he told me. For years, he's been infecting people to keep up the Hyde population. He's even been experimenting on Hydes right here in this basement."

Elliot's throat closed. Iris was not only right—it was worse than she'd imagined.

"But why would he do that?" Cam cried. "And why would he infect *you*?"

Andrew glanced at Elliot, and then slowly turned back to Cam, his fracturing heart slicing his chest like glass. "Because he knows."

Any blood that was left in Cam's ashen face completely dissolved. He stared at Andrew, his eyes like a trapped animal's. "He knows what?"

"Everything."

The three of them spun around to see the Lord Mayor on the stairs, strolling down to the basement's lowest level, holding a gun.

"I'd feel much more comfortable if you would disarm yourselves," he said, as calmly as if he'd asked them to have a seat in a drawing room.

With visibly shaking hands, Cam took his pistol from its holster and slid it across the floor to his father. Everything in Elliot screamed to not give up his gun, but the combination of his own fear, Andrew's pain, and Cam's dread ensured that he would never draw fast enough to beat the Lord Mayor. He gritted his teeth, removed his gun, and slid it across the floor.

"Thank you," the Lord Mayor said, placing their pistols in his pockets. "Now I feel much more at ease."

He did, to a degree. Arrogance and triumph were coming off of him in waves, but Elliot sensed the rage and bone-chilling fear he hid beneath them.

"Father," Cam began, masking his panic with stunned surprise. "I don't know what you think you know, but—"

"I know what you are, Cambrian," the Lord Mayor said as he approached. "You can't honestly have believed you could keep such a thing from me. I've been suspicious for years, and last night, my fears were confirmed." He paused, his eyes darkening. "I saw you and Andrew together."

Cam's stomach plummeted. "I don't know what you mean—"

"I mean you're a deviant, Cambrian. A twisted abomination. Can you even comprehend the shame and horror I felt when I saw you? *My* son, the heir to this city..." He paused and viciously spat on the floor beside him. "A goddamned mandrake."

All the terror and shame that Cam ever felt rose up inside him, and Elliot stumbled backward, gripping a bar to keep upright. Cam turned around and rushed toward him with frantic, wild eyes.

"El, it's not true! I don't know what he—"

"Elliot already knows."

They turned and stared at the Lord Mayor, who sneered and strolled a bit closer.

"Don't deny it," he said to Elliot. "I'm sure you've *felt* it."

Elliot's mouth went dry. "How—how did you know—"

"Because your father told me, of course. It's something we both have in common, you know. Being ashamed of our sons."

"El, what's he talking about?" Cam asked, his strained voice growing shrill.

"Three weeks ago, Elliot injected himself with a serum," the Lord Mayor explained. "He created it from his father's notes after hearing a

189

conversation of ours. He wanted to remove his empathy, but of course he botched it up, and now feels the feelings of those around him like they were his own." He looked at Cam, a shrewd smile spreading across his face. "Everything you've felt for the last three weeks, he's felt as well."

"El..." Cam murmured, his throat going dry. "Tell me that isn't true."

Elliot tightened his jaw. "It is, but Cam—"

He turned away, and Elliot rushed to his other side.

"Cam, you need to know—"

"How could you keep that from me?" he demanded, his chest cracking beneath the weight of his shame. "You're like my brother."

"I know, and I didn't *want* to lie to you. It killed me to do it. But I knew that if you knew what I'd discovered, you'd think—"

"You betrayed me?"

He started to turn away again, but Elliot caught his sleeve. "Cam, listen! You need to know that your father is wrong about you. I've felt what you and Andrew feel, and there's nothing wrong with it. It's pure, good, and exactly the way that Iris and I—"

"That's disgusting!"

Cam shoved him away, sending him stumbling back into the bars. Then he glanced at Andrew and shut his eyes, his soul splintering.

"It's not," Elliot insisted, rising and fighting Cam's agony. "Here," he said, reaching out to take his hand. "I can show you."

"Stop!" Cam shouted, backing away and running his hands through his hair. "Father," he cried, rushing toward him. "I swear it isn't true—"

Without a word, the Lord Mayor snapped his gun across Cam's face, sending him sprawling back against the bars of the cell next to Andrew's. Andrew screamed, and Elliot crumbled down to the concrete floor, paralyzed by the sudden blow of terror, pain, and shame.

"Don't lie to me," the Lord Mayor bellowed at Cam. "That's over now. I know what I saw, and I know what you are."

Cam struggled to stand, and the Lord Mayor drew back his foot and kicked his injured rib, tearing the feral cry of a wounded animal from his throat. Andrew gripped his bars and shook them as if he could break free, and Elliot fell to his hands and knees and vomited on the floor.

"Now look at me," the Lord Mayor growled, seizing Cam by the collar and dragging him up onto his feet. "Andrew is infected, and the law states he must die, as should you for the vile, disgusting things you two have done. However," he said, taking a breath and evening his voice. "I have been merciful thus far, and I will continue to be. I will give you one more chance to prove your worth to me."

Cam sucked in a desperate breath and released a rattling cough, causing a mouthful of blood to spill out and trickle down his chin.

"Go back to the palace, clean yourself up, and meet with Earl Blackwell. We've already spoken; he's waiting for you to ask for his daughter's hand. Marry that girl, get her with child, and you'll prove to me you've changed. Then, in return, Andrew can stay here—imprisoned but alive."

Cam's shoulders slumped, and he closed his eyes, wheezing against the pain, but the physical trauma was nothing compared to the torture he felt inside. Elliot felt something split and finally snap inside Cam's heart, as if his soul had been battered to the point that it detached. He was nothing but a broken shell, a ghost made of pain and shame, so Elliot shouldn't have been surprised when he looked at his father and nodded.

"That's my boy," the Lord Mayor said, so certain of his victory that he reached inside his pocket, drew out Cam's gun, and handed it back.

Elliot still couldn't move, and Andrew seemed equally paralyzed, so they watched in helpless silence as Cam accepted the gun, clutched his side, and limped toward the stairs. He wanted to stop and look back at them—Elliot could feel it. The smallest trace of the spark that once was Cam *begged* him to look back, but the fear won, and he climbed the stairs and left without a glance. Once he was gone, however, so was the burden of his pain, and Elliot climbed to his feet and silently charged toward the Lord Mayor. Unfortunately, he turned around and saw him just in time.

"Hold it right there," he said, raising his gun to Elliot's face.

Elliot froze, sickened by both his own fear and the Lord Mayor's triumph.

"What did you think you were going to do?" the Lord Mayor taunted him. "It's not like your *condition* would allow you to cause someone pain."

"I could," he replied. "I simply wouldn't enjoy it like you do."

The Lord Mayor blanched a little, and Elliot sensed an advantage. Anyone as hungry for control as the Lord Mayor would find someone knowing his deepest, darkest feelings extremely upsetting. If he could just unsettle him enough to drop his guard...

"You say you're disgusted by Cam," he continued. "But I know you're really afraid. Why? Are you frightened that part of you might feel the way he does?"

The Lord Mayor's face reddened. "I think you're forgetting which one of us is holding a gun on the other."

"I think you're forgetting that I know every single thing you feel."

He squeezed the gun tighter, his hand shaking, but then his grimace curled. "You're right," he said. "How silly of me. Tell me, what am I feeling right now when I think of your friend, Miss Faye?"

Violent lust and venomous hatred erupted inside the Lord Mayor, and Elliot clenched his teeth and swallowed the bile in his throat.

"Where is she? What did you do to her?"

"She's unharmed. For now." He backed toward the stairs, keeping the gun trained on Elliot's face.

"Wait!" Elliot cried, desperate to keep him there and talking. "How much does my father know about what you've been doing? Making the drug, infecting people, and experimenting on Hydes?"

The Lord Mayor laughed as he continued to climb the stairs. "Frank? He's as weak as you, even without your pathetic condition. He's been nothing but a wretched, broken man since your mother's death. Keeping all this from him has been a kindness on my part."

"Then why is he still alive?" Elliot called, approaching the steps. "Why would you allow him to continue to look for a cure?"

The Lord Mayor paused, smirking at him. "Because he's not."

A brilliant flash of gold shot through the doorway beside the Lord Mayor, knocking him off his feet and sending him tumbling back down the steps. Elliot looked up to see Iris—alive, whole, and seemingly unharmed—at the top of the stairs. She gripped the knob and pulled at the door, apparently planning to trap the Lord Mayor, but then she caught sight of Elliot beside his crumpled frame. She froze for only a moment—just long enough to meet his gaze—but it was plenty of time for the Lord Mayor to react. He pushed himself up, raised his gun, and fired a single shot, sending Iris flying backward onto the concrete floor.

CHAPTER SIXTEEN

ris!”

Elliot screamed and started to dash up the stairs toward her, but the Lord Mayor quickly swung the gun in his direction. He froze again and watched as the Lord Mayor stood and climbed the steps, seizing a fistful of Iris's hair and jerking her up off the floor. A cry of relief erupted from Elliot's throat when he saw she was still alive, blinking against her stupor as the Lord Mayor forced her to stand. Her shoulder—bared by her strapless gown—was now splattered with blood. But once she was back on her feet, the bullet slipped out and *clinked* to the concrete, and the wound where it had been began to close and heal itself.

“How did you escape your chains?” the Lord Mayor demanded, dragging her down the stairs and throwing her back against one of the cells.

She straightened up and turned to face him, rage flaring inside her eyes.

“I broke my thumbs,” she replied.

Even the Lord Mayor blanched a little, but then he recovered, fueled by rage as powerful as her own.

“I'd so wanted to keep you around for our little experiment,” he said. “But you've proven to be much more of a liability than you're worth.”

He waved his gun and forced both her and Elliot away from the stairs, backing them up to where Andrew stood in the final holding cell. As they walked, Elliot glanced down and noticed the Lord Mayor limping; he must have twisted or sprained his ankle badly when he fell.

"Perhaps it's for the best anyway," the Lord Mayor continued to Iris. "I probably would have grown tired of you eventually anyhow. Healing power or not, you're just a slit like any other."

Elliot stiffened as rage scorched his veins, and the Lord Mayor laughed.

"As for you," he said. "Unfortunately, you know too much. Although, I think you'll agree that putting an end to your pathetic existence would be an act of mercy."

He stopped just before they reached Andrew's cell, and when he dug his free hand into his pocket and drew out a key, Elliot assumed he was going to lock them up next to Andrew. Instead, however, he fiddled with the padlock on Andrew's door, opening the clasp and removing the padlock completely. The door swung open, and Andrew cried out, backing against the wall.

"I think I'll let the three of you take care of my problem yourselves," the Lord Mayor said, pocketing the lock and backing away toward the stairs. "I'd love to watch, but I have more important matters to tend to."

Ice slid through Elliot's veins as understanding dawned. "No—*no!*" he cried, his heart thrashing against his ribs. "You can't do this! Andrew's mother, *my father*—they'll find out what you've done and they—"

"People die and disappear in this city everyday," he replied. "Besides, Elliot, can you honestly say that your father will be anything but grateful to hear you're gone?"

Somehow, in the midst of Elliot's panic, the comment *hurt*, so badly that—against all reason—he charged toward the stairs.

"Why the hell did you want to remove your empathy?" he hollered. "You're already an evil, soulless excuse for a human being!"

The Lord Mayor paused and looked down, quirking his lips into a smile. "It wasn't meant for me," he said. "It was meant for Cambrian. I thought that destroying his feminine weakness would make him more of a man; little did I know the serum would do the opposite. So thank you for that, Elliot," he said, stepping through the doorway. "I must admit this second plan worked out better than the first."

He shut the door and turned the iron lock with a deafening *clang*.

Elliot stared up after him, his lungs frozen in terror, but then he rushed back to Iris, fighting the roar of his pulse in his ears. "Iris, are you all right? What happened? What did he do to you?"

"I'm fine. He brought me here last night and chained me up in a room on the third floor. It's a laboratory, Elliot—a full, working lab. I'm certain it's where he's been making the drug and doing God knows what else. I imagined a hundred terrible things that he might do to me, but all he did was take my blood."

"Your blood?"

"About a pint."

"Why would he do that?"

"I don't know. He took it, and then he left." She clutched his hand, and he squeezed it back in spite of her anxiety. "Why are you here?" she asked. "Why was Andrew locked up in a cell? And what did the Lord Mayor mean when he said we'd solve his problem ourselves?"

Elliot's stomach dropped, and his blood turned to ice again. "Cam and I came here looking for you and found Andrew locked up instead. The Lord Mayor infected him last night. He's a Hyde."

Iris blanched. "Oh God. Where is Cambrian now?"

Elliot took a breath and then explained everything that happened. Iris's face grew more and more pale as she listened to the story, but then a metal clanking sounded behind them, and she jumped. Both of them turned to see Andrew, pulling desperately at his door, trying to find a way to jam it shut without the padlock. They rushed toward him, but once they reached him, he screamed and backed away.

"Get back!"

"Andrew," Elliot said, raising his hands. "It's all right."

"No, it's not! I could change at any moment and kill you both."

"Andrew, calm down," Iris said, stepping closer to the bars. "We just need to compose ourselves and think rationally about this." She slowed her pulse and breathing and then glanced around the room. "We can find another barrier, or maybe a way to bind you. Once that protection's in place, we can focus on how to escape."

"Right," Elliot said. "It's a jail. There must be some handcuffs or chains."

He and Iris separated and searched around the room, but Andrew remained in his cell, tugging urgently at the door. Then, in a corner a few feet away, Elliot found a long, unfamiliar, metal table. A grey, woolen blanket had been draped over the surface, and when he pulled it back, a strangled gasp escaped his throat. A wide array of surgical equipment lay on the table, and most of it—as well as the table itself— was stained with blood. He shuddered, reaching down and picking up a sharpened scalpel. What terrible things had the Lord Mayor used these instruments for?

"Dear God," Iris whispered, coming to stand beside him.

After a moment, Andrew crept out of his cell and looked as well. "Unfortunately, a scalpel won't be helpful against a Hyde." His breathing slowed, and his heart ground to a halt, arrested by a combination of terror, grief, and hope. "A person, however," he murmured.

Elliot spun around to face him. "No," he said, clutching the scalpel and backing away. "Don't think it."

"Elliot, it's the only way. You have to kill me now, before I have the chance to change."

"Like hell I do!" he cried. "Have you lost your bloody mind?"

"Andrew, wait," Iris said. "You need to stop and consider your options. There has to be another way—"

"There is no other way," he yelled. "Face the facts: We're trapped down here, and no one is coming to save—"

He broke off and turned away, choking on his anguish, which rose with such intensity Elliot's knees nearly buckled beneath it. "I *am* thinking reasonably," he continued after a breath, gripping the table to keep his composure as tears swarmed his eyes. "I'm infected. What kind of life can I possibly hope for now? Either the Lord Mayor will kill me, keep me imprisoned, or let me go, but no matter what he does, it won't stop me from being a monster." He gritted his teeth and closed his eyes, his knuckles turning white. "I'd rather die than live with knowing I murdered two of my friends. Besides..." The tears spilled over, and his soul sank into the ground. Elliot clutched the scalpel and turned away, unable to breath. "Since I... now that Cambrian..." And then he couldn't go on. He slid to the floor, covered his face, and sobbed against his hands.

"Andrew," Iris said fiercely, kneeling down on the ground beside him. "Don't give up! All hope isn't lost—not even with Cambrian. I don't believe there is such a thing as a hopeless situation. You always have options, and there is always more than one choice to make."

Andrew sucked in a rattling breath, his shoulders trembling. "You're right," he wheezed, wiping his eyes with his sleeve. "I have a choice."

Iris tumbled backward as he shoved her and leapt to his feet, making a mad dash for the scalpel in Elliot's hand. Elliot jerked his arm away and stumbled against the table, sending the surgical instruments clamoring down to the concrete floor. Andrew lunged again, but Elliot ducked down just in time, causing Andrew to roll over his back and onto the table.

"Andrew, stop!" Elliot cried, clutching the blade to his chest.

But Andrew ignored him, scrambling off the table and springing again. His shoulder slammed into Elliot's chest, and they both crashed to the ground, but the violent influx of Andrew's desperation gave Elliot strength. With double the drive, he shoved him off and started to crawl to his feet. But the moment he stood up, Andrew reached out and caught his ankle, yanking it back and sending him flying facedown onto the floor. He blinked and shook his head, trying to clear his blurring vision, and Andrew climbed onto his back and gripped the hand that held the blade. Elliot clenched his fist as tight as he could, but Andrew bit his wrist, and a bolt of pain shot through his nerves like a blinding electric current. His fingers opened against his will, and Andrew snatched the scalpel. When he rolled over, Elliot saw him raising it to his throat. Before he could draw the blade across his flesh, however, it vanished.

"Stop this madness now!" Iris cried as she snatched the scalpel, shoving Andrew off of Elliot and onto the floor. "Neither of us is going to let you kill yourself, and that's final. Now stop wasting time and help us to find a way out of here!"

Andrew covered his face and rolled over onto his side, flooding the entire room with his pain and desolation. Elliot gritted his teeth against it and crawled up onto his knees, but then Andrew's despair dissolved like water down a drain. Once it was gone, a sharp, creeping hunger crawled into its place—a hot, gnawing ache that snaked through his body like angry vines.

"Iris," Elliot murmured, slowly rising to his feet. "I think... I think he's..." He looked at her, and her eyes grew wide.

"Oh God."

"Come on!" he cried, taking her hand and running to Andrew's cell. Once they made it inside, they grabbed the door and pulled it shut.

"It's going to be all right," Iris said, though her fear was as sharp as his own. "We simply have to hold him off until he changes back."

Andrew screamed, and a wave of vicious hunger seared Elliot's throat.

"Iris, you have to slow your heart," he said, gripping the bars. "Please, lie down and do it now, before he changes completely."

She stared at him, her fear dwarfed by a wave of disbelief. "There is no way I am leaving you to fight him on your own."

"Iris, you have a way to protect yourself—"

"By abandoning you? I'm sorry, Elliot, but that isn't going to happen!"

Andrew shrieked again, and Elliot slumped down to his knees. The hunger was all consuming, and the high was roasting his brain. He raised his head and watched as Andrew's skin became bloodlessly white, his hair sank into his scalp, and his muscles strained the already torn seams of his evening coat.

"Iris, we can't fight him," he groaned. "You have to save yourself."

She bent down beside him and seized the sides of his face with both her hands, filling his veins with tenacity and courage.

"We're not giving up!"

A howl split the air as Andrew rose and stretched out his massive arms, and Elliot closed his eyes and bit his cheek.

He'd fully transformed.

"Use it," Iris cried, dragging Elliot back to his feet. "Use his feelings to make yourself stronger. We can do this!"

Elliot sucked in a breath and clutched the bars to steady himself. That night in the snow, before Iris saved him, he had used the Hyde's hunger to run as fast as the creature. Maybe, with his empathy and Iris's adrenaline, they really could survive long enough for Andrew to change back. He looked at her and nodded, but then Andrew turned around, and his raging desire peaked as he charged toward the cell.

He rammed into the bars with the weight of a wrecking ball, and Iris and Elliot stumbled back, but righted themselves in time. The door opened only an inch before they shoved it back, gripping the bars and straining to keep it closed with all their might. Andrew gnashed his dagger-like teeth and launched himself at the door again, but Iris closed her eyes and flooded her system with adrenaline, and Elliot harnessed Andrew's wild drive and stood his ground. It worked for a while, but eventually the attacks became too much.

"Iris," Elliot cried, "I can't hold it for much longer!"

She looked around, her brow sprouting with sweat. "I have an idea. We'll release the door—"

"What?"

"Just hear me out! We'll release the door, and I'll run out and get him to follow me. You can gather your strength while he chases me around, and then I'll run back, and we'll hold him off with the door again. It will work."

"But what if he catches you?"

"It's the best chance that we've got. I can regenerate my strength, so it has to be me that goes." She paused and nodded toward her hand, which still held the gleaming scalpel. "If I have to, I can wound him— that will give me some time to escape. As long as he doesn't actually get my heart, I'll be able to heal."

Elliot shook his head. It was madness, but what other choice did they have?

"All right," he said. "On three, we let go and you run out."

She closed her eyes and took a breath. "One... two... three!"

They released the door, and it swung back and pinned Elliot to the wall. Iris dashed out, swiping Andrew to make sure he saw her and followed. He turned around and bounded after her like a rabid dog.

Elliot peeled himself off the wall and watched as Iris ran. Andrew crawled on top of the table and launched himself after her, but his strength was so great he flew too high and crashed against the ceiling, destroying an entire row of buzzing, electric lights. The room dimmed and shattered glass rained down onto the floor, but Iris continued running, shielding her head and face with her arms. She tore up the stairs and then down again with Andrew trailing behind her, and then she turned and headed back for the safety of the cell. Elliot sucked in a breath and readied himself to hold the door again, but just as Iris reached the pile of glass, Andrew caught her.

She tumbled forward, face-first into the broken glass, and when she rolled over, her palms, neck, and face were gushing blood. Andrew crawled on top of her, but she wiped her eyes, raised the scalpel, and slashed at his face and neck. The blade made contact, and even more blood erupted from Andrew's throat, but after a gurgling howl, he recovered and lunged at her chest. She stabbed and sliced again, reopening the healing wound, but he pinned her down before she had the chance to evade his grasp. He bared his razor sharp teeth, and the scalpel slipped from her hand. All she could do was raise her bloody palms to his bleeding throat, squeezing as hard as she could, pressing his face away from her chest. Elliot flew from the cell, thinking of nothing but getting between them, but then Andrew jerked back, fell to the ground...

And changed back to himself.

When Elliot watched Will change from a Hyde to himself in the bakery, the transformation had been uneven, gradual, and slow, but Andrew's change was clean, complete, and instantaneous. It was almost as if he wasn't shifting from one state to another, but merely waking up from a nightmare that had ended. Iris sat up, staring and feeling equally mystified, and when Andrew rose from the ground and looked at them, the puzzlement swelled.

"Are—are you two all right?" he asked.

Elliot nodded, crossed to Iris, and helped her to her feet.

"Yes," she said, healing her wounds as she spoke. "But what just happened? I've never seen a Hyde change in the middle of a kill— especially not so quickly and completely."

"Neither have I," Elliot said. "Andrew, how are you feeling?"

"I..." he began, blinking and shaking his head, searching for words. "I feel *different* now. That burn I'd felt inside ever since the Lord Mayor infected me..." He raised his head and looked at them, barely breathing. "It's... it's gone."

"Gone?" Elliot echoed. "Are you sure?"

"Yes, I'm certain."

"And it hasn't gone away since you first swallowed the tablet?"

"No."

Elliot looked at Iris, at the blood on her now-healed hands. "My God," he murmured. "Iris, your blood came in contact with Andrew's wound. You—I mean—your blood... Iris, it could be—"

"The cure."

The words seemed to escape her lips almost unconsciously. The three of them stood in silence, until a gunshot tore through the air. They all jumped and jerked their heads to the stairs, where the shot had sounded. The basement door was swinging open, its iron lock destroyed. Elliot raced up the steps with Iris and Andrew close behind. Once they reached the top, they saw a figure sprawled out on the floor, and when it sat up and shook its head, they gasped.

It was Philomena.

She blinked and glanced at the smoking shotgun lying by her side.

"Albert wasn't kidding," she said. "These things have a hell of kick."

"Philomena!" Elliot cried. "When did you—how did you manage—?"

"Please. One question at a time." She raised an arm and an eyebrow. "Care to help a lady up?"

Elliot parted his lips and then stepped forward to take her hand, and when their skin met, the surge of her proud relief relaxed his heart.

"When my mother barged into my room this morning," she said as he helped her to stand, "it was to inform me that my marriage had been arranged. I knew I couldn't wait any longer; I had to run away. With Jennie's help, I drugged her tea with a massive amount of laudanum. She fell asleep in my room, and Albert and I made our escape. I'd planned to steal my father's pistol, but all I could find was this." She crouched down and, with some effort, picked up the shotgun. "I found Milo before I left, and he told me where you and Cambrian were, so Albert and I took a carriage and drove here as quickly as we could. I followed the sounds of crashing and screaming down here, to the basement door. When I couldn't unlock it, I took the gun and—well, you know the rest."

"Philomena," Elliot breathed, "You truly are a marvel."

"Tell me something I don't know." She grinned. "Now what the hell is going on? Why are you covered in blood?"

She gestured at Andrew and Iris, who glanced at their clothes as if they'd forgotten.

"We'll explain in a moment," Iris said. "Where is Albert?"

Philomena glanced at the floor, guilt pricking her chest. "I was worried about you," she said to Iris. "I didn't know what else to do, so after he dropped me off here, I sent him to look for you. I told him to go to that secret address you gave me when you first moved in."

"That's all right," Iris said, raising her hands. "I understand. And actually, I think the four of us should go there now."

Elliot knit his brow. "Go where?"

Iris set her jaw before turning to face him. "To see my mother."

Disbelief flooded the room as they all turned to stare at her.

"I thought you said your mother was dead," Andrew finally murmured.

"I lied," she said. "My mother faked her death to escape the Lord Mayor." She paused and took another breath. "Her name is Virginia Carroll."

CHAPTER SEVENTEEN

S o, what's your real name then?"

Philomena was the first to speak once the four of them were safely inside the hansom cab. She'd come to Mansion House in a carriage, but Albert had taken the horse with him to Iris's address. The distance was too far to walk, and Iris and Andrew could hardly stroll down the street in their bloody clothes, so Elliot had gone and found a hansom cab to take them. Thankfully, besides the shotgun, Philomena had also stolen quite a bit of money, and a generous tip had persuaded the driver not to ask any questions.

Once Elliot returned with the cab, the other three snuck past the guards, ran out, and joined him inside. The driver took off, and the four of them sat in silence, catching their breath. Once the danger had passed, Philomena asked her question. Iris, who was seated next to her and across from the boys, glanced at Elliot with a twinge of guilt before she answered.

"My name really is Iris Faye, it's just... Iris Faye Carroll."

"And your mother was that female doctor who worked with Lady Cullum? The one who studied with Dr. Jekyll and died—well, I suppose *allegedly* died—in a lab explosion?"

"Yes. The Lord Mayor killed Lady Cullum when she discovered he was making the drug and infecting people, but not before she had the chance to tell my mother the truth."

Elliot glanced at Philomena to see how she took the news about the Lord Mayor infecting the public, but her lack of a reaction—and the fact that she hadn't asked any more questions about the blood—told him that Iris and Andrew had filled her in while he'd gotten the cab.

"My mother knew the Lord Mayor would be coming for her next," Iris continued. "So she blew up the lab, made it look like she'd died, took me, and went into hiding." She turned to look at Elliot. "I'm so sorry I lied to you."

Elliot reached over, took her hand, and shared his feelings with her, and she closed her eyes and let out a breath when she felt his understanding. "You were protecting your mother," he said. "We'd all have done the same thing."

Iris smiled and opened her eyes again, and he released her hand.

"What I don't understand," he continued, "is why she hid your existence. Sometimes, after she and Lady Cullum would come for tea, my mother would say how sad it was that Virginia had no family."

Iris sighed. "She said it was for my protection because of my abilities. And since she wasn't married... well, no one would have respected her as a doctor or a woman if they'd known she had a child."

"But why are we going to see her now?" Andrew asked. "We need to find Cambrian."

Elliot shook his head. "Andrew, we can't. He's at the palace."

"But he needs to know—"

"Have you lost your mind?" Philomena said. "There isn't a place that's less safe for us to go right now."

Andrew sat back, let out a breath, and then turned back to Iris. "Are you sure your mother will even be there?"

"It's Sunday. That's her day off." She glanced at her lap and wrung her hands, her anxiety thickening. "We have to go there. She's the only one with answers to our questions, and this time, she won't be able to refuse an explanation. Not when she finds out that I... that my blood might be..." She trailed off, as if saying the words out loud might somehow jinx them.

Philomena, however, had no such qualms. "The bloody cure." She let out a breath and shook her head. "I don't know that I ever truly believed one would be found."

They rode along in silence, absorbing the thought and the palpable, measureless hope it accompanied.

"Do you think the Lord Mayor knows?" Elliot murmured after a moment. "You said all he did after kidnapping you was take your blood."

Iris knit her brow in thought. "I don't think so. If he thought I was the cure, he would have killed me straight away."

"Then why do you think he wanted your blood?" Andrew asked.

"I have no idea."

"I wonder where he is now," Elliot pondered, biting his fingernail. "What 'important matters' he had to leave us to attend to."

"He's probably meeting my father," Philomena said with a scowl. "Cambrian is the one my parents wanted me to marry." She shook her head and rolled her eyes. "I adore Cambrian—he's loads of fun and a fabulous dancer—but I'll lock myself up in that bloody dungeon before I'll marry anyone, especially a man who doesn't like women to begin with. Sorry—no offense, Andrew."

All three of them turned to stare at her, and Elliot's lungs nearly collapsed beneath the weight of their shock.

"What?" Philomena asked. "I'm not a bloody idiot. They've been gazing at each other as if shot between the eyes by Cupid himself for the last few weeks." In response to their continued silence, she sighed and shook her head. "When will you people grasp the fact that I know everything?"

Iris's lips quirked into a grin. "Did you know Elliot's an empath? He feels the feelings of those around him as if they were his own."

Philomena looked at him, her eyes widening with the surprise that stilled her heart. "Well," she said quickly, glancing away as if bored. "Bully for you."

A few minutes later, the cab reached the Waterloo Bridge and crossed the Thames. They descended into the lower marsh, and just before they reached the old Southwestern Railway Station, Albert appeared, riding a horse in the opposite direction. Philomena stuck her head out the window and called for the driver to stop, and once he did, she waved her arms and hollered for Albert's attention. He saw her and immediately pulled up beside the carriage.

"Alby," Philomena said. "Did you go to the address?"

"Yes, Miss Blackwell. She wasn't there, and the woman who lives there was quite alarmed by my presence and my questions."

"Iris is actually here with me," Philomena explained. "We're on our way back to the flat right now. Will you come with us?"

"Of course."

The driver took off down the road again, and Albert followed behind them. Finally, they reached a tenement building beside the old station. Elliot wrapped his coat around Iris before they stepped out of the carriage, hoping it would hide most of her bloodstained gown from the crowd. Unfortunately, there wasn't much Andrew could do to conceal his clothing, so Albert and Philomena walked close beside him to shield it from view. They climbed the steps to the second floor, and Iris raised her arm and knocked on a door, her anxiety peaking.

Elliot felt the fear behind the door before it opened, and when Virginia stepped into view, the force of it became blinding. He blinked for a moment, but once he saw her, he couldn't believe how familiar she looked for someone he'd only met a handful of times as a very young child. But then, perhaps the familiarity also stemmed from how much she and Iris resembled each other. Instead of gold, her eyes were dark grey, but her delicate face and thick, charcoal curls were exactly the same. The moment she saw Iris and her bloodstained gown, however, those eyes expanded with panic and terror that ruptured her pounding heart.

"Mama, I'm not hurt," Iris began, but before she could finish, Virginia threw her arms around her and pulled her against her chest.

"Iris," she cried. "I didn't know if you were dead or alive!" She stepped back and looked at her dress. "What in God's name happened to you?"

"I'll explain everything," Iris said. "But we need to go inside."

Only then did Virginia lift her head to see the others, and when she saw Elliot, her face grew pale. "Is that..." she murmured, terror closing around her throat.

"Please, Mama, inside."

Virginia looked at Philomena and her shotgun, Albert in his footman's attire, and Andrew in his torn and bloodstained eveningwear.

"My God..."

"Mama, *please*," Iris begged.

"A-all right," she stammered. "Come inside."

Virginia refused to ask or answer any questions until her daughter was no longer covered in blood, so the rest of them waited while she cleaned Iris up and helped her to change out of her gown behind a screen. When the two of them emerged, Iris was wearing a plain brown dress, and her mother's fear and anxiety had softened the slightest bit. She handed Andrew the basin and cloth she'd used to clean Iris's blood, and he thanked her, sat on the floor, and wiped the stains from his hands and neck. Iris sat down on a mattress, and Virginia slid into a chair, so Elliot, Philomena, and Albert seated themselves on the floor.

"Mama," Iris began after pausing to clear her throat. "These are friends of mine: Andrew Heron, Philomena Blackwell, Albert... oh, I don't actually know—"

"Cummings," Philomena provided.

"Thank you. Albert Cummings. And this is Elliot—"

"Morrissey," Virginia interjected, both her eyes and her voice like ice. "What is he doing here?"

"Mama, I know what you're thinking, but all of these people— they're on our side."

"*Our side*?" she demanded, her eyes growing wide. "What have you told them, Iris?"

She shifted against the mattress. "They know everything I know."

The veins in Virginia's neck nearly burst with her panic and rage. "Have you lost your mind?" she cried. "First, you disappear after work, then you send me a letter saying you're living inside *the palace*, then you show up covered in blood with the son of Dr. Morrissey—"

"I know, I know," Iris said, raising her hands. "And I'm sorry for that. But Mama, just listen and let me explain. I have something wonderful, something even possibly *miraculous* to tell you."

Virginia set her jaw and sat back in her chair, and Iris went on.

"Last night, the Lord Mayor kidnapped Andrew and forced him to take the drug."

Elliot jumped as Virginia's fear spiked, and she stood and stumbled against her chair.

"Mama, wait!" Iris cried, rising as well. "Just hear me out. This morning he changed and attacked me, and during the struggle, our open wounds came in contact with each other. The moment my blood met his blood, he immediately changed back. It was instantaneous—like nothing any of us had seen—and he said he feels different now, that there was a burning inside him that's gone. Mama..." She took a step closer, holding her breath. "I think he's cured."

For a moment, Virginia's shock was so strong she almost felt nothing at all. Then, slowly, her frozen lips formed a single word. "Cured?"

"Yes," Iris exhaled, reaching out and clutching her hand. "I don't know how or why, but Mama... I think my blood is the cure."

The room swelled with silence so thick it coated the air like smoke. Virginia sat back down as if unconscious of the movement, staring straight ahead and seeing something far away. Iris's pulse quickened with concern, and she knelt before her.

"Mama... did you hear what I just said?"

"I—I should have known," she murmured, almost inaudibly. "I never thought... I didn't want to think... I should have known."

Suddenly, a well of pain and shame sprang up inside her, clogging her soul and spreading through her body like poisonous bile. Elliot bit his lip and closed his eyes, his muscles tensing. The feeling was almost identical to Cam's agony in the basement—wretchedness and degradation so fierce it devoured the self.

"Mama, what is it?" Iris asked. "What do you mean you should have known?"

Virginia turned away, shaking her head against the pain, and Elliot rose and rushed to Iris's side.

"Give her a moment."

"Why?" she asked. "What's wrong? What is she feeling?"

Elliot let out a breath and closed his eyes, taking her hand. He shared the feelings, and Iris shuddered, her eyes filling with tears.

"My God," she murmured, releasing Elliot's hand and taking her mother's. "Mama," she said softly. "Mama, please. Will you look at me?"

Slowly, Virginia turned her head, and when she looked at Iris, tears swam into her eyes as well.

"Mama," Iris said. "Mama, I love you more than life. I'm here for you, and there's nothing you can say or do to change that."

Virginia closed her eyes, and the tears slipped down her cheeks.

"I know what you're feeling," Iris continued, her voice growing raw. "I don't know why you feel this pain, but I'm here to help you through it. Just like you've been there to help me through everything all my life." She sucked back a sob, squeezing her hand. "I'm strong because of you, because you taught me how to be. Trust me now, and let me be strong for you. Talk to me."

Silence swelled in the room again, but then Virginia opened her eyes and released a trembling breath. "I should have known," she said, "because of how you were conceived."

Iris's heart ground to a halt, as did everyone else's, but no one spoke, and after another breath, Virginia went on.

"I was working late in the lab one night, here in London, when I was a student. And he, my teacher..." She bit her lip. The struggle to say the name was dragging her stomach up into her throat, so Elliot swallowed and said it for her.

"You mean Dr. Jekyll?"

Virginia's nausea swelled, but she nodded and continued. "He came in unexpectedly. I asked him if he needed something and he said no, he was fine, but then he just sat there, watching me as I continued my work. I grew nervous and asked again if there was something I could do, and then he said, 'Well, yes, Miss Carroll. I do have something in mind.' He told me he'd created a new serum a few days ago, and that since then he'd been testing it out, but always by himself. I stopped my work and watched as he revealed a vile and syringe. Then, without another word, he removed his coat, rolled up his sleeve, and injected himself with the serum. I was so stunned I couldn't speak or move from where I stood, and when he was done, he looked at me and said—" She broke off, gritting her teeth as her throat began to close. "He said, 'I think I'm going to enjoy this experiment.'"

Elliot shuddered and glanced at Iris. Her face was pale as death.

"Then he transformed," Virginia continued. "His eyes went black, and his skin turned white, and he became the kind of Hyde that none of you would remember—the kind that didn't eat hearts but committed... other violent acts." She closed her eyes as guilt rose up and joined the shame in her throat. "I was the first to witness the monstrous thing he had created, but I didn't tell a soul what I'd seen... or what he'd done to me. I booked passage for America and left the very next day. I was already back in Kansas when I discovered..." She opened her eyes and looked at Iris. "That I would have you."

Iris stared at her, not breathing. "My father was... Henry Jekyll?"

Virginia nodded. "And you were conceived while he was an active Hyde." She took a breath and wiped the tears from her eyes with the back of her hand. "I thought I could forget what happened, pretend that you were simply a magical gift that came from nowhere, but now I see that in doing so, I blinded myself to the truth."

"Mama, it only makes sense that you would want—"

"No, listen to me." She leaned down and cupped Iris's face in the palm of her hand. "I've never considered you anything but a blessing from God, Iris, but I didn't want to acknowledge the terrible act that brought you here. I knew it was the reason you could do all the things you could do, that the powers of the drug had been transferred into your body, but admitting that meant admitting what had really happened to me, so I told myself—as well as you—that it was a mystery."

She dropped her hand and sat back in her chair, steeling herself to say the words she couldn't manage before. "Dr. Jekyll," she finally said, "wanted to separate good and evil, and now I realize that I've been doing the same thing all these years. But you were right, Iris; potions and formulas aren't always the answer. Evil doesn't exist in a vacuum. It's part of every day life, and darkness can't be fought until you face it for what it is." She clenched her jaw as regret sank into her heart like heavy claws. "If I had faced the evil that had a part in creating you, I would've made the connection between your blood and a cure years ago. It isn't a stretch to imagine that the blood of a person conceived of the drug would have some kind of effect."

She lowered her gaze to her lap and the room fell silent again. Then, surprisingly, Andrew spoke.

"Miss Carroll," he said. "Is it possible that there are others like Iris? People conceived in such a way before the drug was a tablet?"

Virginia raised her head and knit her brow. "I suppose there might be. If any of those isolated, early attacks by Jekyll and his friends resulted in pregnancies, and if those women survived long enough to bring the children to term, and if the children survived, then yes—it's entirely possible."

"But if Iris *is* the only one," Philomena supposed, "could she really cure every Hyde? A person's only got so much blood to go around, you know?"

"Andrew only needed to touch my blood with his wound to be cured," Iris said. "So it wouldn't take very much. Besides, I can replenish my blood supply whenever I need. I did it yesterday after the Lord Mayor took that pint."

Virginia's face paled. "The Lord Mayor took a pint of your blood?"

"Yes," she replied. "And he's the real problem; a cure means nothing as long as he's still the one who's running the city. We have to try and think of a plan."

A creak and then a blast tore through the air as the door burst open. Albert, who was in front of it, flew face down onto floor, and Elliot looked up to see a group of palace guards in the doorway. They rushed inside and tackled Albert, Andrew, and even Philomena, who—in those few seconds—had somehow managed to reach and raise her shotgun.

Screaming, Iris and Elliot leapt to their feet in front of Virginia, but more guards surged in. Soon, all six of them were on their knees. Metal clinked as their wrists were bound behind him in iron cuffs, and when Elliot glanced at the doorway, he gasped.

His father was standing before him.

CHAPTER EIGHTEEN

lliot, Iris, Virginia, Andrew, Philomena, and Albert were crammed together inside a barred carriage, and Elliot could hardly breathe for the fear in the small, enclosed space.

"I don't understand," Iris said as they jostled against their seats. "How did they find us?"

"Anyone could have followed us from Mansion House," Philomena replied. "Perhaps they've been following Albert and I ever since we left the palace." She closed her eyes, guilt swimming up into her throat. "It's all my fault."

"Of course it's not your fault," Andrew said. "If it weren't for you, we'd still be locked in that dungeon."

"It's nobody's fault."

Everyone turned to look at Virginia, who hadn't said a word since the guards burst into her flat.

"It was only a matter of time before they found me," she said softly. "I'm just sorry the rest of you had be a part of this."

She glanced at Elliot, and he winced when he felt her regret. Perhaps after watching his father turn a blind eye to his arrest, she felt guilty for assuming he was the enemy at first. Elliot had screamed for his father's help the moment he saw him, but although his chest had cracked with pain, his father had turned away.

"All hope isn't lost," Iris said. "At least they took us alive."

"Yes," Philomena responded, rolling her eyes. "We're not dead *yet*."

"Where do you think they're taking us?" Andrew asked. "Back to the palace?"

Elliot sucked in a breath, trying to fight the fear and focus. "Wherever it is, I'll talk to my father as soon as we arrive. He has no idea the Lord Mayor's making the drug and infecting the public."

"How do you know?" Iris asked.

"The Lord Mayor told me himself just before you burst into the dungeon, and since he believed I'd be dead soon he didn't have any reason to lie. If I can get my father to listen—"

"But the Lord Mayor also said your father hasn't really been looking for a cure all these years," Andrew said. "I'm sorry, Elliot, but even if he doesn't know the scope of the Lord Mayor's crimes, that doesn't necessarily mean he'll side with us once he does."

"Iris," Elliot said, not ready to face that possibility. "Do you think you could break your thumbs to free yourself from your handcuffs again?"

She nodded. "Yes. They're mostly the same as the ones I escaped before. But I'll wait until the right time, so they won't see me as a threat."

"So our plan then," Philomena said, "is for Elliot to talk to his father and pray he believes his story, and if that fails, for Iris to take out a group of fully-armed guards?"

None of them responded, but the silence spoke for itself.

"All right," she said with a nod. "As long as everyone's on the same page."

Eventually, the carriage did arrive at Buckingham Palace, and the guards pulled them out, lined them up, and ushered them into the empty Grand Hall. Elliot's skin was slick with sweat, but that didn't help him escape the cuffs that bound his wrists behind him. In fact, the more his pulse climbed, the more his bonds seemed to tighten, and something about the Grand Hall only increased his anxiety. Maybe it was the red and golden room's imposing grandeur, or his carefree memories of playing there as a child. Either way, he'd certainly never dreamed he'd be brought there in chains.

After a moment, his father appeared and descended the Grand Staircase, where Iris first collided with the Lord Mayor a week ago. He avoided Elliot's gaze as he reached the bottom step, hurrying toward the guards as if the rest of them weren't there.

"Spread throughout the palace and inform the servants and courtiers to stay away," he said. "No one may approach until the Lord Mayor has arrived."

The guards obeyed, leaving him alone with the prisoners, and as soon as the last one was gone, Elliot spoke.

"Father, please listen—"

"Don't say another word," he said, still avoiding Elliot's gaze, unable to mask the pain and fear in his voice. "Not another word."

"But Father, there's something you need to know," he insisted, starting toward him, but then his father drew and raised his pistol.

"I said don't move." His hand was trembling, and his heart was cracking in two, but he kept the gun at eye level. "You've already done enough."

"What has he done?" Iris asked. "What have any of us done?"

Elliot's father clenched his jaw and shifted his gaze to Iris. "Harboring a fugitive. Treason as well, I suspect."

"What fugitive?"

"You know damn well. Your mother, Virginia Carroll." He stepped a bit closer, looking at Virginia. "You almost got away with it. Until a week ago, I truly believed that you were dead."

"Why is she a fugitive?" Andrew asked. "What's her crime?"

"Unauthorized scientific research, aiding and abetting Hydes, espionage against the Lord Mayor."

"Frank," Virginia said. "You don't know what you're talking about."

"I know more than you think," he replied, anger penetrating his fear. "When I heard Philomena tell this footman to go to Iris's address, I sent guards to trail them both, because I knew my suspicions were right. The moment your daughter opened her mouth she reminded me of you—her accent, her voice, her cool intelligence, even her hair—and I knew if she was yours, she wasn't here by accident. I wasn't surprised you'd try to somehow infiltrate the palace; the only thing that surprised me was whose eyes your daughter had."

Virginia stared at the floor in shame, and Elliot's father stepped closer.

"I knew you were close with Jekyll," he said, spitting the name with disgust, "but I never guessed how close. Perhaps you even helped him to create that evil serum."

"Father, stop!" Elliot cried, wounded by the bolt of pain that shot through Virginia's chest, and his father turned to him, stunned and shaken by the outburst. "You're right," he continued, gritting his teeth against Virginia's anguish. "Iris is the daughter of Virginia and Dr. Jekyll, but that's because Dr. Jekyll raped Virginia when he was a Hyde."

His father's lips parted. "Well, perhaps that's what she *claims*."

"Think about it," Elliot said. "How else could Iris heal herself exactly like a Hyde? It's because she was conceived while her father was on the drug. Virginia had no idea what Dr. Jekyll had created, or what a monstrous person he really was until that night."

Pity swarmed his father's heart. As a scientist, he couldn't deny the logical explanation, but he strove against it, setting his jaw and gripping the gun even tighter.

"That doesn't change the fact that Virginia broke the law. And so did you, by helping her daughter to infiltrate the palace."

"I had no idea who Iris really was until today. But even if I had, I would have helped her however I could, because she came here to prove the thing that I've been trying to tell you." He paused and took a breath. "The Lord Mayor's been making the drug and infecting the people of London."

The blood drained from his father's face. "Elliot, how—how dare you? That's not only absurd, it's *treason!*"

"It's true, and we found proof this morning, over at Mansion House. He's also been experimenting on Hydes in the old jail cells."

His father shook his head. "That can't be true. There's some mistake."

"No mistake. He told us himself, and then he tried to kill us."

Ice slid through his father's veins, and Elliot shivered but clenched his fists behind him and pushed through the fear.

"The Lord Mayor locked Iris and me in the basement with Andrew this morning. He thought that Andrew would kill us, because he infected him last night."

His father's panic spiked just as Virginia's had at the news, and he swung the gun in Andrew's direction.

"Andrew is a Hyde?"

"Not any more," Elliot said. "That's what I'm trying to tell you. He *was* a Hyde, but now he's cured, because of Iris's blood."

"What?" his father breathed, his eyes going wide. "Did you say... cured?"

"Iris's blood is the antidote," Virginia explained, feeling strengthened. "Because she was conceived while her father was infected."

Elliot's father blinked and lowered his gun in disbelief. Then, slowly, his heart erupted with something Elliot hadn't ever felt from him before:

Joy.

But then, almost immediately, a wave of grief rose up and devoured the newfound bliss, and his father embraced the pain and fought the joy with all his might.

"Why are you doing that?" Elliot asked.

"What?"

"Fighting your joy."

His father's face reddened. "Stay out of my feelings."

"You know I can't."

"Then at least have the decency to shut your mouth and ignore them!"

Silence swelled between them, and his father turned away, but then Elliot sucked in a breath and spoke.

"I'm sorry, but no."

His father turned around, his blood running cold. "What did you say?"

"You've been ignoring your feelings ever since Mother's death," he said, wincing as the word passed his lips and sliced through both their hearts. "And ever since I injected myself with that serum, I've done the same thing, but I'm through ignoring my feelings and the feelings of those around me. I don't want to live the cold, half-life you've lived for the last five years."

"How—how dare you."

"When feelings get buried, so does the truth," he continued. "The truth is what I want and what I am going to give to you. The Lord Mayor told me you didn't know he'd been infecting the public, but he also said you haven't really been looking for a cure."

His father froze, his face going pale, and Elliot's stomach sank, but he kept his voice and his gaze steady.

"Father, is it true?"

Silence filled the room again, and his father glanced at his feet. Then, after a moment, he gritted his teeth and murmured, "Yes."

Elliot's throat went dry, and he shook his head. "Why not?"

"Because they don't deserve it!" his father shouted, flushing with rage. "After all the lives they've taken and all the misery they've caused, why should they be allowed to simply return to their everyday lives?"

"They didn't *choose* to be monsters."

"Elliot, one of them murdered your mother!"

"But, Father, a cure—"

"Would be a reward for the beast who took her away!"

The world slowed to a halt, and Elliot parted his arid lips. His father's grief was as massive and torrential as a hurricane, but rather than clouding his vision, the storm made everything suddenly clear.

"Oh God," he murmured, almost to himself. "I understand."

"You understand what?"

"Why you've pushed me away and tried so hard not to love me."

His father's face blanched. "Elliot, shut your mouth right now."

"It was your grief. It was so intense, so terrible and devastating, that you were afraid of feeling the same way again if you lost me."

"I told you to stop!" he cried, raising his gun with a trembling hand.

"Father, I loved her, too. I know exactly how you feel."

"You have no idea—" his father began, but then he clenched his jaw.

"I understand why you've done what you've done," Elliot continued. "But do you honestly think that she would want you to live this way? To push me away and reject the only part of her that's left? To avenge her death by denying a cure to a desperate, suffering city?"

His father gripped the gun tighter, but his eyes were filling with tears.

"You tried not love me," Elliot said, stepping closer. "But you do. You couldn't stop, just like I couldn't stop loving you, or Iris, or Cam, or Andrew, or Philomena, or any other person who's bound to my heart. I used to think that made me weak, but I know it's the opposite now. Real bravery is facing and embracing what you feel." He walked even closer, stopping only inches away from the gun. "I've always looked up to you," he said, looking straight into his eyes. "And I know deep down you're brave enough to accept the things you feel, to face your fears and finally do the right thing for this city."

"Only one person in London decides what's right or wrong for the city."

The air stilled as they all looked up to the top of the Grand Staircase, where the Lord Mayor was resting his arm against the bannister.

"Virginia Carroll," he said as he started down the stairs, his confidence and triumph so bright they nearly blinded Elliot from where he stood on the floor. As soon as his vision cleared, however, he noticed something strange: the Lord Mayor's gait as he descended was smooth and even. Only a few hours ago, he'd been limping in terrible pain. How could his ankle have possibly healed in that brief amount of time?

"I must commend you," the Lord Mayor continued to Virginia. "I truly thought you were dead. No one else has ever fooled or evaded me for so long." He reached the first floor and strolled toward her, a dark smirk on his face. "Of course, I can't imagine what kind of life you must have been living, the terrible ways you must have had to degrade yourself to survive." He stopped and glanced at Iris, who was standing right beside her. "The guards informed me that this is your daughter," he said, his smirk deepening. "I must admit I didn't see the resemblance until now. Although I suppose it only makes sense for one bitch to beget another."

"There's only one bitch in this room, and it's you," a fearsome voice rang out, and everyone turned to see Philomena glaring at the Lord Mayor. He chuckled and strode toward her.

"Now, now, Miss Blackwell," he said with a tsk. "I will not have such language from my future daughter-in-law."

"That will never happen."

"I assure you that it will. You'll marry my son and bear me titled grandsons within the year." He looked her over and shook his head. "Of course, we'll have to do something about that mouth of yours." He sighed. "Even well-bred horses have to be broken, I suppose, and if Cambrian can't do it—"

But he didn't get to finish, because Philomena raised her chin and spat right into his face. He stumbled backward and wiped his cheek, too stunned to react at first, but then rage flooded his veins, and he snapped the back of his hand across her mouth with brutal force. She flew to the floor, spitting blood, and Albert screamed and charged toward them. The Lord Mayor drew his gun and fired at Albert's chest. The shot tore through the air, and Albert collapsed immediately, his blood spilling out all over the lush, red velvet carpet. Philomena shrieked, "Alby!" and Elliot's father rushed toward him, but then the Lord Mayor turned and swung the gun in his direction.

"Leave him be."

"Harlan, you just shot an unarmed man!"

"He was about to attack me."

"His wrists were bound behind his back! And he only did it because you assaulted a little girl in chains!"

"I'm growing rather tired of your squeamishness, Frank." The Lord Mayor sighed. "It's a nuisance that's beginning to outweigh your usefulness."

Elliot's father froze, fear and horror stilling his heart. "For God's sake, Harlan, let me help him. It might not be too late."

"The penalty for attacking one's king is death."

"Attacking one's... *king*?"

"Toss me your gun, Frank. Now."

Elliot's father glanced at his hand as if he'd forgotten his pistol. He looked back up at the Lord Mayor, who still had his gun trained on him, and after a beat, he swallowed and tossed the weapon at his feet.

"Thank you, Frank," the Lord Mayor said, retrieving the gun and sliding it into the pocket of his coat. "If there's one thing I've always liked about you, it's your practicality."

"What did you mean by 'king'?" he asked again.

"Just what I said. London belongs to *me*. I am its total and absolute ruler."

"You are a coward!" Elliot cried, looking up from Albert's crumpled frame and glaring at him.

"And you," the Lord Mayor replied, "should have been dead four hours ago." He started toward him, but then he changed his mind and walked to Iris, who was standing on the other side of Albert and Philomena. "Both of you should," he said, raising an eyebrow as he approached her. "I must admit, I'm interested in knowing how you escaped, and why in the world you dared to bring a Hyde to your mother's home."

He smiled and glanced at Andrew, who was standing to Iris's right, but then his mirth and self-assurance suddenly dissolved, and he creased his brow and turned back to Iris, studying her face.

"But you wouldn't," he murmured, almost to himself. "You aren't mad. Perhaps you'd risk your own life, but you wouldn't endanger your mother's. You wouldn't have let Andrew near her unless..."

His blood cooled as he glanced over his shoulder at Elliot, whom Cam had always accused of being a hopeless, open book.

"Christ," he breathed, turning back to Iris. "I'm right. He's cured." He strode to Andrew and stared down into his face. "But how is that possible? What on earth could have cured you while you were locked inside that basement? Nothing was even down there but my tools and the three of you..." His voice died, and his face blanched as he slowly turned back to Iris. "Unless the girl who can heal herself can heal other people as well."

The silence that filled the room was all the answer the Lord Mayor needed.

"Well," he said, breathing a stupefied laugh as he approached her. "I suppose that's one more reason to rid myself of you."

Virginia screamed, and Iris jumped as the Lord Mayor raised his gun.

"I'm sorry, my dear, but I don't think you'll heal from a bullet wound to the head."

He cocked the gun, and Elliot bolted toward him, blinded by terror, but the Lord Mayor flew to the ground.

Tackled by Elliot's father.

The two men howled and screamed as they grappled for the gun, which Elliot's father eventually managed to smack from the Lord Mayor's hand. Elliot dashed toward it and kicked it out of the Lord Mayor's reach, but he kicked too hard, and it soared through the air and landed behind a sofa. He looked back down at his father, who had nearly succeeded in snatching his own gun back from the Lord Mayor's pocket, but the then Lord Mayor struck a massive blow to his father's face, knocking him onto his back with nearly supernatural force. Once he was free, the Lord Mayor rose, drew the gun, and aimed it at Elliot.

"No!" Elliot's father cried. He leapt to his feet and lunged between the Lord Mayor and his son, his love so strong that Elliot nearly stumbled in its wake.

"Step aside, Frank," the Lord Mayor said, his voice as hard as his eyes. "I could kill you for what you just did, but I don't want to do that. We've known each other a long time, and there are still some ways in which you could make yourself useful to me. But Elliot knows too much, and he's proven he can't be trusted."

Elliot's father straightened his back. "You'll have to kill me first."

The Lord Mayor laughed and shook his head. "You're both pathetic. This is the perfect example of how compassion makes men weak." He cocked the gun and aimed at Elliot's father. "Have it your way."

In the graveyard on the night that Iris and Elliot first met, Iris attacked the charging Hyde by jumping onto its back and slitting its throat with a knife from her boot, and at that moment—as Elliot stared at the Lord Mayor over his father's shoulder—the same scene unfolded like a dream before his eyes. Iris, who had apparently freed her hands during the fray, leapt up onto the Lord Mayor's back and dragged the scalpel from Mansion House across his open throat.

Elliot and his father stumbled backward as blood sprayed the air, and the Lord Mayor dropped the gun and clutched his throat in his hands. He slumped to his knees, emitting a strange and horrible gurgling sound, and then his body went limp. He collapsed facedown on the floor and lay completely motionless in a pool of his own blood.

Iris let out a strangled breath, staring down as if she couldn't believe what she'd just done. Elliot stared as well, his chest swelling with stunned relief, and then his father spun around and clutched him, compounding the feeling.

"Are you all right?" he murmured, and Elliot nodded, unable to speak. His father drew back, reached inside his pocket, and pulled out a key. "I'm going to look at the footman," he said, inserting the key into Elliot's handcuffs and freeing his tender wrists. "Here, take this and unlock the others." Then he ran to Albert.

Still dazed, Elliot rushed to Andrew and Virginia, released their bonds, and tossed the open cuffs onto the floor. Then he approached Philomena, who was on still her knees beside Albert, her face streaked with tears, and her lower lip caked with blood. He sucked in a breath, fighting her pain and fear as he freed her wrists. Once he was done, she reached for Albert, but Elliot's father stopped her.

"Let's get his hands free first," he said, taking the keys from Elliot and unlocking Albert's cuffs. Once they were off, he turned him over and slid his coat from his shoulders, then bunched it up to firmly press the fabric against the wound. The blood, however, was everywhere, and Albert's face was pale and slack. Elliot lowered his head and closed his eyes.

It was too late.

Philomena covered her face and sobbed into her hands, and Iris wrapped her arms around her and pulled her against her chest. Elliot stood and stepped away, consumed by the rising grief, but then a low groan sounded just a few steps behind him. He furrowed his brow and turned around, but there was nothing there—nothing but the Lord Mayor's bleeding, lifeless body. Shaking his head, he turned back, but then he heard the sound again, and this time when he looked, he froze.

Because the body moved.

He opened his mouth, but nothing came out at first—not even air. His throat was dry, his lips were numb, and his feet were off the floor. He watched, completely paralyzed, as the Lord Mayor started to rise, crawling up out of the pool of his own blood and onto his feet. Once he was standing erect, he wiped his eyes with the back of his sleeve, staring out at Elliot through the mask of blood.

And smiling.

"F—father!" Elliot cried, finally finding his voice, and the blast of terror behind him let him know they'd all looked up.

"How," his father choked. "How in God's name—"

"It's simple Frank." Smirking, the Lord Mayor lifted his chin and wiped the blood from his throat. The flesh that Iris had just sliced open was now completely intact. "Miss Faye—I mean, Miss Carroll," he said, "is no longer the only person in London who can heal."

"My God," Virginia murmured, edging forward. "That's why you took her blood."

"How very astute, Virginia," he said. "You may be a treacherous bitch, but I must admit you're a sharp one."

"What do you mean?" Iris asked her mother. "What did he do with my blood?"

"Fashioned a serum," the Lord Mayor replied. "My own creation. For years, I've been trying to find a way to obtain a Hyde's abilities without becoming infected. I've crafted other serums out of the blood I've taken from Hydes, but every time I tested them on people who weren't infected, the subjects simply ended up becoming Hydes themselves. One of them was the younger brother of that stable boy—the one who killed Andrew's father—which I probably should have seen coming."

Elliot trembled as violent rage erupted in Andrew's heart, and they started forward, but then the Lord Mayor picked up the bloody gun.

"When Iris fell into my lap," he continued, wiping it off on his trousers, "I knew that she could finally be the answer to my prayers. Once we'd tested her powers and made certain she wasn't infected, I took her blood and used it to make her abilities my own."

"You are a monster!" Elliot cried, unable to fight the rage around him and too disgusted to care. "A thousand times more of a fiend than Dr. Jekyll ever was!"

The Lord Mayor laughed. "What I am is invincible. Throw in immortality, and I'm very nearly a god." He raised the gun and aimed it at Iris. "And I am a jealous god. One that will not only have no others before me, but none at all."

At that moment, Elliot formed one final, desperate plan. He lunged forward and grasped the Lord Mayor's free hand in his own, pushing every feeling in the room into his body—Iris's panic, Virginia's fear, Andrew's rage, Philomena's grief, his father's horror, and even his own wild and frantic despair. Eventually, he even managed to dredge up Cam's crippling shame, closing his eyes and sharing every last bit with the Lord Mayor. He knew that once he felt the pain and misery he'd caused, he would have no choice but to reconsider his actions. When he opened his eyes, however, the Lord Mayor was sneering down at him, completely unmoved and feeling nothing at all but vague disgust.

"You fool," he said, shaking him off. "You think I care what you feel?"

Elliot stumbled backward, all the air in his lungs dissolving. Iris was right—empathy couldn't solve heartlessness on its own. A person could know exactly how another person was suffering and still choose to look the other way and do nothing about it. The scent of blood hit his nose as the Lord Mayor raised the gun, pointing it directly at the spot between his eyes. His father screamed, and Iris's distant figure started toward him, but he knew that there was nothing she could do to save him now. He clenched his teeth and closed his eyes, and a gunshot split the air.

But then... nothing happened. No sudden blow, no oblivion.

Elliot blinked and opened his eyes to see the Lord Mayor still before him, but the gun slipped from his hand, and he slumped down onto the floor, his body completely inert.

And the back of his head blown away.

Slowly, as if he'd stepped inside a dream, Elliot raised his head, and there—at the foot of the Grand Staircase, with a gun in his hand—was

Cam. As soon as he saw Elliot, he dropped the pistol, leapt over his father's body, and rushed straight into his arms. Relief, regret—but more than anything, love—consumed them both, and Elliot clutched him back with all the strength he had left in his body.

"El, I'm sorry," Cam cried.

"No, don't be—"

"No, listen to me." He stepped back and looked into his eyes, gripping the sleeves of his coat. "This morning I abandoned the two people I love most in this world."

"You had no choice, and you couldn't have known what he'd do."

"I should have known. And I should have listened to you, because you were right about everything. I don't deserve you, El—your love, your acceptance—"

"Cam, shut up!" Elliot shook his head and laughed, nearly drunk with joy and relief. "You saved my life—all our lives. Give yourself a break."

For once, Cam was too stunned to speak, and Elliot touched his arm. *"Aller à Andrew,"* he said, smiling. "Go to him. He wants to see you."

Cam flushed and stared down at his feet. "How do you know?"

"Because I can feel it myself, remember?" Elliot quirked up an eyebrow, and when he saw it, Cam spit with laughter.

"Christ, you're smug now," he said with a sigh. "This power is going to make you bloody impossible to live with."

Elliot smiled again. *"Je t'aime."* I love you.

"Well, who doesn't?" Cam grinned, let out a breath, and then hurried over to Andrew, and once he was gone, Elliot's gaze fell on Iris across the room. She beamed at him, and he felt the force of her love from where he stood, so he crossed the floor and swept her into his arms, sharing his own.

EPILOGUE

Elliot held Iris's hand as they climbed over the pebbles and cobbles of Brighton's rocky shore. The air smelled of salt and fish, and the setting sun had spread a blanket of gold out over the beach. Elliot's heart had been racing since the ocean first came into view, and now that they were nearing the water's edge, he thought it might burst. Iris's excitement only amplified the feeling, but just as he had every moment he possibly could for the last two months, he kept his fingers entwined with hers, clasping her hand even tighter.

The quarantine had been officially lifted the day before, but they hadn't had the chance to get away until today. Even though the Hyde menace was now considered eradicated, a few people were still trickling in to Frank and Virginia's clinics, which Elliot and Iris had been helping to oversee. Today, however, they'd finally boarded a train at the newly opened King's Cross, and in less than an hour, arrived at the nearest seaside city.

"Is it like you remembered?" Andrew called to Iris over the crashing waves. He and Cam were walking beside them, holding hands as well. The beach was out on the edge of Brighton—more rocky, but also deserted—which made them feel safe enough to behave as they would at the palace.

"It's even better," Iris said, smiling. "Everything is."

"So, this is the English Channel, then?" Philomena asked. She and Jennie had been strolling arm in arm behind them, but now Philomena was hurrying up to the front, dragging Jennie along. Elliot let out a breath of relief as Philomena shot past him; at least for the moment, her joy had caused her grief for Albert to wane.

"What do you know?" Cam asked Andrew. "Miss Blackwell has a basic, working knowledge of geography."

Philomena only paused long enough to stick her tongue out at him. "What I meant," she said, "is France is on the other side. There's only a stretch of water between us and a different country."

Elliot looked out over the sea, now just a few meters away. He and Iris had talked about going to Paris for him to study art and her ornithology, but both of them wanted to stay and help their parents a while longer. Cam and Andrew would also remain in London for the time being, at least until the government had fully transitioned back. Only Philomena had definite plans to move away; she and Jennie were sailing for New York in a couple of weeks. They'd grown quite close in the last few months, especially after Albert's death, and though Philomena's parents had promised to cut her off if she left, she remained determined to pursue her dreams on the stage. Together, she and Jennie could find work and support themselves, at least until Philomena became an international star, which Elliot had no doubt she would eventually be.

Finally, the six of them reached the edge of the rocky shore. The sea stretched out before them, blue and endless as the sky, its salty spray filling their lungs as the waves lapped at their feet. They stood in silence, and then, softly, Jennie began to cry. Philomena wrapped her arms around her, resting her head on her shoulder, and Andrew did the same to Cam, who reached up and touched his cheek. Iris squeezed Elliot's hand and leaned closer.

"Are you all right?" she whispered. "I mean, with everyone's feelings right now. Is it too much?"

Elliot sighed and closed his eyes as love and hope washed over his heart like the waves along the beach.

"No," he said, opening his eyes. "It's not too much."

ACKNOWLEDGMENTS

I first have to thank my agent, Jen Linnan, not only for taking a chance on me in the first place, but for understanding me (and my writing) on pretty much a soul mate level. Next, all of the people on my team at Curiosity Quills, who have not only made my dream come true, but made me a better writer – especially my editor, Claudia Carozza, and my acquiring editor, Vicki Keire. I am so happy to be a part of the CQ family.

To my incredibly supportive family: My parents, Vicki and Scott Price, for always reading my work and never judging me for it (at least not out loud). My sister, Megan Coberly, who has always been my number one reader, cheerleader, and friend, and my brother, David "the raptor" Price, who always provides the enthusiasm (and expletives) I need.

I also have to thank my amazing beta readers, most of whom are former students and/or fabulous writers themselves. Nancy Horner for understanding me without ever even meeting me and giving me the strength and confidence to journey on, Grant Urban for being there for me as a person and a writer, Kaitlin Hicks for her hilarious, stream-of-consciousness responses, Alyssa Marr for her French tutoring, and Kylie Groom, Jordan Lolar, Kaycee Kellogg, and Nicole Cummings for their indispensable fangirling.

Thanks to my former professor and constant mentor, Darcy Zabel, for being the first person – other than my mother – to tell me I could be a writer and help me pursue it. To my uncle and fellow author, James Bryan Smith (or Uncle Jimmy), for always making time for me and supporting me as well. To Dr. Marv Hinten for appreciating my passion for justice and introducing me to Victorian/Edwardian England. To Dean Hall for helping me get to a place where I was strong enough to finally tackle a novel. To Darham Rogers for his crucial historical knowledge, Xan Mattek for unknowingly providing inspiration, and Scott Newland for blowing my mind with his awesome facts about zoos.

And finally, to my husband, Matt Berthot, who is not only the love of my life and the best father in the world, but also the biggest supporter of my writing and my dreams. I couldn't have written this book if not for his constant love and encouragement, and also if not for his help in taking care of the next person I have to thank: My oldest son, Maximus, for showing me more love than I have ever known before. And lastly, to my youngest son, Leonardo, who – at the time of this writing – has yet to join us out in the world, but whom I already love with every fiber of my being. I want both of you to know as you grow up that you can achieve your dreams; all you need to do is trust your heart and never give up.

ABOUT THE AUTHOR

Andrea Berthot's last name has a silent "t," like the word "merlot" - which fits, since that is her favorite drink to have at the end of the day.

Back when she was born in Salina, Kansas, her last name was Price, and she grew up loving singing, acting, reading, and of course writing. By day she teaches high school English, creative writing, forensics, and directs the yearly musical, and by night (or rather, by early morning, as her brain is more alive at 5am than 5pm) she writes Young Adult stories involving history, romance, magic, literature, and some good, old-fashioned butt-kicking.

She lives in Winfield, Kansas with her husband and their two sons, Maximus and Leonardo.

THANK YOU
FOR READING

Please visit http://curiosityquills.com/reader-survey to
share your reading experience with the author of this book!

The Deathsniffer's Assistant, by Kate McIntyre

The sensitive and mannered Chris Buckley has spent six years raising his magically talented little sister, Rosemary, on the savings that his once-wealthy family left behind. But that money is drying up, and Chris finds himself with no choice but to seek out work in Darrington City as it spirals into a depression. The only employer willing to consider his empty résumé is Olivia Faraday, the manic Deathsniffer. Olivia's special magical gift gives her a heightened intuition which makes her invaluable in hunting down murderers.

Burning Bright, by Melissa McShane

In 1812, Elinor Pembroke wakes to find her bedchamber in flames—and extinguishes them with a thought. Her talent makes her a desirable match in Regency England, but rather than make a loveless marriage or live dependent on her parents, Elinor chooses instead to join the Royal Navy. Assigned to serve in the Caribbean, she turns her fiery talent on pirates preying on English ships. But as her power grows, Elinor's ability to control it is challenged. Could her fire destroy her enemies at the cost of her own life?